Victim

Victim

A NOVEL

Andrew Boryga

DOUBLEDAY NEW YORK

This is a work of fiction. Names, characters, places, and incidents either are the product of the author's imagination or are used fictitiously. Any resemblance to actual persons, living or dead, events, or locales is entirely coincidental.

 Published in the United States by Doubleday, a division of Penguin Random House LLC, New York, and distributed in Canada by Penguin Random House Canada Limited, Toronto.

www.doubleday.com

DOUBLEDAY and the portrayal of an anchor with a dolphin are registered trademarks of Penguin Random House LLC.

Book design by Anna B. Knighton
Jacket illustration by Victoria Sieczka
Jacket design by Emily Mahon

A cataloging-in-publication record has been established for this book by the Library of Congress.
LCCN: 2023946796
ISBN: 978-0-385-54997-4 (hardcover)
ISBN: 978-0-385-54998-1 (ebook)

MANUFACTURED IN THE UNITED STATES OF AMERICA

10 9 8 7 6 5 4 3 2 1

First Edition

To my family for your
unconditional love and support.

To the BX.

And to all the ghetto nerds worldwide.

Perhaps the turning point in one's life is realizing that to be treated like a victim is not necessarily to become one.

—JAMES BALDWIN

Victim

One

I WASN'T TRYING to play the victim until the world taught me what a powerful grift it is. Believe it or not, all I wanted was to be successful. To hustle like my Pops but keep my life and freedom in the process. My desperate chase after your approval was really all about that. I needed that approval to be considered successful. I needed it to feel like my life mattered.

The truth is, I didn't create this racket. I was put on. I peeped game and realized I happened to be uniquely equipped to thrive in it. You see, there are many ways to go about it, but the absolute easiest starting point is to actually have had some tragic shit happen to you.

It gives you something to pull from. A leg to stand on. *I survived this . . .* If you don't have that but you have the right shade of skin, you'll be okay, for now. If you don't have the tragic story or the right skin color but you grew up in the right kind of place with the right kind of poverty, and have the right kind of people to back up that story for you, you might be able to work something out.

But if you don't have the tragic shit and you don't have

the right skin color and you don't have the right geographic background, you're fucked. Get out of the game entirely—it is just not for you. Take your privilege, earn your cash, invest in your stocks, and for the love of God, stay off social media.

Lucky for me, I had the trifecta: the right skin color, the right birthplace, and tragedy to mine—thanks to my Pops.

There is a lot I could tell you about him. But that's a whole book in itself. For our purposes, the last days I spent with Pops before he died are enough.

I was twelve years old and on a plane to Puerto Rico to see him. A few months earlier, Mom and Pops had broken up for like the three hundredth time. It had happened right after the cops showed up at our door looking for him while he hid out in a secret room in the building's basement. Mom said she was tired of lying to the police. "I told you from the start that I ain't going to jail for your ass." Pops pulled me aside shortly after, got on a knee, and gave me his spiel: "I love you, mijito. And I'll always be your Pops. But I gotta go." I was long past the point of tearing up or even getting upset. I figured they'd be back together in a few months, Pops would be back in the Bronx, and the world would keep spinning. I patted Pops on the shoulder and conned him into breaking me off with a hundred bucks before he left.

When the plane landed in Puerto Rico, everything was bright, as if God had placed the entire island under a lamp. The flight attendant led me to another woman. I sat in her golf cart as she drove me past a gift shop full of coffee, T-shirts, and fake machetes. In the pickup area, a few people waited with signs. Pops wasn't one of them. He leaned against a column near the baggage carousel, talking up a woman. His jeans were tight, and his tank top showed off his bulging arms.

I directed my guide to Pops, and he pretended to be excited to see me. "Macho!" He hugged me, then quickly spun me around to show me off to the woman he'd been talking to. She put a hand on her cheek. "So adorable."

"I make beautiful kids," Pops said.

The heat outside slapped me up like a schoolyard bully. Pops led me to a parking garage with paint-chipped walls and put his arm around my shoulder like I was a little boy. Normally, I would have shaken him off. But he'd missed me. And it felt nice.

I can't say I hadn't missed him. The way his thick mustache brushed against my face when he hugged me. His stupid jokes. The way he'd sometimes decide to splurge after a big hit, buying me new gear and video games just because. Then there were the things I didn't miss: his booming voice when he yelled, the thunder after he'd slam our front door, the way Mom cried and smoked all those cigarettes, the heavy knocks from police.

We stopped in front of a shiny blue Mustang.

"Te gusta, macho?"

I'd liked his old tinted-out Accord better. It had made me feel like I was in a spaceship. But I didn't want to hurt Pops's feelings. He was clearly in a good mood.

"It's tight," I said.

"*Sí,* nene, sí," he said. "Estamos en PR. If you're my son, you can't be some little gringo kid, entiendes?"

"What do you mean, 'if'?"

He flicked my ear and threw my bags inside. I melted on the blistering seat. When the engine came on, I blasted the AC, but Pops immediately turned it off and rolled down the windows. "Do you pay for gas?" he asked.

I wondered what the point was of him being a drug dealer if he was going to be such a fucking cheapskate. He might as well have cleaned toilets or stood outside fancy Manhattan buildings like all the other dads I knew.

A cigarette hung from the side of his mouth and wobbled like an antenna. His gold chain hid in the thicket of his chest hair like a vine in a wild forest. "Your mom seeing anybody?"

"Not that I know of." She talked all day about the white doctors at her job, the ones she answered phones for. But only as a fantasy. She wondered out loud sometimes what her life might have been like if she'd met one of those guys and resigned herself to being his hot Puerto Rican wife, instead of getting knocked up by Pops at nineteen.

Pops put the car in gear, turned around, and started to reverse out of the spot. When he was halfway out, he stopped, put the car back in park, and pointed his cigarette at me.

"You'd tell me if she was seeing somebody, right?"

I leaned my head out the window, trying desperately to pick up a gust of wind to cool me off.

"Yes," I said.

"Sí."

WE PULLED UP to the McDonald's just before the city center turned into a maze of small streets. I smiled. Mom didn't let me eat fast food, but when I was with Pops, it was what I subsisted on. Inside, salsa played on the speakers. The woman at the counter was young and cute, and Pops got to flirting immediately.

"Why is someone as beautiful as you working here?"

She responded as you'd imagine.

I asked for a Happy Meal and looked at a display showing off the plastic toys I might get. All *Lilo & Stitch* themed. I stared at the Stitch figurine and prayed for it. Then I realized who I was with.

"I want that one, Pa."

"Cómo se dice?"

I sighed. "Yo quiero eso."

"Por favor," Pops said, pretending for the pretty young thing that *he,* of all people, cared about fucking manners.

Pops ordered chicken nuggets and a soda. He pulled out the thick wad of cash he always seemed to be carrying around. A wad so thick it could knock someone clean out. He peeled off way more bills than the meal cost and winked at the girl, pointing at the Stitch toy. The girl's smile revealed bright braces. Before we left, she scribbled her number on a paper bag with a pink pen and signed it with a heart.

We ate in the car with the windows down. Pops sipped his soda and matched the conga beat coming from the radio with taps on the steering wheel. As I bit into my cheeseburger, a man approached my window. His hat looked like it'd been run over a few times, and his T-shirt had holes in it. In his hand was an empty large soda cup that he jangled around.

He rested his hands on Pops's car. "Señor, me regalas unos chavitos para comer?" He smelled sour, like the drunks and fiends I was used to seeing in the Bronx. He rattled his cup of change once more and was just about to go into his spiel when Pops shushed him.

"Cállate, cállate. No más. I don't want to hear it. Get the fuck away from my car before I shoot you."

The man was undeterred. He must not have believed Pops. He shook his cup once more. "Por favor, señor . . ."

Pops reached under his seat and pulled out a black pistol. In a split second, it was cocked and aimed. "Qué te dije, cabrón? Muevete."

The man put his hands up and slowly backed away from the car. I took another bite of my cheeseburger.

When the man had moved on enough to Pops's liking, he put the gun back under his seat.

"Me cago en tu madre." He looked over at me. "Never be like that, Javi."

I scrunched up my cheeseburger wrapper. "What? Homeless?"

He pushed the side of my head with his finger. "No, smart-ass. A beggar." He pointed out the window at the man dragging his feet, heading toward another parked car in the lot. "Ese tipo, he's got no chance. Tú sabes? He goes around feeling sorry for himself instead of taking shit into his own hands. Entiendes? You can never live like that. You don't feel sorry for yourself. Si te caes, te levantas. Así es. That's how I live my life. That's how you need to live yours." Pops seemed pleased with his speech. He reached into my bag and stole a fry. He looked at his gold watch. "Vamos."

Pops drove on narrow streets that were theoretically two-way. I stared up at the electrical wires crisscrossing the sky, creating something like a mosquito net. We pulled up at a faded concrete house by the water wrapped in thick metal gates. A man I didn't recognize sat on the patio, rocking in a chair. I never recognized the dudes Pops visited. They always just seemed to appear from nowhere. Faceless people who handed him wads of cash and spoke a few mumbled words.

The man scratched his belly and waved us in. Near the entranceway, a little girl sat cross-legged on a Winnie the Pooh blanket playing with Barbies. She was seven or eight, tops.

"Juega con ella," Pops said, depositing me next to her.

"What am I, a babysitter?"

"Cállate."

I missed the Bronx immediately. Although I'd had high hopes for this trip on the plane—the mall for new sneakers, maybe a new gold chain, tons of Pokémon cards, maybe a new Game Boy, a beach where I could actually see my toes through the water—I was instantly reminded of what life in Puerto Rico was really like with Pops. Driving from house to house while he conducted business and I was left to interact with random strangers and confront my wack-ass Spanish.

I sat on a corner of the girl's blanket. She gave me a skeptical look. I showed her my Stitch toy. She squinted, then rifled through a bucket and pulled out another Barbie.

"La esposa de el," she said in a singsong voice.

She handed me the Barbie, and I held the two toys in my hand, unsure of what to do. I heard a chicken cluck and a motorcycle engine pop. Everything felt slow on the island, like God was playing life at half speed.

The girl, annoyed, put her hand on her hip like she was twenty-five. "Que se besen, chico."

In the distance, I could hear Pops laughing in a back room. Like an idiot, I brought the toys together in a kiss. The girl rolled her eyes and snatched them from me. She brought the tiny plastic lips of Stitch and Barbie together mad hard but twisted the toys slowly and sensually.

"Así. Bien tranquilo."

I looked at her stringy arms, tan like dark wood. Bright purple beads were scattered throughout her short braids. I wanted to ask how she knew so much about kissing, but I didn't know how to say that correctly in Spanish. I was too afraid of making a grammatical mistake and exposing myself as a gringo. So I remained quiet.

Eventually, Pops whistled, and I was saved. The girl didn't look at me when I left, but she made the Barbie give Stitch a peck on the cheek goodbye.

After Pops pulled out of the dirt driveway, he dug into his pocket and retrieved a wad of crumpled bills spun into a ball like a Fruit Roll-Up. "Put that in the cosita."

I opened the glove compartment and saw a silver pistol under some papers and CD cases. I put the money on top of the gun. I always knew Pops to ride around with at least one. More than one was new.

"How many guns do you have in this car?"

"It's probably better that you don't know the answer to that, mijito."

I leaned my face into the choppy wind as Pops drove. I watched waves crash in the ocean alongside the road. I wanted to get to our house already. Grab my boogie board from the garage. Eat some alcapurrias and wiggle my toes in the sand.

"Are you done now?"

Pops turned down the radio. "Nope."

I sucked my teeth.

He kept one palm on the steering wheel. With his free hand, he reached over me to get to the glove compartment on his own now, as if it were somehow safer, driving eighty miles an hour, to do this at this moment rather than when we were stationary. The smell of sour beer on his breath reminded me of times in the past that you might call good. Family parties where he'd be drunk and happy and there'd be too many people around for him to fight with Mom. Sunday-afternoon Mets games where he'd get three Coronas in before the first pitch and badger outfielders from the opposing team every inning until they'd turn and give him the finger.

Letting both hands off the steering wheel for a moment, Pops peeled off a few fifties from his wad of cash and handed them to me before righting the car. He pulled my head close and planted a kiss on it. "Mira. For your birthday. I'm probably gonna miss it this year."

POPS MADE A LEFT off the main road and onto a skinny dirt road that meandered through a thicket of bushes. The car bumped up and down, looking like the cars Mexicans in California drove on television. It eventually stopped in front of a blue house with a crack running down the wall on one side like it had been struck by lightning.

"How many more stops you have?" I asked.

"As many as I want. I'm working."

He retrieved the pistol from under the seat and shoved it into his waistband. Historically speaking, this meant he was visiting somebody he expected to be short or have some excuse he didn't want to hear. He knocked on the door, and a skinny man opened up. He seemed reluctant to let us inside. Nonetheless, Pops told me to sit on a couch in a dim living room that felt like it was a thousand degrees. Sitting across from me in an armchair was an older woman with gray hair pulled back into a bun. A preacher on the radio went on about how Satan was everywhere. Pops and the skinny man spoke in another room. The woman took two puffs of a cigarette and stared at me as I rocked my feet back and forth.

"Mira, chico, tú quieres comer?"

There were a lot of things I hated about Puerto Rico, but one of the things I loved was the food. Everywhere you went, someone, usually an older woman like her, was ready to shove it down your throat.

As the woman got the food together, I heard muffled voices. Pops said "cabrón" over and over, then "hijo de puta." Nothing seemed out of the ordinary. I'd heard him shake down a million dudes. The woman returned with a steaming plate of rice and beans and bacalao guisado. On the side were tostones the size of a Discman and two large slices of avocado that looked like young moons plucked from the sky. I took two delicious bites. Then I heard a loud *thwack*.

The woman stared down the hall. I stared, too. Outside, somewhere in the distance beyond the trees and sand, a horse neighed. The woman rubbed my head. Two forkfuls of rice later, Pops emerged from the room, stuffing his pistol into his waistband. "Vámonos."

"But I just got this food."

He shot me a look, one I remembered from his time at home, where I often felt like I was walking in a minefield. There were the good days, good times, and then there were days and moments where anything I said or did seemed like a distraction from something more important to him—like the baseball game on TV or the beer in his hand or the cigarette in his mouth.

I ate one last forkful of rice and beans.

"Espérate," the woman whispered. She rushed into the kitchen and came back with the food stuffed between two paper plates. She even included a plastic fork rolled up in a napkin. I almost kissed her.

Outside, Pops ground his cigarette under his shoe and watched me as I strolled to the car with my bounty. "You just ate. That's why you're getting fat. That right there."

I looked down at my stomach, hidden under my Charizard T-shirt. I hadn't thought of it as big until Pops said something. But after he said it, I couldn't think of anything else. As I buckled my seat belt, the skinny man stood on the porch. The side of his face was red. His eyes were pointed like he wanted to do something about it.

"Qué pasó, mano? Si tienes algo que decir pues dímelo, puñeta."

The man remained quiet but nodded, as if confirming something for himself.

Pops ripped the food from my lap and flung it at the front steps of the house like it was a Frisbee. The top plate flew off, and the rice and beans trickled down the concrete like blood. "Mamaguevo!" he shouted.

WHEN WE FINALLY pulled up in front of our house, Tío Pito was out front leaning on a car. Whenever I came to Puerto Rico, it seemed like somebody was always leaning on a car in front of our house, waiting. Often, it was Tío Pito. Tío Pito wasn't technically my tío. Pops was an only child. But they were best friends and "associates," as Pops liked to say, in his terrible accent so that it sounded like ass-so-shits.

Tío Pito walked over wearing gold frames, a black vest, and khaki pants. "Papo! Look at how big you are." He gave me a hug. The scent of weed on him was like a familiar cologne.

Pops collected more wads of crinkled bills from Tío Pito and mimed how he'd smacked the shit out of that last guy. Tío Pito doubled over. I went inside.

Our house was nice, by Puerto Rico standards. It was white, and the paint wasn't chipping anywhere noticeable. But compared to the houses Mom would show me in Riverdale sometimes, it wasn't shit. It didn't have AC, and the power always went out. The water, too, which is why there was always a big trash can full of water parked in the corner of the shower. On too many occasions to count, I'd had to bathe using a bucket to scoop cold water out of it. One scoop for washing, one scoop for rinsing. Anything more warranted an ass-whooping.

I went straight to the back room and found big garbage bags in the corners. I decided not to look through them. It was too hot. I put my suitcase on the bed and started to unpack my things. When I opened the first drawer of the dresser, there were stacks of cash inside and no space for clothes. I threw my bag on the floor, turned on the fan, and lay down. The fan blew hot air back at me. After some minutes staring at the ceiling and sweating, I went out to the backyard. I stuck my nose in the lemon plants. In the far corner were Pops's chickens, hemmed in by wire. They jumped on top of each other and bristled, looking like Fordham Road in the summertime. I loomed over their cage and stared into their small, beady eyes.

THE NEXT MORNING, Pops woke me up with a whistle from the threshold of my room. He held a cup of coffee. Light streamed through the back door. I understood why Mom said she was swept off her feet as a young girl in New York. She always said Pops was so pretty that it made it easy for her to look past the things she didn't like about him.

While we were eating eggs at the small table, he asked if I wanted chicken for dinner.

"It's like ten in the morning, Pa."

"Just answer."

"Sure."

He grinned. "Hurry up and finish eating, then. We have work to do."

I figured we'd spend another day driving around and picking

up money, which is how he seemed to spend most of his days. It sounds cooler than it is. One time, while we were driving on a long road shaded by trees, I asked Pops if he'd always wanted to be a drug dealer. He turned down the radio. "No, I just wanted to make money," he said. "Now I make money." He turned the radio back up. It was one of the deepest conversations we ever had.

Pops left me baking in the driveway for a few minutes and eventually returned to the car with one of his chickens in a cage.

"What's that for?"

"You'll see."

We drove to the caseríos, the large, towering buildings that were just like the projects in the Bronx. They were where Pops kept all his drugs and all the men who worked for him. The apartments were stacked on top of each other like little boxes. Chipped courtyards and faded green basketball courts were scattered throughout the complex. At one of the courts, flowers and candles were arranged below the hoop, as well as a picture of a man named Bonano. I knew enough to know he wasn't being honored for his dunking ability.

Pops drove slowly, passing a group of men in long, flowing shirts and large baseball caps. They nodded at him when he whistled. I stared up at the fenced balconies of the apartments and saw brown and black arms dangling out like loose noodles. Pops parked in a corner, near where Tío Pito and another group of men played pool on a table shaded by a tarp. Pops grabbed the chicken and sauntered over. They spoke in fast, grating words that were too hard for me to follow. But I knew Pops had said something about me, because by the end they were all smiling and staring.

Pops led a group of us through the courtyard, cutting straight through a pickup basketball game. The guys stopped dribbling and looked away as Pops and his friends passed. As soon as we were all off the court, they continued like nothing had happened.

Pops walked to the very back of the caserío, to a large grassy field. In the center was a tree stump stained with blood. Pops laid the cage on the ground. Everyone stood around in a circle, and I suddenly felt like I had in kindergarten right before I had to get onstage for a school play. Pops whistled, and one of the men handed him a long machete that glinted in the sun.

He wrapped my hands around the handle just like dads on the Disney Channel did when they taught their kids how to hold a bat. He bent down and grabbed the chicken. I watched it squirm and flutter its feathers. I caught its beady eye.

Pops spread its wings flat like paper and laid his crisp sneaker on the tip of one wing. The bird kept trying to wiggle but eventually stopped. I watched its chest rise and fall, slowly, accepting its fate in a way I found noble. I felt like a hole had been opened up in my own chest and I was falling inside it. Tío Pito crouched down in the grass and offered advice.

"Nice and quick." He made a cutting motion with his hand. "*Fwakata.*"

I stared at the machete. I crept forward and looked into the bird's eye. I raised the machete over my head and felt my arms tremble. Pops's friends laughed, but Pops became dead serious.

"Let's go, Javi. Tú eres un hombre. Tú eres mi hijo."

I hesitated.

He narrowed his eyes. "Ahora mismo, Javi. I'm not going to ask you again."

I winced and brought the machete down. The tip hit at an angle and caught part of the chicken's neck, causing it to snap like a tree twig but remain connected. Blood squirted like water from a small sprinkler. I dropped the machete and stepped back. The tears came fast.

As his men doubled over in painful laughter, Pops sighed. He picked up the machete and brought it down swiftly. The chicken's head rolled clean off. The chicken stood and jumped off the stump. It ran in circles. It came close to me, and I stared into a red gaping wound. Pops shook me off his leg. He manhandled the cage and stomped back to the car, muttering.

Later that night, he bought us a bucket of Kentucky Fried Chicken. We ate in silence at a small red booth. When we got home, Mom called to speak to me. As soon as I was on the line, she asked me if Pops had a girlfriend.

"No."

"So you haven't seen any sucias around, you're telling me?"

"No."

"Are you telling the truth? I don't believe you."

I sighed.

She asked if I was okay. "Are you having fun?"

I twirled the phone's cord and looked at Pops, sitting on the couch, immersed in a novela. He leaned forward, cupping his chin in one hand. "Honestly, Pops fucking sucks. I hate him."

"Hey. Watch your mouth," she said. "He's your father."

I WAS STILL PISSED at Pops the day he died. I've never been able to reconcile that. It was the day of the big Tito Trinidad fight that summer. Pops hosted a party in the beat-up concrete plaza just a few blocks from our house. A projection screen and speakers were erected. Food vendors handed out free bacalaitos, pastelillos, and beers. Everything was on Pops, and everyone kissed his ring, like he was a king.

There must have been over a hundred people. Many came and hugged me and told me what a great man Pops was. I smiled stiffly in return. I figured they were either lying or didn't really know him.

As the undercard fights started, I sat with other abandoned kids near the grass. They all understood that I didn't speak the language and, more so, that I wasn't interested in trying. I just wanted to get back to the Bronx. But one boy with a tight line-up just wouldn't take the fucking hint. He kept coming up to me and counting, "One, two, three," clearly the only English words he knew how to say. He'd leave for a few moments when I didn't respond, only to return minutes later to see if I'd changed my mind. "Hey. One, two, three."

I ignored him and reorganized my stack of Pokémon cards in the grass. The grunts of the fighters echoed for miles. I looked over at Pops, who was drunk. I knew because he looked happy. After the second undercard ended, he came over to where I sat. He asked me to put my hands up like we were fighting and his hands were mitts. I played along, swinging harder when he goaded me because I did actually want to hit him. He stopped. He looked like he wanted to say something, but he didn't. He just rubbed my head and walked off.

After each subsequent fight, salsa music played. People twirled. The air was hot and thick, making everyone sweat in a way that felt unifying. Tito Trinidad walked out on the screen, draped in a Puerto Rican flag like a superhero. The camera panned around Madison Square Garden, where a sea of flags waved. Everyone in the plaza shouted. Even I stood up to get a better look at the screen, feeling a swelling of pride that I hadn't even known existed. They stripped his robe off. Tito raised his fists and looked around at the thousands of faces screaming his name. Imagine having all that attention, I thought. All that love.

Tito's thin body glistened as he fluttered warm-up punches. He smiled wide, like he knew the fight was in the bag. It was. At the end of the third round, the other guy clutched a swollen eye the color of a prune.

I softened up and started showing off my Pokémon cards to the boy who kept counting to me. I laughed at the way he pronounced Bulbasaur (*bull-bee-sour*) and Pikachu (*peek-at-ju*). He laughed, too.

Then, out of the corner of my eye, I saw Pops yelling at someone. He'd been sitting on a foldout lawn chair surrounded by his friends near the screen. But now he was standing and screaming right into the face of a man. It took me a moment or two to recognize him as the one Pops had smacked the day I arrived.

Everyone yelled in Puerto Rico—especially Pops. I figured that was just how our people communicated. But after Pops pushed the man, I noticed a maniacal look take hold on the man's face. I watched in slow motion as he reached into his waistband and quickly aimed a pistol at Pops. I remember thinking how old the gun looked. Like it was from the 1800s. But the bullets flew out just fine.

The sound pierced the sky, and I watched Pops wilt to the ground like the chicken after it finally died. I stared into Pops's wide eyes. The sound in the plaza vanished. More shots were fired, chairs scattered, tables toppled. Cords were ripped from the speakers, and Tito disappeared in a flash.

The kids around me were snatched up like fumbled footballs. My eyes remained fixed on Pops, who was twitching on the ground. I wanted to run over to him, but my legs felt as if someone had dipped them in cement. All I could do was stare.

Eventually, Tío Pito rushed toward me huffing and puffing with a gun in one hand. He grabbed me by the collar and pulled me with him. "Vamos, vamos!" he yelled. I followed him into his car, and he sped through the tiny streets and stopped abruptly at a house I didn't recognize. He slammed the steering wheel a few times.

It took seeing Tío Pito, someone I'd always thought of as tough, beginning to break down in front of me, to show real emotion, for me to really feel the weight of what had just happened.

"Tío? Is Pops okay?"

Tío Pito huffed.

He noticed the tears on my cheeks and used his thick finger to wipe some of them away.

"Wait here, okay?" he said. "It's going to be okay. No worry, okay? No worry."

He ran inside the house, and I sat in his Civic in the dark. The only thing I heard was the sound of the coquis in the trees. I looked around for Pops on the street, as if he might be out on a stroll. As if he might have shaken off that shot. To me, he was Superman. Larger than life. I believed that if anyone could do it, it would be him.

Tío Pito came back and shuttled me inside the house. A woman wearing a hairnet and a bata stood there looking confused.

"Cuídalo," he said to her.

He bent down and stared at me. "I come back for you, okay? This my friend. You stay here. I come back. Entiendes? We get you back to New York."

"What about Pops?"

Tío Pito wanted to say something, wanted to give me some kind of comfort, some kind of hope. I could tell. But he didn't. He just rubbed my head, kissed the top of it, and rushed out. I listened to his tires squeal on the pavement as the woman and I stood on the threshold and watched him go. She shut the door and looked at me.

"Tu papá era un buen hombre," she said.

The "was" in the sentence told me everything I needed to know.

The woman shuffled her feet on the concrete and scratched under her hairnet. "Quieres comer?"

When I didn't respond, when I kept staring at her closed door, she bent down to my level. She cupped her hand to her mouth. "Eat?"

I'd stuffed my face with food at the party. So much that my body couldn't physically accept more. But in that moment, all I wanted was something that seemed familiar. Something that would make me believe that everything actually was okay. That everything actually would be fine.

"Yes," I said. I thought of Pops's admonishments. His ear flicks, head smacks, grins, stupid speeches. The things I'd always found so annoying, but perhaps because I always thought they'd continue, because I figured they'd be as constant as the sun rising and falling.

"Sí, I mean."

TWO

IT'S HARD TO DESCRIBE how I felt after Pops died. It's hard to describe losing a person who was only *kind of* there. A person who appeared and disappeared like a ghost. It was not, I imagined, the same thing my best friend, Gio, felt when his mom died. That was his mom. But Pops, and dads in general where I'm from, were not like that. If they were around, present and in your home, you were lucky. For most of us, dads were like my Pops. People who dropped in and out of our lives for various reasons.

I don't know if Pops's dying was really the beginning of it all. But I do know that when I got back to the Bronx after his murder, I got my first taste of the high that comes from being a victim.

In short order, I learned that I was no longer just a poor kid from the neighborhood like anyone else. I was one of those *tragic* kids. One of those kids who'd had something terrible happen to them, even by our high standards. In school, teachers suddenly gave me more attention than I was ever used to. They constantly asked if I was okay after classes, as if I'd just survived an earthquake. They let me take time off at home—which was nice, except that I didn't want to stay home because it only made me think about Pops more. A glance at his leather jacket hanging in the closet or his baseball bat signed by Bobby Bonilla standing by the door was enough to send me spiraling.

The best thing my teachers offered me was a free pass to go to the nurse. On one of my first days back at middle school, my homeroom teacher, Ms. Williams, and Principal Nelson sat my mom and me in his office and told Mom about this "mental health break" I could take whenever I needed one. They said they'd already alerted all of my teachers to what had happened and that I didn't even need to tell them if I was having a "moment." I could just get up and go to the nurse's office. "You don't need to explain," Principal Nelson said.

For the first time, I realized my tragedy could translate into personal gain. A skirting of the rules. A perk. Mom seemed confused by the offer but thanked my principal. She turned to look at me. "I don't expect Javi to be needing that. I think it's important for him to be staying in class and learning. Right, Javi?"

The thing is, Mom couldn't keep tabs on me while I was at school. So I used my get-out-of-class-free card often. Particularly during math and science. In the beginning, the nurse, Lillian, would ask me how I was feeling and if there was anything I wanted to share with her. She'd attempt to do her job. At first, I'd pretend like I was bothered. Say things like "I feel like I want to cry." Sometimes I really did want to cry. Sometimes I had real tears. Sometimes I'd be sitting through a lesson and have a sudden memory of Pops and then the crushing realization that I'd never see him again. Instead of having to suck in that feeling and hide it, sometimes it was nice to go to Lillian, cry a bit, and lie down on the little hospital bed in her room.

But there were many more times when I felt nothing, when I

showed up because I wanted to get out of class, or because I was tired and wanted to nap. It became such a habit, and happened so often during the same times of the day, like clockwork, that eventually Lillian would just wave me into the room and nod at the bed.

After some months, Mom was finally called in to talk about these frequent visits. Not because I was in trouble, but because Ms. Williams and others were concerned that perhaps I was depressed. Perhaps I needed serious medical attention. "Maybe medication," she said to Mom.

"None of that will be necessary," Mom said. "We'll be taking care of this at home."

On the bus ride home that afternoon, my prescription was a smack to the back of my head that stung for three stops. On top of that, a grounding for the rest of the school year and a warning that there would be more to come if I kept up my act. "Stop the bullshit, Javi," Mom told me. "Go to class."

Mom wasn't the only person mystified by what I was doing. Gio was, too. He'd known me since we were both babies crawling around the legs of our teenage moms as they chain-smoked and talked about their man problems in each other's apartments. He knew how I really felt about Pops's death. He, more than anyone else, even then, could see the hints of my charade. When I told him I'd been punished by Mom, he only laughed at me. "I told your ass you were overdoing it."

From the beginning, I was more mystified by Gio. I didn't understand why he didn't want to follow my example. After all, as far as I was concerned, his tragedy was worse than mine. He'd lost someone he was actually close to. Someone who was always around. Someone who didn't miss his birthdays or prompt the cops to come knocking on his door all the time. And yet, he never seemed to like the idea of using that for his benefit. He was, I thought, a dummy.

I tried to persuade Gio by talking up the benefits of my perks while I had them. The naps helped me think more clearly. I had less acne. And because I was missing math and science for a seemingly legitimate reason, my teachers in both classes gave me half the work and expected half the effort. If anyone deserved this, I thought, it was Gio, given that he *actually* brought his mom up all the time.

"I don't want any of that," he'd say. "I just want to be left alone."

I DIDN'T REALLY UNDERSTAND Gio's reluctance to take advantage of his dead mother until the very last day of middle school. From the cracked steps of our school building that day, our tired teachers, happy to send us packing, yelled, "Go home!" into their megaphones. No one listened. I pushed through my classmates and the churro sellers with hands cloaked in plastic gloves and found Gio waiting at the end of the block.

Instead of going right home, we stopped at the playground. Gio whipped out his handball, and we played against the wall, stopping to admire the crews scattered around the park, the girls getting macked on, the ballplayers trying their hardest, but mostly failing, to dunk. The elevated train ran by every few moments, slicing through the sky and scattering sparks in the air. Cars cruised along the avenue, and sweaty hands hung over the sides of the doors, tapping out beats to congas and 808 machines.

Gio bragged about watching channel 59. "The things I saw," he said, closing his eyes for a moment. He rubbed in the fact that I still had to jerk off while sitting on the toilet and keeping my eyes trained on the bathroom door. "How do you even bust a nut?"

"I don't," I said.

"That's sad."

"I know."

I checked my watch and realized it was time to get back before Mom did, time to scatter my books around the floor, fill a cup halfway with something to drink and make it seem like I'd been home since school let out. As we walked, Gio kicked an empty Heineken bottle on the ground and watched it ricochet off the concrete. Its green glass glinted in the sun like an emerald. He asked me to stay over at his place that night. "We can watch as much channel 59 as your horny ass wants. I think there might be a WWE pay-per-view, too. You know my bootleg box gets those."

"Okay, okay. You can quit bragging."

As great as that sounded, I had to remind him about my punishment.

He bounced his ball as we walked. "Still? For the nurse shit?"

"Still." I slapped the ball away and stole it from him. "Has your grandma ever punished you?"

"Nope."

"And you get a bootleg box. Unlimited channel 59. Playboy. The movies. Didn't she buy you a bunch of games for Christmas, too?"

Gio nodded. "Yeah."

"Son, you have the life."

Gio cracked a forced smile that disappeared almost instantaneously. "Maybe. But at least you still have a mom." Gio always defended Mom. Always took her side in shit. And always hit me with this same line.

"What's the use of having a mom if all she does is nag you and punish you for dumb shit?"

Mom had always been strict. But everything intensified after Pops was killed. It felt like she wanted to control my every move. Like she wanted me to be her little robot. She seemed to only speak to me in commands: *Javi, don't stay outside late; it's dangerous. Javi, play the numbers for me. Javi, turn off the lights; do you think I'm sleeping with someone from Con Ed? Javi, do your homework. Javi, get good grades. Javi, don't watch too much TV. Javi. Javi. Javi.*

"It's annoying," I told Gio.

He bounced the ball on the asphalt. "I guess that does sound wack. My grandma don't tell me shit."

"That's what I'm looking for."

We walked under the elevated train tracks until we reached our block, eventually changing subjects to argue about who was a better wrestler: the Rock or Stone Cold Steve Austin. In the lobby of our building, we tried out their moves on each other, then progressed to socking each other with the large packs of circulars stacked on the floor.

Anna, a woman with long dreadlocks who lived on the third floor and whose apartment always smelled like funky seasoning, pushed a shopping cart into the building and made us snap out of our shenanigans. "Hey, hey. You chicos be careful with the roughhousing. Don't neither one of you want to break a bone. You know how much a ride in an ambulance costs?"

"Yes, Ms. Anna," we said in unison.

Gio and I huffed and puffed as we each held a pack of circulars over our head. "So what's good? You tryna sleep over tonight or what?" he said. "It's technically the end of the school year today, right?"

He made a strong point. "I need to ask my mom."

" 'I need to ask my mom,' " Gio mimicked in a whiny voice.

"Fuck you. Come with me upstairs. When she gets in, I'll—"

"Javier?" The voice was muffled from outside the lobby door, but I knew instantly who it was. The clack of the heels down the building's entranceway only provided confirmation.

"Damn, son. You fucked up," Gio said.

Mom burst through the door. "What are you doing, Javi? You're punished. You should be upstairs." She looked me up and down. "And why do you still have your book bag on? Don't tell me you didn't come straight home."

"We just went to the store." It was not my best work. I hadn't prepared. Mom was home thirty minutes earlier than she was supposed to be.

She looked at my hands. "I don't see no food, nene. Where did you go? You didn't go to the park, did you? Didn't I just tell you about the boy on the news who got his face all cut up the other day? They sliced it like a damn pumpkin on Halloween."

"Yes, Javi remembered, Sonia," Gio said, saving me. "He told me when I suggested it. Which is why we played a little bit of handball, right outside. Where it's safe. Right, Javi?"

I nodded. "Right. Exactly. We weren't at the park."

Mom eyed me.

I took a breath. Recovered. "I know I'm punished, but you keep telling me I need to stop watching TV and playing video games at home. So Gio and I were just getting some healthy activity in. Isn't that right, Gio."

Gio nodded.

Mom raised her eyebrow. "'Healthy activity.'" She opened the door. "Get your ass upstairs, pendejo, before I give you some 'healthy activity' upside your head." I sighed and walked inside. Mom looked at Gio. "Did you eat, Giovanni? Do you want food?"

Gio gave Mom that doughy smile he always gave her. Like he was in love or something. "I would love some food."

UP IN THE APARTMENT, Mom started cooking, and Gio and I went to my bedroom. He sat in the beanbag chair while I turned the radio on to Hot 97. He asked about the books on the shelves and told me to tell him about the last one I read.

"You could read them yourself," I said.

"No thanks. This way is a lot easier."

I told him about the fantasy novel I'd just finished. About a fictional world where dragons ruled over humans and inserted chips in their brains to get them to do what they wanted.

"Like *The Sims*?" Gio asked.

"Exactly."

"Interesting."

I told him that over the past weekend, Mom had taken me to Barnes & Noble, and I'd run into the writer there, sitting at a table signing copies of his books. The writer looked to be in his fifties, and had nicely styled gray hair. He seemed surprised to see me when I appeared before him, ushered over by the events coordinator, who excitedly said that a "young reader" was interested in speaking with him. "I told you someone would show up," the coordinator said.

The writer gave me a strained smile. "Well, hello, young fella," he said. "Thank you for coming out. How'd you hear about this?"

"I didn't," I said. "My mom brings me here on the weekend."

The events coordinator walked away. The writer peered at him as he left. He asked if I had a book to sign, but I'd left my copy at home. I got him to sign a napkin from the coffee shop instead, just so it felt like he was doing something. Then I hit him with the real reason I'd walked over. To ask him what I'd been wondering ever since my teachers had started to tell me in the fifth grade that I was good at telling stories, that I was good at writing, that maybe I should try writing a book one day.

"So how much money do you make?"

The writer smiled. He told me some shit about focusing on my art and characters first. But I pressed him. I remembered what Pops had always told me: *Money makes the world go round, Javier.* "But you have to make money, though, right?" Eventually, he folded, telling me he'd gotten a hundred-thousand-dollar advance for his book. He tried to explain how it was paid out over time and so on, details that I didn't care to listen to. Details I didn't bother repeating to Gio in my room.

"One hundred stacks just for one book."

I thought that seemed like a lot of money. Naturally, I imagined it in cash, in bundles, sitting around in my room the way I used to find bundles of cash wherever Pops stayed. These were my earliest literary dreams: Writing a book of my own. Having all that cash around me. Throwing it up in the air like the rappers on *106 & Park*.

"That's aight," Gio said, seemingly unimpressed. He fidgeted in my beanbag chair on the floor. "There are easier ways to make more than that and without all that work."

I was skeptical of Gio's answer. I wanted to know more. But I didn't get a chance to interrogate him because Mom burst into the room.

"Lower that porquería music," she said. "And come eat. Dinner is ready." She slammed the door on her way out.

"See what I'm saying about her?" I told Gio.

He sniffed the air. "At least she cooks for you. Good, too."

MOM HAD MADE rice and beans and chuletas. Some juice on the side. I devoured my food, trying to finish as soon as possible so Gio and I could go to his place. Where we were free to do what we wanted. But Gio ate slow, chewing with this euphoric face like he was eating filet mignon.

"This is so good, Sonia. Thank you."

"I'm so glad someone around here appreciates my cooking." She shot daggers at me, and I ignored her.

"I wish my grandma cooked for me more," Gio said.

Mom looked at him with soft eyes. "Hey, your abuela has a lot on her plate, okay? Don't forget that. I know she loves you very much."

Gio nodded.

I cleaned my plate and pushed it forward.

"So can I sleep over at Gio's tonight?"

Mom folded her arms. "And your punishment?"

"Technically, the school year is over. You said for the rest of the school year."

She smirked. "Well, technically, yo soy tu mamá, so I can do whatever I damn please. Including tell you to stay home because what you did was serious. Tú tenías a toda esa gente pensando that you're some depressed loco. Then they were asking me all this stuff about if I was ignoring you y no sé qué. Do you know you could have ended up in a foster care? Then you really would have had something to cry about."

"So that's a no?"

Mom looked at Gio. "You see what I have to deal with, Giovanni?"

"I said I was sorry already," I added.

Gio cleared his throat. "You know, Javi also told me today that he is very sorry. I think he's very embarrassed for being so disrespectful."

"Easy," Mom said. "I get it, he's your boy. But you're overdoing it now."

Gio gave me an encouraging look.

"So can I stay over?"

Mom shook her head. "Fine. But don't give Mercedes any headaches. That lady has enough to worry about."

MERCEDES OPENED the door cradling a thin cigarette between her lips. She was a small woman with a dime-sized mole below her left nostril and short hair like a boy's. She leaned in to kiss me on the cheek, and the smell of menthol filled my nose. She kissed Gio, too.

"You eat? I can give you money to go down to Kennedy Fried Chicken."

"I ate," Gio said. "Good food. Food that Sonia cooked with love."

Mercedes rolled her eyes. "Bueno. Good for you. I just finished a ten-hour shift. So here." She dug into her back pocket and gave Gio a twenty-dollar bill. Cash to buy whatever snacks he wanted, without her scrutinizing the grams of sugar on the back of the package like Mom would. He pocketed the bill like it was nothing. Some people, I thought, just don't realize the luxuries they have.

A long, thin hallway ran down the apartment, leading to the living room. Among the photos lining the wall was one that always made me stop. Gio's mom, Raquel, in front of a train station, holding Gio by the hand. He must have been eight or nine. He had that boyish smile that I hadn't seen in so long. But Raquel looked like a shadow of the woman I'd always known her to be: boisterous, loud, always moving her hips to a beat. Her cheeks were sunken. Her arms looked wasted. There was a dead look in her eyes, a cloudy haze, like perhaps she wasn't even there.

A thick black sheet hung off the archway at the end of the hallway, blocking off the living room. Gio and I pushed through and into what had become his room after Raquel died. There was an air mattress on the floor and a tangle of sheets. A television close to the mattress and a couple of video game controllers next to it. Gio's clothes and things were in blue plastic bins stacked one on top of another on the floor. Bundles of shirts and shorts were scattered in mounds.

"You're so lucky."

"Why would you say that?"

"Mom would kill me if my room looked like this."

"At least you have a room."

I picked up one of the controllers. "Never mind. I can't say shit without you saying something back, yo."

We played for a while. Eventually, Gio pulled out the crinkled bill Mercedes had given him and held it up. I could see there was something happening behind his eyes. Some machine back there working overtime. "I was thinking. Let's get drunk tonight."

"Why tonight?"

"Because we can."

"True." The logic was sound. "How we gonna get it? That'd be too hard to steal from the bodega. Also, to remind you, I'm on thin ice. You want me to have to stay home all summer?"

Gio waved the bill in his hand.

"Who will buy it for us? Papo at the counter is cool, but he ain't that cool."

Gio smiled. "I know somebody."

Outside, Gio led me past the normal bodega we shopped at and around the corner toward the one I hardly ever went to—especially at night. Even though the block was geographically so close to my own, it was not my own. It was understood by everyone that it belonged to the collection of men that hung out in front of the other bodega. As long as I'd known Gio, we'd been on the same page about these men: Stay away.

"Since when do you go here?"

Gio shrugged. "It's just another bodega. I don't see the big deal."

The men blocked the front door, laughing and cutting up the air with the jagged motions of their hands. We were neighbors of a sort, but we never spoke. First because I had been told I shouldn't speak to them, would hear Mom whisper, "Zánganos," under her breath when they'd pass by. And second because after Pops died, I became deathly afraid of gunshots breaking out at any moment and decided to stay away from people who reminded me of him. People like these guys. People with lots of time on their hands who wore nice jewelry, drove nice cars, and had loud laughs they unleashed with abandon.

From month to month, the number of men seemed to fluctuate. But you could always tell who the leader was. Just by the way he carried himself. The way everyone listened at attention when he spoke. The leaders changed depending on the year. Some got locked up; some saw worse fates. The leader on this night, though, I knew, had been installed for some time. I'd seen him my whole childhood. Watched him evolve from an older kid with a cool bike, to a teen who sat on a lawn chair on the block, wore nice clothes, and tongued down girls, to a man who was to be feared. But I'd never spoken to him. Never gotten close enough to even know his name.

"That's Manny," Gio said as we approached. "He's cool."

"He's cool? Since when?"

I had many questions. How had Gio gotten this guy's name? When had they spoken? But I didn't get a chance to ask. Gio pushed me hard in the chest, nearly knocking me down, and marched over. He gave Manny a wide smile that I realized I hadn't seen in a long time. A smile I could only remember from times when we were real, real little. Like when his mom and my mom took us on a sweaty-ass bus trip out to Six Flags one summer day and we rode the roller coasters over and over.

Manny looked over at me. "I know you. Schoolboy."

"Schoolboy?"

There were some snickers in the circle that had now formed around us.

"That's my name for you," Manny said. "I always see you with your fine-ass mom. And always carrying that big old book bag." A couple of the men laughed like this was the funniest thing they'd ever heard.

"It's just a normal book bag with books."

Gio shot me a look, like I'd said something out of turn. "It's kind of a big bag."

"What?"

"Forget it, Javi. It's just a joke." Gio turned to Manny. "We need some help."

"What's up, little G."

Little G, I thought. Why did Gio get a cooler name? Why had he gotten a name to begin with?

Gio explained the situation, our intended goal for the night. But before he could finish, Manny stopped him. "Say less." He pulled open the door of the bodega, releasing a cascade of bachata. He stuck his head inside and said something over the music. Within a minute, a lanky dude with a sharp fade and a rope chain came out with two 40s. Manny sucked his teeth. "Come on, son. They need bags to go with them. They kids, dumbass." He shook his head, disappointed. "Think. What did I tell you about thinking?"

The dude looked annoyed, and reminded me of Pops's employees, the ragtag group that was always around him. How often when he was yelling at them about something, I could tell that they didn't really want to hear it. I could tell that behind their shades or their glassy eyes, they were saying something about him, cursing him out. Maybe even, I thought after his murder, plotting on him.

The dude went back in for our bags. Before I knew it, Gio and I were strolling back to the building with the beers.

"What was that about?"

"What? Getting free beers? How about a thank-you."

"Since when have you been chilling with 'Manny'?"

Gio shrugged. "I don't know. I see him around sometimes when I go out at night to the bodega and shit. He's cool. You'd know if your bitch ass was even allowed out past sundown."

"Shut up."

We crept back into Mercedes's apartment. Through the gap at the bottom of the door to her room, I could see the flicker of light from her television and smell her cigarettes. Gio barged into the living room and put the beers on the floor like the apartment was his. Immediately, he started playing music and opening his can.

"Shouldn't we wait a bit? What if your grandma comes out?"

Gio laughed. "She ain't coming out. Those novelas are watching her right now. She'll be asleep till work in the morning. Besides, she don't care."

I tried to imagine the same scene at my house. I'd never drunk anything there aside from at family parties, when my titi Nilda would sneak me half a beer every now and then when Mom wasn't looking. She'd wink and say, "You're my favorite nephew" even though I was her only nephew.

Gio handed me my beer. I cracked it and heard the crisp hiss. I thought about how at those family parties, there would always be lots of calls for saluds as everyone raised their glass to something to praise, something to drink to, as if they were even looking for a good reason.

"What are we drinking to?" I asked, raising my beer toward Gio.

But he was already feverishly sipping his, the liquid running down the side of his mouth.

Gio killed the entire 40 in what seemed like seconds. I struggled. The beer kept making me burp. By the time Gio slammed his can on the ground, I already felt woozy and had trouble focusing on the television screen. Gio pressed pause on the game and lay back on his air mattress. He groaned and stared up at the ceiling.

"You good?"

"We should get more, right? Manny will get us more if we want. He's cool, isn't he?"

"Seems like a run-of-the-mill thug to me. I also didn't appreciate that 'Schoolboy' shit."

"He's not. He's cool. He's a self-made man."

"A self-made man? He's a fucking drug dealer. And, what, in a gang, right? I'm assuming those guys aren't just his best buddies from day care."

"He's a businessman. You see how he dresses. He got a nice car. Jewelry. Girls. What's wrong with that?"

"My Pops had shit like that, too. And you see how he ended up."

"He ain't your Pops," Gio said.

"Sorry. I didn't realize you were his number one fan."

Gio sat up on the mattress. "Fuck you. Anyway. We getting more beer or what?"

I shook my can, sloshing around the remainder. "I'm good."

"Nah. We should get more."

"I think we're good."

"I think you're a bitch," he said, but not in a playful way.

"What's your problem?"

Gio patted his bed for the remote. "Nothing, man." He changed the channel to 59. Then he grabbed my beer and chugged it, too.

A white woman with razor-straight hair appeared on the screen.

Her body was bare apart from a small fur coat that covered her from the bottom half of her breasts to her thighs. The entire screen was engulfed by ice. The music in the background sounded like the *Sonic the Hedgehog* theme song. The woman looked around, lost. The camera panned out. A white man on the left side of the screen, unseen by the woman, walked in her direction. He was built like a sturdy house in Riverdale, with bulging forearms and calves. Long dirty-blond hair tickled the small of his back.

"He looks like Tarzan on steroids."

Gio didn't laugh.

The man and the woman looked at each other. Their gaze was hungry. The man stroked the woman's face and ran his fingers through her hair. She took in long, sensual breaths and moaned. As the man's hand moved from the woman's hair to her arms and down to her breasts, my mouth dried up. With one wild, easy motion he threw off her fur coat and unveiled large breasts that he palmed like they were basketballs.

"They gonna?"

"Just watch, will you."

The man traced his lips down from the woman's cheeks to her neck. He circled her dark nipples with his tongue like he was trying to tie a knot. The woman moaned louder. Gio lowered the volume. The man looked up, and the camera focused on his piercing eyes for a moment. He grabbed a handful of the woman and lifted her off the ground, laying her down on a slab of ice as tall as my desk at school. His lips roved to her belly button. He looked up into her eyes, which blinked magnificently slow. Then he shoved his face between her legs. The woman moaned and tightened her limbs.

I felt like an ember. The stirring in my cargo shorts grew. The man lifted his head from between the woman's legs and removed the cloth shorts he wore. It was the first time I'd ever seen what

I'd heard all the boys talk about in school. The words I'd even said myself though I did not know what they meant. *Piping, smashing, hitting, fucking.* The words sounded violent, but the action on the screen seemed even more so. The woman shifted to a seizure-like noise. Her eyes bulged. I wondered if I'd be able to do the same thing to a woman.

"You get to just watch this every day? You really have the life."

I had stopped paying attention to Gio's presence. I was so lost in everything else. But when I didn't get a response, I looked over to find him staring past the screen.

"The life," he repeated. He was dead-eyed. Drunk. He chuckled to himself. He lifted the empty beer can up in the sky like he finally had something to say salud about.

I'd always thought his mom had died in a freak accident in her bathtub. Something crazy, bizarre, that caused her to suddenly drown. It seems obviously suspicious now, but being so young, I didn't question it. I went to the funeral, and I watched Gio cry over the casket in a way that left an imprint on my mind.

"You know, my mom didn't die by accident, Javi," Gio said.

"Your mom? What do you mean? Somebody killed her?"

"No. It was on purpose."

"What do you mean, 'on purpose'?"

"She wanted to die. Don't you get it? She didn't want to be here no more."

I sat there confused, watching Gio's face become graver than I'd seen it in a long time. I could see him fighting to hold back tears, until one came. One that he wiped away quickly. Then it hit me. I finally understood.

Gio turned off the television. "I'll get the sleeping bag out for you."

"Okay." I wanted to say more. But I couldn't.

I WOKE UP EARLY the next morning. The apartment was silent. I heard Papo raise the security gate on the bodega, the loud crash it made when it reached the awning. I gathered my things, including the beer cans. I stared at Gio, sprawled on his mattress, hugging his pillow. I'd known him my whole life, but I felt like I was seeing him for the first time.

I threw the cans down the trash chute and walked over to the other side of the building. I rang the doorbell to our apartment. Mom answered, still in her pajamas and looking skeptical.

"Why are you here so early?"

I hugged her tight.

"Are you okay?"

"Yes," I said. "I just want to hug you." She hugged me back. Then she pushed me away and looked at me serious for a moment.

"You're acting weird. If the cops come knocking, just know that I'm going to kick your ass."

"They won't," I said. "They won't."

"Good." She brushed my hair to the side with her hands and led me inside the apartment. "You want pancakes?"

Three

I KNOW WHAT you're thinking: *Okay, so maybe you did actually have some rough shit happen to you and your friend. But what do we care? What you did is still wrong. You're still an asshole. When did that start?* As my Pops always used to say whenever I asked him for McDonald's on his money runs, espérate.

How I came to be did not involve some single light-switch moment. Despite what everyone likes to think—despite what Twitter likes to think—change doesn't happen that easy. In my case, a big chunk of my origin story can be traced back to Mr. Martin.

I first met him at the beginning of my senior year. My school had just gotten a grant to partner with Groverdale High School in Riverdale, the elite private school that cost somewhere around fifty thousand dollars a year. Once a week, they sent one of their guidance counselors to our school in the South Bronx to advise seniors in the honors class in an attempt to save us from what everyone expected our course in life to be: a couple of kids, a criminal record, and a menial job somewhere.

I was one of the lucky few to be blessed by Mr. Martin's presence. I used to be in the bottom class, where teachers paid me no mind because they assumed I was brain-dead just like they figured everyone else was. It was only after I did what I thought were the basics—completed my homework on time, did reasonably well on tests, and had a pulse in class—that I was moved up to the honors class.

The honors class moved at a speed I didn't know school was capable of operating at. Homework was more involved. There were projects. Presentations. Field trips. Guest speakers. Instead of being multiple-choice, the questions on tests were open-ended and required written responses. Each test, it seemed, was set up to actually prove whether I knew what I was doing instead of whether I was good at cramming. I started studying daily just to stay on top of things, making index cards, highlighting passages in books, researching. It took me the first half of my junior year and a couple of concerning report cards until I hit my stride. I even went to my former English teacher, Ms. Rivas, at one point, telling her she'd made a mistake by pushing for me to get moved up. "You need to be around better-quality students," she told me. I was flattered. Gio was offended. "I'll show her quality," he said after I told him, grabbing his balls. But Ms. Rivas was right. By the end of that year, I had better grades than I'd had the two years before.

It was a development that likely changed everything. For my first session with Mr. Martin, I was directed to a small office on the third floor that everyone had previously thought was a janitor's closet. On my way, I passed an old classmate named Victor, who asked me about Gio—as did everyone else who noticed his absence in our senior year. They all knew that for the three years before that we were essentially attached at the hip.

"Where is that fool?"

I broke the news to him, just like I'd broken the news to the rest: He'd dropped out. He'd taken up selling drugs for Manny full-time.

"Dope, weight?"

"Not sure," I said. "But he seems happy. And he's making money."

If it were someone other than Victor, someone I was close enough with to confide in, someone like Gio, I would have shared my true thoughts: My best friend was headed down a destructive path. A path I knew well enough, and knew only led to one of two places. I'd have shared that I thought Gio was better than that. That I *knew* he was better than that. That I wished he hadn't come to see Manny as someone to emulate. Of course, I'd already said all this to Gio. I'd pleaded with him one afternoon that summer when Manny took us to Orchard Beach. I noticed Gio taking orders like a miniature soldier, noticed his eyes sparkle at Manny's chain and his ride. But Gio told me to mind my own business. "Let me live my life, and I'll let you live yours," he said as we bobbed in the dirty water.

Victor stabbed the side of his cheek with his tongue. He nodded like he thought Gio's choice was a good idea, like maybe he should have thought of that, too.

When I opened the door to Mr. Martin's office, I was greeted by university posters on the walls. The campuses boasted lush grass, buildings that looked like they used to house Roman dudes with togas back in the day, and huge, ornate libraries without a masturbating homeless person in sight. Mr. Martin looked up with a harried expression, like he had been dwelling on a deep problem and was startled by my presence.

"Javier, right? Come in, please."

The bookshelf behind him was full of SAT prep books. I recognized the yellow one that Ms. Rivas had bought for me at the end of the previous school year, pleading with me to study and take practice exams to boost my score. I tried to take one in the library one weekend when I was off work from my summer job, but I gave up halfway. I couldn't stomach staring at a book while everyone else was outside strutting the block in their flyest summer gear and eating ices.

Mr. Martin flipped to a clean page on a legal pad and wrote my name. He asked what schools I planned on applying to.

All the city schools, I told him.

"Solid safety choices." He waited for more.

"That's it."

"I see."

Before I met Mr. Martin, I hadn't thought much about college. It was the next step in the process. The next grade level. There was no doubt I would go, but I'd never thought about going anywhere that looked like the places in those posters on the wall above his head. I figured I would end up somewhere local. Take a job in the city afterward. Mess with my writing on the side until it eventually got noticed by the right people and I got paid like that writer I'd met at Barnes & Noble.

Mr. Martin's brow furrowed. His shirtsleeves were rolled up to his bony elbows. His tie was loose. That he wore a tie at all stood out and made me wonder if that was how things went in Riverdale. "Javier, you have really good grades. It's also a good sign to the admissions committee that you were moved up to the honors class and that you've responded so well. Not to mention that your teachers speak very highly of you and the progress you've made.

"Your SAT scores could be higher, though," he said. "You're taking the test again, right?"

"I've taken it twice."

"You really should take it again."

"That's what everybody keeps saying. But I ain't doing it."

Mr. Martin was now deep in thought. I decided that he looked too young to be a guidance counselor. I decided that on the bench of counselors at Groverdale, he was probably near the end. I decided that he was like twenty-seven, that he drank craft beer in Brooklyn when school was over. He knew a few Jay-Z songs, could quote Plato and Tolstoy, and rode a skinny bike.

"What kind of college experience do you want?"

"Experience? I don't know. I want to study writing, get a day job, and become a famous writer who makes bank one day."

Mr. Martin sat up, seemingly shocked that I had ambitions. "A writer? How interesting."

I smiled. It was the same reaction I'd gotten from the white people at the summer job I'd worked at in Manhattan, delivering packages for an advertising firm. Titi Nilda cleaned their offices at night and hooked me up. The widened eyes of my coworkers conveyed the same message as Mr. Martin's: *Oh, you're one of those* smart *brown boys.*

"I don't really care about where I go to school all that much. Or where I get a job. I just need to get my degree and get going."

It sounds naive, but this is how I thought. I knew little to nothing about the kind of writer I wanted to be or how to get there. I didn't know, for example, if I wanted to be a poet, or a journalist, or a novelist. I just knew I wanted to write books and have a lot of people read them and get a lot of attention for them and have a lot of people think I was smart and, hopefully, get some girls who liked nerds to sleep with me. College was a means to an end. I'd study writing, learn some stuff, write my masterpiece at night, and shoot off into the stars once I got my big break.

"College is more than just the next step," Mr. Martin said. "It's a place of discovery. A place to challenge yourself. It will probably be the best four years of your life." He stared off into the distance for a bit, then returned to me with a deep sigh. "I really think you should be applying to more prestigious schools, Javier."

"What do you mean? Aren't the schools on my list good? That's what all the teachers told us."

"They're fine, Javier. But they're not very selective. At the schools I'm talking about, you'll be among top-tier peers. You'll be challenged in ways you can't even imagine." He pointed at my list. "These are easier schools. You can stroll into them, kick back, and get a degree without really trying all that hard."

"That don't sound too bad."

Mr. Martin smirked. "Sure, I admit, that sounds nice. But in the long run, it won't pay off. Going to a better school will lead to better opportunities, better networks to take advantage of." He looked at me and seemed to be able to tell he was losing my interest, quickly. "You want to be a writer, right? Well, usually, great writers come from great schools. They grow there, they learn, they study with the best professors. And when they show up for a job, they impress people. Javier, you should want to go to a school that when you say the name of it, people pay attention. That's how you get ahead."

He rifled through a filing cabinet and dropped a brochure for a school named Donlon University in front of me. On the cover was a building with tall white columns and short, broad steps. Students lounged on blankets on a great big lawn. In the distance was a Gothic clock tower. Beyond that, trees with fall leaves, a glimmering lake.

"Where is it?"

"Upstate New York. Only a four-hour bus ride away."

I looked at the grass, the students, and the scenic views. It looked *too* peaceful. Boring, even. Would there be the sorts of things I enjoyed? Concert venues, movie theaters, late-night train rides with entertaining crackheads? "I don't know. This doesn't seem like my kind of place."

Mr. Martin leaned forward. "Why? Because you think you don't *belong* there?"

I could tell he wanted me to say yes. So I did. But I swear it was only because I thought it might speed up the meeting. I was still naive to the power of telling people, especially white people, what they really wanted to hear.

Mr. Martin seemed so pleased. "This is why I'm here," he said, more to himself than to anyone else. "This right here." He pounded his table. "I understand why the world might make you feel that way. I can only imagine what it's like for someone like you to go through life. But it is my job—my *privilege,* actually—to tell you that what you're thinking isn't true, Javier. The truth is that you can go to college wherever you'd like, even to the best schools our nation has to offer. And you know what else is true? Those schools would be lucky to have a student like you on their campus, Javier. In fact, those schools *need* students like you. Desperately."

Mr. Martin waited, as if he expected me to clap my hands or something. Silence fell over the small room. I listened to the sound of an ambulance flying by, siren wailing. When it was out of earshot, I scratched the side of my face. "That school looks expensive, too," I added, trying to poke another hole in his plan. "I probably couldn't afford that. I think a city school is probably just fine."

"This school is extremely expensive, actually," Mr. Martin said, thumbing the brochure. "Obscenely expensive. But for a student like *you,* help is available. With your grades and even with your middling SAT scores, you have a shot. It all boils down to the essay. Which is great for you, Mr. Writer. All you have to do is nail that essay and you can win over the admissions committee."

The phrase "admissions committee" made me think of a tribunal of people wearing burgundy cloaks and sitting in a cave before a fire. I imagined them reading applications, meditating on them, murmuring. Then flipping their thumbs up or down and tossing rejected applications into the flames.

"Do you have the sheet?" Mr. Martin asked. I handed him the worksheet I had been given ahead of this meeting to brainstorm college essay topics. We were supposed to write short summaries of three potential topics, but I'd only come up with one that I figured was good enough. It was about working in Manhattan over the summer making deliveries for the advertising firm. I wrote about how the job had taken me to other parts of the city I'd never seen before to personally deliver corny-ass pens, hats, and T-shirts. I had been sent to Wall Street, the South Street Seaport, the Village, the Upper East Side—neighborhoods so clean and organized and full of so many people walking around looking like they had somewhere to be that it would blow my mind that they were only a thirty-minute subway ride from where I lived. I wrote about how these mini adventures "expanded my mind." I didn't really know what that phrase meant, but it sounded like something that belonged in a college essay.

"You're concerned with escape," Mr. Martin said, after reading the summary. He scribbled on his notepad. "Let's explore. There is probably something there that is more compelling."

So this is what a real guidance counselor is like, I thought. Up until then, I'd only had the briefest of encounters with the counselors who actually worked for my school. They were always tied up with more important drama concerning girls who'd gotten pregnant, boys who'd brought knives to school, and the kids who everyone knew had some real mental problems because the way they acted out in class wasn't even funny.

"What do you think about your neighborhood?" Mr. Martin asked.

"I don't know. It's where I live."

"Yes. But how does it make you feel? Or, rather, how do *you* feel about your neighborhood?"

"Isn't that the same question?"

"Indulge me."

I thought about telling him about working in Manhattan over the summer a little more. Zeroing in on the differences I noticed. Like the fact that everyone in Manhattan seemed to wear clothes that looked tailored and pressed. That when they got on the train drunk, they talked about Broadway musicals and plays instead of what gang sets they repped. It all seemed so foreign compared to what I saw on my block, in my world. The dichotomy was already beginning to spark thoughts I'd never had before, vague dreams about what my future could look like, but I wasn't ready to explore them yet. And especially not with someone I'd just met.

"My neighborhood is fine," I said. "Very average."

He clicked the button on his pen. "Is it dangerous?"

I thought about a day back in August, when I was coming home from a supermarket run Mom had demanded of me. I was carrying five heavy bags and was only half a block from the entrance of my building when I had to stop because I saw a man in a tank top being circled by two other men like sharks. I thought maybe they were playing and almost walked by, until the man on his own whipped out a switchblade. I wasn't afraid. I was annoyed because the bags were so heavy with cans of beans and corned beef. I stood there, arms straining, and waited. The man in the tank top made a few swipes in the air, but not like he really wanted to stab anyone, maybe just to scare them away. I put the bags down. Eventually the other two men spit in his direction and left him alone. When the man put the knife back in his pocket, I finally walked by. When I got home, I put the groceries away and didn't even think of mentioning to Mom what had happened.

"Sometimes my neighborhood is dangerous. But it could be worse."

Mr. Martin laid his pen on the pad and ran a hand through his messy hair. "Javier, you're a smart kid. I'm just going to be up-front with you. You have to understand what these committee people are looking for from applicants like yourself. If you give them what they're looking for, you could go somewhere like Donlon—for free."

I perked up. "What do you mean, free? Like, free, free?"

"Free, free."

"Nah. You lying."

"I'm not. These schools have scholarships. Particularly for poor, underserved minority students. If you come from certain backgrounds, they also, how should I say this . . . *value* some aspects of your application over other parts."

"What does that mean?"

"It means they take things into account besides just your SAT scores or your grades being perfect like those of everyone else who applies there. If you're from a certain demographic background, come from a tough place, or maybe survived some difficult circumstances, and you have good enough grades, you have a real chance."

This sounded a whole lot better than what I'd been told up to that point: that colleges only cared about SAT scores and I didn't have high enough ones to bother worrying about going anywhere but the schools in my own backyard. The only problem with what Mr. Martin was saying was that none of the words he'd used to describe me lined up with the words I would have used. *Poor*? *Underserved*? *From a tough place*? As much as I liked attention and people feeling bad for me about my Pops and stuff like that, I had never thought of myself in those terms. Gio had a tough background. Naomi, a girl I'd dated for a month my sophomore year, who'd told me about the horrors of foster care, had a tough background. Shit, even Chris, a Chinese kid in my honors class who worked eight hours a day *after* school at his parents' restaurant in the hood, had it worse than me. I knew I was poor—certainly poorer than the people I worked around in Manhattan, who seemed to have unlimited money to spend on shit—but the actual word *poor* was something I associated with the people in commercials with flies in their face. My neighborhood wasn't as nice as the Upper East Side, yeah. But I had a big apartment. My own room. Food. Decently fly clothes. A good mom, as Gio was always saying, even if she could be annoying. A free MetroCard. Life wasn't all that bad.

Mr. Martin looked at his watch. "We don't have much time left." He pushed a fresh worksheet my way. "Just please give this another go."

"So I have to write what?" I asked. "How 'poor' I am or something?"

Mr. Martin eyed the closed door. "No. No. I didn't say that. Right? I didn't say that?"

I shrugged. "Kinda sounds like what you're saying."

"Well, that's not what I'm saying. I know this might seem odd. And I am in no way saying you need to, like, *look* for pity. You know? What I am saying is that, for someone like you, writing about any challenges you've had, things that you've overcome, helps. It helps *a lot*."

"Okay. But what if I'm not actually that poor?"

Mr. Martin smiled again. But this time, like I was a cute toddler trying to say his first words. "Why don't we do this? Get a piece of paper at home and make a list of some obstacles in your life that you've had to overcome. Challenges. Be as specific to you and your family as possible. Write as much as you can about each thing on the list, and be as vivid as you can. Bring that in for our next meeting, and we'll work off of it. Deal?"

ON THE BUS RIDE HOME, I thought about what "challenges" I had faced in my life. It was an odd exercise. I'd looked for sympathy after Pops died, but that was to get out of things, and to get the attention I wanted. Through high school, I'd mostly dropped that gambit because I quickly realized that the people whose attention I suddenly wanted most—girls—did not react how I'd hoped when I talked about my Pops. Which is to say, they did not find me attractive because of my trauma but rather odd, lonely, sad, and unfuckable.

But even through that period just after Pops died, it didn't feel like a "challenge" to me. It was something bad that had happened in a world where I already knew that a lot of bad things happened. Where worse things happened. And besides, I knew, and had always known, in my heart of hearts, that someone like Pops kinda had it coming.

The assignment before me felt different. It entailed commodifying all the shit I'd been through to see if it was worth anything to some committee hundreds of miles away. It was a new exercise that would soon become as normal to me as breathing. But as a naive high school student, I was simply intrigued by Mr. Martin's words, by the opportunity he was selling me on. Prestigious sounded good. Free sounded even better.

I started my list with the obvious: dead Pops. But then I thought,

Yeah, so? You know how many people I know who have no dad? I moved on. Poor. But poor*ish,* really. The lights had never gone out in our apartment. Although we sometimes ate the same dinner a couple of times a week, there was never a time when dinner wasn't served. We'd never spent a night in a shelter or on the streets. Okay, the rent. Yeah, Mom was often late with it, drawing the ire of our Albanian landlord. But it always got paid—eventually—and it never got bad enough that we had one of those embarrassing eviction notices taped to the front of our door.

The more I thought about Mr. Martin's question, the more I thought about Gio. About that night we'd stayed up late and he'd told me the real story about his mom. That look in his eyes. The pain I'd never before realized was there, under the surface. Dealing with that? Now, *that* was a challenge. I thought it was just too bad Gio had zero interest in going to college. Anytime I'd ask him about it, he'd say a version of the same thing: "Why would I willingly sign up for more school, and pay for it? That's some sucka shit."

When Mom got home from work that day, I decided to pick her brain as she peeled off her flats and rubbed her feet.

"I met with the new guidance counselor today. To talk about college."

"Did he tell you that it is dumb to study English in college because you already speak English?"

"No. He did not."

"He sounds like a bad counselor already."

"He said I can get into a really good school. A top one. The kind of school that can impress people and get me a fancy job."

Mom looked at me like I was trying to sell her a glow-in-the-dark yo-yo on the D train.

"For free," I added.

She ran her fingers between her toes, grimacing. "And the catch? Nothing in life is free, Javi."

"He said it all depends on my essay. If I write a good one, I'm straight."

Mom rubbed her eyes. I could tell she was only half listening. She was probably thinking about dinner. About what she could throw together from what was in our cabinets with the least amount of effort. "Well, your teachers do say you're a good writer. Even though I don't know how you expect to pay bills doing that. You should study something that pays money. Like engineering. Or medicine. Don't you want to be a doctor? They make a lot of money at—"

"I'm not gonna be a doctor, Ma. I'm going to be a writer."

Mom rolled her eyes. We'd had this discussion many times already.

"You know, if I would have known that all those books I bought you would lead to this, I would have just let you play video games."

"I tried to tell you. But now it's too late."

"Oh, shut up."

"Anyway, the thing about this getting-into-college-free business: I need to write about how poor I am so it looks good to the 'committee.' The guidance counselor basically was trying to say that if I make myself sound really poor, they'll let me go to these fancy schools for free." I pulled a notebook out of my book bag. "I need ideas. He said I could use stuff from my family."

Mom twisted her face in disgust. "We're not poor, Javi. *You're* not poor."

"Yeah, I know. But I mean we're not, like, rich either. And you always talk about how your childhood was bad."

"My childhood was not bad. I had lemon trees in my backyard.

I rode horses and went to the beach. I went out dancing. My childhood was incredible."

"I mean, yeah, but sometimes you also tell these stories about walking, like, miles to school, or about hurricanes blowing everything down, or about your grandpa who was a drunk and hit your grandma in front of you all the time, and those stories sound *pretty—*"

Mom stood up. "Do you have clothes to wear every day, Javi?"

"Yes."

"Do you have a bed with clean sheets to sleep in at night?"

I stared at her, wondering if she really wanted me to continue.

"Well? Answer me."

"Yes, Ma."

"Tá bien. Then drop this crap. We ain't on some handout line. I work for everything we have, and we are doing *just* fine."

I clicked my pen a few times. "Okay. I don't have to write about being poor. But if you don't wanna pay for college, then I'm gonna have to write about some obstacle or challenge, according to this guy."

Mom laughed. "Qué challenge? You grew up with everything, Javi. You want to talk about challenges? Go interview your abuela. She'll tell you how she used to sleep on a dirt floor in Puerto Rico. But, oh, of course, you'll have to call her first. Which you never do. And which you'll regret the day that she dies."

"That right there," I said. "Grandma on a dirt floor." I started to write. Mom slapped the pen out of my hand.

"Do you know your abuela? She'd die if you thought of her as some poor, defenseless thing. She's a warrior. She never begged nobody for nothing. Write that."

I sighed. "Never mind."

"Yeah. Exactly. Never mind."

Mom carried her shoes to her closet down the hall. She stopped on the way to smash a cockroach crawling up the wall with her bare hand.

" 'Challenge,' " she muttered. "Unbelievable."

BEFORE MY NEXT MEETING with Mr. Martin, I scrolled through the Donlon University website. On my worksheet, I mentioned a few professors I'd like to learn from, classes I'd like to take, and clubs I'd like to join. What I had seemed decent. It showed that I had done my research on the school. But Mr. Martin was still not impressed.

"This is good for the end of your essay," he said. "We still need something to grab them. Something to separate you from the pack. There will be thousands of students who are also"—he mimed quotes—" 'looking forward to new doors of opportunity.' "

"Listen, I know you want me to write about being poor and stuff, but that was too hard."

"Again, that's not what I said, but continue."

"Whatever. I asked my mom for help, and she got mad at me. She said her life on the island wasn't all that bad, and that—"

Mr. Martin looked at me quizzically. "Island. Where is your mom from?"

"Puerto Rico."

"Puerto Rico. So she immigrated here, correct? Did she happen to come here on a boat or something harrowing like that?"

"Seriously?"

"Sorry if I'm mistaken."

"No, man. Puerto Rico is basically a colony. She came on a plane."

"Right, of course." Mr. Martin nodded, disappointed. "And your dad? What did he say about the assignment?"

"Nothing. He's dead."

Even years after Pops's shooting, it still stung to tell people about it. It still made me think about him lying there in the plaza twitching in a pool of blood. It still made me wonder what was running through his mind in those final moments as the man raised the gun, as he stared down the barrel. Was he scared?

Mr. Martin sat up as if he'd been shocked by a bolt. "I'm sorry to hear that." He looked around. "If you don't mind my asking—"

"How he died?"

He nodded, eager.

"He got shot. Right in front of me. I was a kid."

Mr. Martin blew out the air in his mouth. He sat back for a moment. I expected him to say that was sad, or tough. Expected him to maybe tear up because he seemed kind of like a softy. At the very least, I expected him to say, "My condolences," which is what most people said to me after Pops died—as if that meant anything or would bring him back.

"That is some great material to work with, Javier."

"What?"

"You're a first-gen student, son of a single mom who is, like, kind of an immigrant, and on top of all that, you're a witness to your father's tragic murder. I mean." He pushed his glasses up the bridge of his nose. "You need to emphasize *all* of this. The sacrifices your mom made for you. What it was like watching your dad die before your eyes. What it was like growing up without him. All that. That will blow the committee away. It blows me away."

"I'm still not sure what I'm supposed to write, though. What, a timeline of my life?"

"Just get down as many details as you can. Take your time. When we meet next week, we'll go from there. I just know you'll come up with something great."

LOOKING BACK, I probably would have come up with something good. Not great. But good enough. I probably would have done it secretly, too, not telling Mom, and certainly not telling Gio, who I already knew would likely disapprove, would likely tell me I hadn't learned my lesson from middle school. Would this effort have still put me on the same trajectory I ended up on? Would the currency of my life experiences up to that point have been enough to buy me the right entrance ticket? I'll never know. Because as luck would have it, my riches—by which I mean my material—were already starting to grow.

Four

AFTER GIO DROPPED OUT of school, I started buying a copy of the *Daily News* or the *New York Post* each morning. The stories I read felt useful to my education as a writer. They also made up for the silence that accompanied me on the bus ride now instead of Gio.

To decide between the two papers, I chose whichever cover seemed more dramatic. The catchier headline. The picture that made you want to know more. You could say that it was my first real education in clickbait. My first experience understanding what kind of writing, what kind of stories, attracted the most eyeballs and how to replicate it.

The *Post* won me over most days. But on this morning, almost a week after my meeting with Mr. Martin, the cover of the *Daily News* stood out. The story was about a drug raid that had been pulled off in the Bronx, which wasn't all that special. What was special, according to the story, was that this particular drug raid was historic. It had resulted in the arrest of over a hundred people. A "Mafia" operating right under the nose of the law.

Mafia stories intrigued me. Reading about what people

got away with, reading about their ingenuity in making money in a system all their own made me think about Pops and see his ventures in a new light. See him not as some lowly drug dealer but as a businessman, as a start-up founder.

STING WASHES STREETS OF GUN-TOTING GHETTO 'MAFIA'

On Sunday afternoon, a citywide drug sting resulted in the arrest of over 100 people in the Bronx. The suspects are all alleged to have been part of smaller drug-trafficking cliques with intricate networks tying them to large suppliers outside of the country. Police said the suspects, ranging in age from 16 to 24, were known to terrorize neighborhoods, apartment buildings and public housing with violence and intimidation. In addition to the large quantities of drugs they were allegedly moving through younger drug runners all across the city, these thugs have also been linked to at least 12 murders over a two-year period, including those of two innocent bystanders.

I paid the quarter for the paper and stood at the bus stop. I turned to the full spread of the story. The large collage of young men being led out of apartment buildings and housing projects in shiny cuffs. Stretched-out shirts covered many of their faces, exposing their bellies. Most wore basketball shorts or sweatpants, as if they'd just been rousted out of bed.

The bus arrived. I got on and continued reading. A picture in the far-right corner of the page caught my eye. I looked closer because of the familiar green building awning. I looked at the four men being led out and recognized them as men who'd been at Gio's recent birthday party—the last time I'd seen him. I saw that one of them was Manny. Then I saw it: Gio's face.

EVER SINCE THE SUMMER of that year, when Gio told me that he would be dropping out and working with Manny full-time, the two of us had stopped seeing each other as often as we had since, basically, we were born.

It was only natural. Our interests had diverged. I was thinking about getting a decent score on my SATs, getting into college, how to launch a writing career. Gio was thinking, it seemed, about money, jewelry, throwback jerseys, and the Honda Civic he'd recently bought and pimped out with illegal tints and a thunderous sound system.

After he left school and moved in with Manny a few blocks away, we traded lazy texts every few weeks because we felt like we had to. We made featherweight plans to chill that we followed through on 10 percent of the time. Whenever we did see each other, Gio seemed put off by my life updates. "Why you always talking about school?" Even when I told him about my nascent plans to be a famous writer and the research I'd done into the seven-figure book and movie deals others had signed, he always found a way to divert attention back to his exploits. "Chump change. I bet me and my boys become millionaires long before you ever will. And we'll have more fun doing it."

Despite the fraying ties between us, when Gio invited me to his birthday party that fall, I knew I had to make an appearance for old times' sake.

When I got to his new building, I heard the thump of the music from the staircase. Outside Gio's door on the third floor, a guy sweet-talked a girl in the hall. She giggled while he sidled up close. She pretended to push him away. A woman in hair rollers walked down the staircase with an empty shopping cart and ice-grilled me—like I had some control over what was happening. I rang the doorbell three times before the guy in the hall, who'd progressed to making out with the girl, looked up and said, "It's open, yo," before sticking his tongue back down her throat.

Hordes of people crowded around the kitchen counter inside. The sink and stove were covered with glass bottles of liquor and plastic jugs of juice. I slinked by two girls huddled around yet another man I didn't recognize who was frantically trying to spark a blunt as the girls rolled their eyes. In the living room, two speakers taller than me were set up near the television. People were grinding in the darkness, staining the walls with their jeans. Nobody looked familiar. For a minute, I wondered if I'd walked into the wrong apartment. Then I saw Gio, sitting on the couch with his arm wrapped around a girl.

From where I stood, I could hear him, even over the loud music, laughing at something someone had said. The laugh sounded forced. Fake. That's how everything sounded to me when he tried to describe the upsides of his new life: *protection, cash, loyalty, brotherhood.* Empty words that were almost certainly force-fed to him by Manny.

I pushed past the crowd and tapped Gio on the shoulder. His eyes lit up in a way that made me feel bad—almost as if he had expected me to bail. "Happy birthday," I said, handing him a card.

He shook it. "How much money you give me? I bet nothing, you cheap fuck."

"It looks like you've probably gotten plenty of gifts." I scanned the room. "Who are all these people?"

Gio smiled and stood. "My brothers. My people." He clapped me on the back. "You're my brother, too. Thanks for coming." He motioned to the girl on the couch. Her hair was razor straight, and her breasts were smashed together like people on a train fleeing the Bronx after a Yankees game. "Jessenia," he said, "this is my boy, Javi."

She flashed me a fake smile and went back to bobbing slowly to the music.

I leaned in to whisper, "Is that your girlfriend?"

Gio laughed. Bellowed. "No." He pointed me to the kitchen. "Get a drink. Let me know if you wanna smoke. I'll roll you a blunt myself."

Near the kitchen counter, I saw Manny surrounded by a few men. Manny held the chain around one man's neck with two fingers and struggled to get words out through his resounding laughter. "What is this? An anklet?"

Everyone laughed with him. I remembered Pops. How he commanded attention, laughter, even if it was forced. Manny had gone from being the mysterious older guy Gio talked about in school to the man who'd replaced his absent father. Along the way, Manny and I had managed to establish a begrudging friendship, despite his continued reservations about the size of my book bag, my knowledge of large words, and my intention to become a writer, which he discovered one day when Gio and I were smoking a blunt in his car and said: "So you want to do homework . . . forever?" When he saw me, Manny yelled: "Schoolboy!" He gave me a pound. "You dropped the books to bless us with your presence. How nice of you."

"I am amicable with both the illiterate and literate alike."

Manny repeated the word *amicable* to himself. "Listen up, fellas," he said to the men gathered around. "See this big-word-using motherfucker right here? He's our very own BX Einstein, you understand? One day he's gonna write some famous book and shit. We ain't gonna read it. But it's aight. 'Cause he's probably gonna fuck around and become president and then we'll have this party in the White House with white butlers lighting blunts for us."

I felt proud for a moment. I almost told Manny about Donlon, my meeting with Mr. Martin, and my plans to make up an essay so traumatic that I would go there for free. Being the hustler that he was, I thought he might appreciate it. Might even see that I was smart on a level beyond books and big words, on a level that he understood. But I thought better of it. I poured a drink instead, heavy on the soda.

"What is that bitch-ass shit, Schoolboy? Take a shot. Drink like a real man."

Manny passed out empty plastic cups and poured hefty amounts of Hennessy into each. I stared at the other men in the circle, their eyes red, faded, glazed into another dimension. They reminded me of the night Pops died. The people all around him, praising him, celebrating him, telling me how much they loved him. They all scattered once the bullets started flying. I never heard from them ever again. They all disappeared almost as fast as Pops did.

We lifted our cups to the sky. Gio barged into the kitchen. The circle whooped. Some of the men ruffled Gio's hat and rubbed his shoulders. Gio smiled as Manny poured him the biggest shot by far.

"Happy birthday to the lil bro," Manny said, raising his cup toward Gio. "Familia. Para siempre." Gio looked serene. He tilted his cup and downed the entire shot.

I didn't stay much longer. Gio and I smoked half a blunt together. We attempted to have a conversation. I told him about Donlon, and he nodded and said, "Oh, word," which told me he didn't want to know more. I tried to tell him more anyway, about Mr. Martin, the essay, the cheat code he'd described. But I could barely get a few words out before we'd be interrupted by people handing Gio drinks to down and throwing their arms around him for pictures. Eventually Gio disappeared. After standing against the wall for a while, feeling out of place in the darkness with all those squirming bodies, I put my cup on the windowsill and left. I'd see Gio later, I thought. Maybe we could get pizza, catch up properly. Then I'd tell him about college. Maybe even get him interested in getting his GED and going somewhere with me.

But I should have already learned that life doesn't work like that. I should have known that just when you least expect it, everything you thought was sacred and constant can vanish before your eyes.

I ZONED OUT of my first two classes after reading the story about Gio's arrest. I imagined him in a cell somewhere as words from the article—*thugs, savages, terrorizing, murderers, ruthless*—ricocheted in my head. If someone had ever bothered to write about Pops, it probably would have sounded similar. And even though the descriptions might have been technically right, they'd still have been wrong.

During third-period science, there was a knock at the door. My teacher told me there was someone outside for me. Illogically, I thought it was the cops. Maybe even the FBI. I had a flashback of life with Pops around. The hushed tones Mom spoke to me in, reminding me to keep my mouth shut, the lies I told to detectives' faces when they came around looking for him, showing me pictures, asking me if I knew of his whereabouts. I reminded myself of the refrain taught to me, the one I'd repeated countless times: "I don't know nothing." Thankfully, it was just Ms. Rivas.

"My usual cast of knuckleheads were talking about Gio this morning. I'm assuming you've heard?"

I stared down the hallway at the blue lockers lined up against the wall. I looked at Gio's old locker. I wondered if it still had drugs in it. If the cops would be bursting into the hallway any minute to bust it wide open. "I did."

"You okay?"

I said yes, but it wasn't convincing. She knew me too well.

Unlike some of our other teachers, she hadn't come from some faraway state with a mission to save us that blew up in her face once we started throwing chairs. She'd grown up on blocks just like ours, gone to schools just like ours, and pronounced *ask* like it was an instrument to chop people's heads off with. "It's tough when people you love go through things like this. I know. But you can't let it throw you off, okay? You have to stay focused. Gio made his choices. You have to make yours."

I nodded again, the words not really registering, just floating through me.

"Keep your appointment with Mr. Martin tomorrow. It might help if you talk some things out."

THE NEXT MORNING, I told myself I wouldn't go on about what had happened. I would keep my head down, agree to write whatever Mr. Martin wanted, and dip. I didn't give a fuck anymore. I just wanted to get away, and a free ride to Donlon, to upstate New York, seemed like the perfect out.

One period before the meeting, I hurriedly wrote down some stuff about how going to college in the United States would fulfill a long-standing dream my Pops had had. How he'd mouthed, "Get an education, Javi, do it for me," just before he took his last breath. How a star had then streaked across the sky, making it clear to me that this request was something I could not ignore. It was my first real attempt at playing with the truth. My first attempt at wholeheartedly fabricating some shit to make the story sound even better. And like most first attempts at anything in life, it was flaming-hot basura.

Mr. Martin read it. He gave me a long look. "I want to say, I'm really sorry to hear about your friend. Giovanni, was it? Ms. Rivas told me."

"Yeah."

"I understand you two were close?"

"Close" seemed like such a distant way to describe my relationship with Gio. "Yeah. But I don't wanna talk about it." I pointed to the paper I'd given him. "Is this good enough? This going to get me into that school?"

"No, Javier. Because it's not true. Right?"

I leaned back in the chair. "I did see my Pops die. I saw everything."

"I'm very sorry, Javier. That's quite the tragedy." He drummed his fingers on the table. "Are you sure you don't want to talk about what happened to your friend? I'm here to listen."

"No."

"How about this?" Mr. Martin pulled out a clean legal pad and a pen. He pushed them both my way. "You're a writer, Javier."

"I want to be one."

"Well, you already are one. So here, take the pen, sit there in the corner, and write. Just get your thoughts down. All your feelings. Can you do that?"

"Like a journal entry?"

"Exactly."

I had always loved journaling. Writing freely without the constraints of thesis statements and supporting paragraphs. I loved the little notes teachers left in the margins. I pretended not to read them like everyone else when I got my notebooks back. But at home, I lapped up the encouragements to keep going, to write more. I reread the parts they'd underlined and felt an immense sense of pride.

I don't know what to think. I feel numb. Like after Pops was killed. But worse. Pops was a ghost. Even when he was alive. Gio is always there. He's always been there. Even now when we're not chillin' like we used to.

Now he's in jail. He might be there for a long time. Just gone like that. And for what? Dumb shit.

I told him. I told him mad times. I still think I could have stopped it. I saw everything. All the signs. I knew. But after a while, I figured nothing too bad would happen. Gio would be aight. He's Gio. All he was doing was selling a little weed. Besides, he made it seem like he was so happy. In some ways, I think he was.

But gangs, murder, thugs? That can't be true. That ain't the Gio I know. It's fucked up.

I don't know what to think. I'm hollow. I don't know if this is the sort of thing you're looking for. I don't know what more to say. I just know none of this feels right.

I handed the pad over to Mr. Martin. Even before he read it, I felt a little better. If I could write about what had happened to Gio to get into college, I thought, if I could write about it in a way that felt real and honest, then maybe this whole essay thing wouldn't be so hard after all.

Mr. Martin stared at the pad for a long time. I heard sneaker squeaks against the hallway floor, the muffled sounds of kids talking on their way back from a bathroom break, the scratchy voice on the other end of a security guard's radio mumbling gibberish.

"I can only imagine the amount of pressure and unease you're feeling right now, Javier," he began. "It's very, very sad, what happened to your friend. And obviously, this is all so raw for you."

"So what I wrote is good?"

Mr. Martin gave me that smile again. Like I was a little kid trying to say big-boy words. "Yes. What you have to say is very important, and it will be very powerful for the admissions committee once we get it into shape."

"I can write more."

"I'm sure you can," Mr. Martin said. "But before we do that, I want to talk to you about structure. Have you ever heard of a narrative arc?"

"In English class. But that's for stories, right? Movies."

"Not exactly." He gestured at the pad. "See, what you have here is a lot of raw emotion. It's fine to start with. But for our purposes, we need more control. You only have five hundred words. You need to tell a story with a beginning, middle, and end. A story that hits certain notes the committee wants to hear. Does that make sense?"

"Not really."

"You need to contextualize things. Make it about the true goal here, which is getting into college. Getting access to more opportunities. So yes, your friend is part of that, but more important, for our purposes, is why *you* didn't end up like him. Where did your paths diverge?"

"I thought this would be about Gio, though. Not me."

"He's part of the story. But he's not *the* story. You are. You and your qualifications to go to this school." Mr. Martin clasped his hands. "Listen, Javier. I'll level with you. I've never had a friend of mine go to prison. Or someone in my family. I'm a privileged white man. But I'm not blind. I know the truth. And the truth is, people from communities like yours get sent to prison all the time. No one wants to admit it, but the world is just rigged for someone like you to end up dead or in prison. In a lot of ways, you're just desperately crawling your way through a sick obstacle course. While people like me just stroll through. And that's not your fault. It's our fault." He sighed. "I mean, it's my fault.

"Here's my point, Javier. We need to write something about how you, specifically, growing in this same messed-up, quicksand-like environment, didn't end up just like your friend."

"I mean, he sold drugs. I didn't. My Pops told me I didn't have the heart for it. And I believed him. He wasn't right about a lot of stuff, but he was right about that. I'm as soft as baby shit. I accept that truth about myself."

"But it's more than that, right? For example, I'm sure, in a neighborhood like yours, you were prey to the same forces as your friend. The guys with the money. The guys who had the nice cars and, what, the rims, right? The 'spinners'? Those things are so cool, aren't they?"

"Spinning rims? They look aight. But they seem like a waste of money, honestly."

"Sure. But my point is, this gang Gio was in—"

"That's the thing. It wasn't a gang. Like there are real gangs, you know? There's a reason I can't wear red and blue and, well, now green and tan, too, come to think of it. But Gio didn't have all that. He got to wear whatever colors he wanted. It was just some guys from the neighborhood he started chilling with. Selling some drugs here and there."

Mr. Martin leaned forward. "So you saw them around? Did they ever try to recruit you? I'm sure you must have thought they were cool, too."

"I hung out with them sometimes. But they're kind of assholes. And dumb. Manny, the guy who runs stuff, he thinks I'm some kind of genius because I can correctly use words with more than five letters in them. That's probably why everyone is in jail right now."

"See, Javier. Wow. This is what I'm talking about. You were right there. You could have been just like your friend. That's what we need. You, dodging all these things to get here, to where you are now."

I felt tugged in so many directions. "I thought you said last time I was supposed to write about how poor I am. Which one is it?"

Mr. Martin laughed uneasily. "That's not exactly what I said, Javier."

"You said a lot of stuff. But basically—"

"Just don't tell anyone I said that. Okay? We're cool, right?" He stuck his hand out for a fist bump.

I limply tapped my fist against his. "I guess, man. I just don't know what you're talking about anymore."

Mr. Martin seemed relieved. "I want you to write about challenges, yes, but also to write about how you overcame them. Your intellect, your creativity, your genius, really, to evade all this stuff. You dodged metaphorical bullets. Maybe you even dodged real bullets?"

"Are you asking if I've been shot at?"

"Well, it seems that technically, you were in the vicinity of shots . . . Anyway. Not the point. The point is, you could have been trapped like your friend, but you weren't. You were smart enough to make it out, Javier. Which is why you deserve to go somewhere like Donlon—even if you don't have the right SAT scores and so on.

"The early decision deadline is a week away," he said. "It's your best chance. We can do it. Because you know what? You don't just deserve a spot at a school like Donlon. You've earned it." He looked me in the eye. "You're a fighter, Javier. You've overcome so much. And you shouldn't shy away from that. You're not like most college applicants. You have something a lot of them don't have. Something that is in demand."

"What?"

"*Experience. Hardship*. And real hardship, too. Not the fluffy stuff."

"There are fake hardships?"

"I tutor kids all over the city. Mostly rich kids like the ones who go to my school because, well, the money is fantastic. When I ask them to think about challenges they've faced, or hardships, I usually get a kid who writes about being called names in school or, like, their parents getting divorced. Which is bad, but it's nothing compared to the sort of stuff you've been through. You see, I do this here, at a school like this one, to work with kids like you, because it makes me feel like I'm able to give back." Mr. Martin's eyes became watery.

I had a realization. The dude was genuinely moved. The little bit I'd shared about my life was akin to some sort of great Oscar acceptance speech to him. I'd made him feel something, and with his help, I could make things sound even better—at least to people like him. The fact that people like Mom, Pops, or Gio would find it absurd no longer mattered as much.

Before Mr. Martin, I'd never attempted to put labels on things that simply happened to me or people close to me. To put them on scales and see which experience, which hardship weighed more. I had never attempted to list these experiences, arrange them, and make them into a good story with a "narrative arc."

But in that little office of his, I began to piece all of this together. Realized an ounce of what I really had at my fingertips—just by the virtue of how I grew up, where I grew up, and the color of my skin.

Currency. Money. Just like the stacks Pops used to keep in my room. With people like Mr. Martin, I was rich. People like him wouldn't call me Schoolboy. They wouldn't tell me to stop whining. To them, I was starting to learn, I was like Tito Trinidad in that ring the night Pops died. My fists raised in the air.

Five

MY LIFE HAS LONG FELT *like one unending race. A marathon. Along the way, many of the people I was closest to have dropped out. People like my father, like Gio now. But I'm still going. I'm still running.*

And even if I were to gain acceptance to Donlon, I know the marathon will continue.

But here is what you need to know about me: I'm equipped to keep running. My grit, determination, and drive to defeat all the seemingly insurmountable forces against me is precisely what I'll lean on at Donlon when the going gets tough. I'll keep running—for me, for my family, for my ancestors, and for all of those who'll come after me, those who are running their own races right behind me and don't even realize it yet.

Mr. Martin pulled back the curtain. But my real transformation began at Donlon. It makes perfect sense now. Donlon was a whole new ecosystem where I could hone my new superpower.

In fact, it was in one of my very first classes there—a required sociology class about race and ethnicity—that I learned something profound: I am a victim of systemic oppression. Or, I guess I should say, I *was*. Now I'm in some liminal space. Existing in some sort of reverse perjury. My immutable characteristics and "lived experience" no longer count for much. Never did I see that coming.

On that fateful morning in a Donlon lecture hall, Professor Gleeson, a rail-thin, balding man, stood at a lectern in front of over three hundred students. He asked us all to stand, too. He waited until the sound of chairs folding up had ceased. "Please take a seat if your parents are still married," he said, in a voice that surprisingly carried well, despite his fragile appearance. After looking at each other for a confused second, a large number of us sat. "Please take a seat if you have ever attended a private school at any point in your life." Another large group sat. There were rumbles of giggles. People shrugged. Some shook their heads. My seat was near the back of the room. I counted about fifty others standing. "Please sit if one or both of your parents have a university degree." The group was cut in half. The giggling stopped. All eyes scanned the room, identifying those who remained standing. "If you have always felt comfortable walking around in your neighborhood at night and have never once feared for your safety, please sit."

I could have sat. The truth was, I *did* feel comfortable walking around my neighborhood at night, but only because I'd learned—after a couple of unfortunate jumpings—*how* to walk in the neighborhood. Cross the street when you see a group in front of you, stay in the light, go the wrong way if you have to as long as you immediately remove yourself from anything hairy, start to run if anyone behind you follows at least two of your turns, start to run even faster—sprint as hard as you can—if they start to run after you. Simple rules. Nothing crazy. But I still decided to remain standing in the auditorium.

After a week of being on the enormous campus, a week of feeling like an ant among the thousands of students, a week of realizing I was at a severe disadvantage with girls because I hadn't done anything cool over the summer like backpacking or sailing and because I didn't play any sports or have any connections at the frats that threw the parties, I knew that I needed some way to stand out. As I stood there in the auditorium, I saw that I was one of only five people remaining. All eyes were on me. Just where I wanted them to be.

"If you have never had any of your family members experience being arrested or incarcerated, sit," Professor Gleeson said.

Everyone else sat. I almost fist-pumped. There I stood: the winner. Tito. I expected the auditorium to burst into applause. But the room was so quiet that if I'd farted, everyone would have heard. I wondered if I was supposed to make a speech or something. But Professor Gleeson simply motioned for me to sit.

A number of people turned their heads to look at me. One of them was familiar. I'd seen her around the dorms and the dining hall and could tell immediately that there was something different about her. One of the most obvious things was that she had an ass that stood out among all the pancake butts I'd seen on my milky-white campus. Her ass was the kind I recognized. The kind that was hard to contain, even in baggy sweatpants. She had a light brown complexion and vaguely Latino traits—curly hair, a perpetual scowl early in the morning, a gold nameplate necklace. She looked like someone who could be from my neighborhood, which felt unique given that everyone else I'd met during my short time at Donlon was from places that sounded like whole other planets to me.

The girl turned back around. I zeroed in on the Apple laptop in front of her. It was not only the latest model, it was covered entirely in stickers that seemed to demand vague but intense action: *Fight the Power! Disrupt! Pay Your Fair Share!* I decided she was not of my kind. And yet she was. I was intrigued.

Professor Gleeson continued his lecture. He began to explain the term I was vaguely familiar with thanks to Mr. Martin: "privilege." Then he introduced a new term that would prove arguably more powerful for me: "systemic oppression." Together, they would soon roll off my tongue as easy as my name and phone number. But at that point, I might as well have been learning a new language.

To explain the terms, Professor Gleeson described a race in which the grand prize was the American dream: a house, a nice car, a family. He drew two vertical lines on his chalkboard to represent a starting line and a finish line. Then he drew dots at various places in between, including one dot far behind the starting line. "I would like for us to imagine something. Together, as a class," Professor Gleeson said. "Take a look at these dots. They are, in a sense, you and me. Here we are, all of us, in this race of humanity, which, for the sake of this example, has yet to begin.

"Each of these dots is akin to a runner. Waiting there at the starting block, waiting for the gun to go off. Can you see it? Good. Now I want us to focus over here." He moved closer to the starting line, closer to the dot far behind it. "Imagine these runners way over here. What will happen to them when the gun goes off?"

Professor Gleeson waited as chair creaks and coughs answered his question. Finally, the girl I'd been looking at raised her hand.

"Those runners will lose. But it wouldn't be their fault. Because their life, in fact, has been rigged from the beginning. Just as it was intended to be rigged by their scheming overseers over there near the starting line. Those white people. The people with the real power that shape this world to their liking and that also control this so-called race on the board." She stopped and looked Professor Gleeson up and down. "But I'm sure you know all about that."

I watched as people around me rolled their eyes. I felt like I was missing out on an inside joke. Professor Gleeson nodded his head approvingly. "Thank you for sharing. Really, thank you."

"I'm just speaking the truth," the girl said.

"That you are," he said, clearing his throat. "She is right. Some people will easily finish the race ahead of others and reap the rewards first. Wouldn't it make sense, then, for those people and their families and their future families to have an advantage over everyone else as each successive generation lines up again for the race?" Professor Gleeson walked over to my side of the room. "Wouldn't it make sense that we, as a society, would be required to help the people way in the back of the start line? The people who never had a chance to begin with? Those people who desperately need our help?" He looked me in the eyes.

I stared at that lonely dot behind the start line. I realized that he, and probably everyone else in that room, thought that little dot was me. They all thought I needed . . . support? Special attention? Gifts? Money? I wasn't sure what, exactly, but it all sounded good.

At the end of the class, Professor Gleeson called me down to his lectern. He crossed his arms over his chest and fidgeted. "Thanks so much for participating. I hope that was okay. Are you okay? Do you want to talk about anything?"

The only thing I wanted to do was thank him. But he didn't let me get a word out.

"I just want to let you know that I'm really glad you're here. Just know that the exercise was by no means meant to single you out or, like, target you, okay? You don't feel targeted, do you?"

I shrugged. The word *target* made me think of the red laser Pops used to have on one of his guns. Made me remember how I woke up one morning in Puerto Rico and saw the laser there on my forearm and watched it trace its way slowly up my torso. Pops laughed so hard at my shocked face when I realized what was going on.

"No," I said.

Professor Gleeson exhaled. "Good. Well, just to reiterate, we are lucky to have you here." He leaned forward. "This school needs you."

Mr. Martin was right, I thought. What foresight he'd had.

I left the room with my chest out. I walked back to the dorms, passing luxuriously manicured lawns. Since driving onto campus with Mom a week before, I hadn't yet found my footing. In addition to all the activities, all the icebreakers, the constant repetition of my hometown and major, which became monotonous and felt so useless, there was also the sheer size of the school, which felt overwhelming. Thousands and thousands of students. Like the entirety of Orchard Beach on a blazing summer day. But in this case, the people seemed so different from me.

They drove Mini Coopers around campus, bragged about ski trips, played lacrosse and water polo (which is apparently a real sport), and knew Jay-Z as simply a rapper with a few songs they sort of remembered—not as Hova—and they loved to walk and get lost in the woods like they were trying to find some hidden civilization. Among them, I often felt left out. Whenever I thought about sharing what I'd done that summer—lugged around boxes in Midtown, watched my friend get sentenced to a decade in prison, tried and failed to use my acceptance to Donlon as a ticket to getting laid by girls I knew back home—it all felt so worthless, so foreign. And when I did share some of the tragic things about myself those first few days, like Pops dying or Gio being in jail, when I tried to frame myself as a survivor like Mr. Martin had taught me to, I was often met with a solemn silence. A glance around confirmed that I had absolutely killed the vibe.

So for the most part, I stayed quiet. I became this mouse of a person. The sort of person I never wanted to be.

Which is why I walked with a bounce in my step leaving Professor Gleeson's classroom that afternoon. I felt like I'd finally been noticed. I was no longer just the average freshman trying to find his classrooms and desperate to make friends. I was no longer the kid who hadn't traveled much, who didn't understand how colors corresponded to the difficulty of ski slopes. I was someone special. Not just a survivor, but a victim of systemic oppression. Someone who *deserved* things, like perks, gifts, and grand prizes, just because. Someone entitled to these things.

WHILE STANDING IN LINE at the dining hall pasta station later that day, I felt a tap on my back. I turned to see the girl who'd caught my eye. The girl I'd already decided I would try to talk to next class, now that I was feeling good about myself. But there she was, beating me to the punch.

"That was such a shitty thing for Professor Gleeson to do in class today," she said. "Not to mention *racist* as fuck."

I'd later come to use variations of the word *racist* as often as simple pronouns. But at this moment, I was still blind to its all-encompassing power. At this moment, the word *racist* still made me think of the KKK, segregated lunch counters, and protesters being sprayed with a water hose. What Professor Gleeson had done, I thought, was teach me something useful. But the girl in front of me seemed genuinely upset. Perhaps, I thought, she didn't understand what had happened.

"I'm not sure it was racist."

She looked concerned. She touched my arm. I felt a nice tingle. Human contact. "Don't make excuses for an asshole like him. Trust me, it was racist. And there will be more where that came from. Especially in a place like *this*."

She looked with disgust at the gleaming dining hall, complete with couches, stylish chairs, clean tables, and more food stations than a Sizzler in the suburbs. She scooped steaming linguine onto her plate and covered it with pesto sauce. She introduced herself. Anais Delgado. A sophomore from Albany. I looked more closely at her complexion, her features. I wondered if she was Dominican or Puerto Rican—a type of Latino I was familiar with. Because one of the most insightful things I'd learned when I got to Donlon was about the wide range of Latinos or Hispanics or whatever the hell they wanted to call us. There were white ones, poor ones, dark ones, and rich ones who, despite their heavy accents, knew exactly what color ski slope was the hardest to go down. They were from countries I'd never met anyone from before: Colombia, Peru, Argentina, Chile. Some of the rich ones were from Puerto Rico, too, but when I tried to claim a shared heritage with them, and told them about the town my family was from and my childhood in New York, they quickly told me they were real Puerto Ricans and I was something different: a "Nuyorican." All the different categories separating us were hard to grasp and keep track of. Before Donlon, everyone in my orbit was either from PR or DR. And to anyone else who wasn't one of us, we were just "Spanish."

As we sat down at a table together, Anais told me that her dad was half Puerto Rican and half Dominican. She looked at the wisps of hair on her forearm. She was the color of coffee with too much creamer. "He's much darker than me," she said, with authority. "I'm only light-skinned because my mom is white." The last part came out like it was some grave sin.

"That's okay."

"I know it is." She flared her nostrils. It excited me.

"What do you do around here for fun? I don't think I've ever seen you at any of the parties."

She slurped a strand of linguine. "Depends which parties you're talking about. Which ones have you been to? Let me guess. The frat parties?"

"I'm guessing those are not the ones you go to?"

"No. That's where all the desperate freshmen go. Not that I blame you. That's all POC like us know when we first get here. Too many of us are blinded and led astray."

Anais seemed like she could keep going, but I had to stop her. "POC?"

She seemed taken aback. "Come on. *You* know. POC. *People of color.*"

I did not know. I'd never heard the term before or used it to refer to myself. At first, I thought it sounded like a tribe. Or perhaps an early '90s hip-hop group, back when people were wearing funky patterns and rapping about incense and Africa.

"You've really never heard that before?" Anais squinted at me. Looked deep into my eyes and seemed to figure something out. Something that made her smile. "What are you doing on Thursday night?"

"What are *you* doing?"

I thought the line was slick. Anais rolled her eyes.

"You should come to the LTC."

"I don't have a fake."

She pushed me and smiled for real. I couldn't believe how well this was going. After being drier than gas station nuts for months, I felt like I was on the verge of a breakthrough.

"It's not a bar. It's the Latino Thriving Center. It's a space for POC like us to gather and just be. For us to talk about things, like the *fuckery* in class today."

A bar sounded better. But I was intent on taking what I could get.

"Will you be there?"

"I'm always there."

THE LTC HAD A GRAND NAME, but it was only a ramshackle house on the farthest stretch of campus. I took one of the campus buses to the last stop and walked what felt like a mile. On either side of the leafy street were homes that had names affixed to their fronts. The American Indian Safe Haven, the Black Liberation Project, the Asian Diaspora Sanctuary. The LTC was the final one on the block before you hit a dead end. It was a white house that looked like a light wind could blow it down.

The porch creaked. The walls of the hallway inside were completely covered with flyers for events; pictures of Cesar Chavez, Che Guevara, Dolores Huerta, Roberto Clemente; brown fists, black fists, yellow fists; the words *La Raza* and *Chinga la Migra* in big letters. Every square inch seemed to be screaming at me to do something, say something, and stand up for something—just like Anais's laptop. What was much more comforting to me was the hip-hop music I heard streaming from a speaker somewhere. Aside from the music I played alone in my dorm room, it was the first time I'd heard any hip-hop—real hip-hop and not the sugary pop stuff that was becoming increasingly popular—anywhere on campus. I felt myself immediately relax, immediately become more comfortable, which made me realize, perhaps for the first time, how *uncomfortable* Donlon could be.

Donlon was cool, but it was also fucking weird. I tried describing it to Gio in the letters we started sending each other after he was sent upstate, at just about the same time I started school. We'd spoken on the phone twice since he was arrested. But the calls were short and expensive. Never long enough, for example, for me to tell him much about how I'd gotten into Donlon, or my essay about him, which I'd mentioned, to which he'd only responded, "Cool," before going on, in a distraught voice, about his case and the time he was staring down and the hints he'd gotten from his lawyer and prosecutors that everyone in the gang was snitching on each other, that a plea bargain might be his best hope.

It was Gio's idea to switch to letters. They were cheaper, and, he said, he liked the fact that he could hold on to them, that he could revisit them and remember what life was really like. When I asked him what he wanted me to write about, he said it didn't have to be special. He wanted to know all about Donlon. About the kids who went there. The parties. The campus. I told him it was the kind of place that made me question why I always packed up all my stuff whenever I needed to use the bathroom in the library when everyone else seemed totally fine leaving their expensive computers and headphones spilled on a table for hours. The kind of place where all of a sudden it was weird to know all the lyrics to "Lean Back" but totally normal, and even as customary as reciting the Pledge of Allegiance, to know all the words to "Wonderwall." But none of that sounded all that bad to Gio, particularly when it was contrasted with the details he slipped into letters about his life, like getting shaken awake by guards at odd hours of the night. "They bum-rushed the room at 3:00 a.m. Threw all my shit around. Then left me to get it together like nothing. And the worst part is, if I do anything to them, say one peep, they'll throw my ass right into solitary." He wrote about washing dishes for hours a day, and the meager wages he earned. "Fifty cents an hour. Can you believe that shit? Never been more broke in my life, son." Then there were the lines that were just too sad, the lines I didn't even know how to respond to. "Some dude a few cells down tried to off himself last night. Craziest part is that he started crying when they brought him down. Not because he was happy, but because he was mad he didn't get to finish the job."

WHEN I HEARD the music in the LTC and saw the faces of other people that looked like they could be my neighbors back home or even members of my own family, I felt like maybe I could turn my brain off for a bit, stop trying to navigate everything else that was so foreign to me on campus, stop trying to make sense of it, and just chill.

The large living room held a dozen or so people gathered on a couple of big, beat-up couches. Near the kitchen was a table piled with trays of pizza, wings, chips, and soda. I looked around and saw Anais on one of the couches chatting up a tall, lumpy guy who introduced himself to me as Luis.

"Your boyfriend?" I asked when he got up to grab some chips.

"No," Anais said, in a quick and decisive manner that made me smile.

Luis, who was in earshot of us, frowned as he scooped more Doritos onto his plate.

I looked Anais up and down. Without her book bag, with her hair up in a bun, and wearing a university sweat suit that fit her snug in just the right places, she looked fine as fuck.

"Excuse you."

"What?"

"I'm not a piece of meat, mister."

I hadn't even realized I'd looked her up and down, much less that she'd noticed. Doing that to an attractive woman was second nature to me. Like breathing. I didn't know if I should apologize or how angry Anais—whose face was unreadable—really was. Luckily, Luis returned.

"He's from the Bronx, too," she said.

Instead of giving Luis his seat next to Anais back, I moved closer to her and made space for him next to me. He almost nodded in respect at my judo. It was obvious that we were both vying for the same prize, and I wasn't about to lose.

Luis and I did the New York thing, comparing streets and avenues. I went first. When Luis found out which neighborhood I came from—which by no means was one that was respected citywide, essentially a code word for "Don't fuck with me," but was certainly one where it was clear that you'd have some pretty constant contact with hairy situations—he admitted that he was from Riverdale and had gone to the fancy private school there. When he said this, I breathed a sigh of relief. I'd hoped he wasn't from a neighborhood harder than mine.

"Where did you go to school, though?" Luis asked, perhaps hoping I was one of those prep school scholarship kids who might have come from a rough area but inside was about as white as the middle of an Oreo cookie.

I smiled. I said the name of my high school, known, if known at all, for metal detectors, gangbangers, and a tiny honors program that, while good, wasn't worth the headache of attending the school if you had any alternative available to you.

"Oh yeah," Luis said, slurping down his drink. "Yeah, yeah, I know that place."

"Is that close by to where you went, Luis?" Anais asked.

Like most other people on campus, she assumed everyone in New York City lived near each other.

I cleared my throat. "Not really. Luis's school is in a much nicer area. Kind of like the suburbs of the Bronx. Very affluent. Right, Luis?"

"Yeah," he said, conveying a look of defeat.

When he got up to join a group of people talking and eating on another couch, I thought I finally had my window of opportunity to get some alone time with Anais. But within moments, another guy in the room walked into the middle and sat on a colorful rug that I hadn't noticed was there until he sat on it. Almost immediately, conversations began to wind down until everyone was silent.

"It looks like we're all settled in," the guy on the carpet said, introducing himself as Ricardo. He wore a baggy sweatshirt and a beanie. "Thanks for joining us at Dentro de la Familia. I see a lot of familiar faces." He looked at Anais and smiled.

A new challenger had appeared.

"For those of you who don't know, this is a weekly session for us to have an open dialogue about life on campus. Vent frustrations. Vibe. Be in community with our hermanos and hermanas. Which, as you know, is important in this hegemonic landscape we find ourselves in."

A few people snapped their fingers.

"Preach," Anais said.

I didn't know what the word *hegemonic* meant. But I made a mental note to look it up later and add it to the collection of words I had been gathering since my arrival on campus—not only as an exercise to get along better with others and understand what the fuck my professors were talking about but also because these words, like *hegemonic, diaspora,* and *modernity,* sounded weighty and important. They sounded like the sort of words you could beat people over the head with. The sort of words that could silence and enrapture a particular sort of crowd, sort of like a good yo mama joke back in the Bronx.

We went around the room and introduced ourselves. When my turn came, I said, in a dramatic tone, that I'd grown up in the Bronx.

Before college, the Bronx was just a patch of earth I happened to be born on. It had its intricacies and beauty and terror, things that I'd always assumed were probably the same everywhere else in the world. But once I got to Donlon and had to repeat where I was from over and over those first few weeks, I realized that to most others, the Bronx evoked images of burning buildings, wild shoot-outs and car chases, rappers, and a zoo where it was rumored that the animals actually ran things.

The reveal usually elicited dumb questions: *How many times have you been shot? How many rap videos have you been in?* But it also elicited an odd sort of respect—even if the people didn't really seem to want to get to know me better, or even hang out with me. Depending on the person, they vacillated, it seemed, between looking at me as some sort of mob boss to be feared and regarding me as a sad refugee from some war-torn part of the world to be ignored.

It was clear that to the people in the LTC, I was the refugee. But the way they slowly waggled their heads was different. It conveyed empathy. Understanding. Solidarity. As if they, too, had migrated from similar war-torn lands. Ricardo, who'd already given me a worried look when he saw I was sitting next to Anais, noticed the reaction in the room and clenched his jaw.

"Excellent," he said, quickly brushing past me. "The floor is now open. Anyone want to share?"

Immediately, a girl who'd introduced herself as Claudia lifted her hand. "Okay. I mean, if no one else wants to, I can go." She told a story about a small group project for her Italian class. She had been paired with two white people. "White men." The room let out a collective groan. While they were discussing the outline for the project at the café on campus two days before, Claudia said, one of the boys had asked why she was even studying Italian. "If I were you, I'd take Spanish and skate by," she recounted him saying, contorting her voice into a nasally staccato.

Anais sneered.

Ricardo shook his head with a look of disgust. "Wow. Just wow."

Claudia breathed in and out, slowly, as if she were telling a heart-rending tale of barely escaping death. "Like, right? One, you just assume I speak Spanish, which I don't. And two, what, because I'm brown I can't educate myself and learn something new? I was so hurt."

Anais reached over and rubbed Claudia's shoulder. "It's okay, girl. Let it out."

Ricardo thanked Claudia for sharing. I took mental notes. I'd never before seen someone make something so seemingly small so dramatic. The artfulness impressed me.

A few more people shared, recounting similarly benign injustices with riveting "narrative arcs," as Mr. Martin would say: anger at having to check the "Hispanic" box on university forms, which didn't seem like the kind of thing that merited applause for "getting through" the "triggering" experience; disgust and "severe mental fatigue" from a Colombian girl who said she was constantly asked about Pablo Escobar by everyone. (I held in the fact that he was my only reference point for the country, and that I probably would have asked her about him, too.)

After a few more people shared, the room became quiet. Anais raised her hand. "Something horrible and, honestly, probably the most racist thing I've ever witnessed on this campus so far—which is saying a fucking lot—happened this week." The room sat in rapt attention as Anais recounted our sociology class exercise. "He made us stand up and singled us out one by one, showing off our oppression for the delight of all the other whites in that room. He made poor Javi stand all alone at the end. Stand there for everyone to gawk at. Like he was a slave on an auction block or something. *Look at me. Look at how hard my life has been.* Like some sort of fucking token poor boy."

The room turned to me, aghast.

Even Ricardo looked disturbed. "That sounds pretty bad. Are you okay? How did that make you feel?"

Anais put an encouraging hand on my shoulder. I thought about telling them how I really felt: noticed, and elated about it. But I wanted to try out the moves I'd been studying while listening to everyone else. "I did feel uncomfortable," I said, dipping my toe in. The sighs and nods in response felt like a hug.

Anais rubbed my back. "Go ahead. It's fine."

"Well, it *was* embarrassing," I said, with feigned anguish.

"What a fucking asshole that guy was," someone said.

"We should get his ass fired," another chimed in.

"We should!" Anais said.

I didn't want Professor Gleeson to go up in flames. The man was a legend in my book. "He called me down after everyone left and apologized," I said in his defense.

Anais blew a raspberry. "Sounds just like a white man to ask permission *after* the fact." She leaned closer to me. "Remember what I said: *Don't* make excuses for him, or for any of them. Never."

In my eighteen years of life up to that point, I don't think I'd ever blamed white people for anything. Aside from the Irish and the Italians and the Albanians and the Jews who also lived in the Bronx—all of whom I barely considered white because they were just as foulmouthed and poor as everyone else—I'd barely interacted with them. But I picked up on the cues around me. I saw the wide-open layup before my eyes. And I knew enough to take it. "I guess you're right," I said to Anais and the rest of the room. "I *shouldn't* make excuses for them."

Six

I FOUND MYSELF at the LTC a lot that first semester because I really wanted to get into Anais's pants, and I thought my best hope was to spend as much time with her as possible. After each LTC meeting, I walked her home, despite the fact that her off-campus house was far and in the opposite direction of the bus stop. In sociology class, we sat next to each other and shit-talked Professor Gleeson. I even nodded in agreement when she called him names that made me wince inside, like "white devil."

We smoked in her room often. In the beginning, when we were alone, I asked her questions about all these strong opinions she held. She was fascinating. Bold, ready to share her thoughts at a moment's notice. Confident in those thoughts, as if she were all-knowing. But at the same time, some of what she said when she expounded on her favorite subjects—racism, sexism, colonialism, a whole lot of isms—sounded preposterous to me.

Once, I asked whether she really believed white people controlled the lives of "people of color" as if we were chess pieces they could move around on a board. "You make them sound superhuman. I feel like they're really not that smart." We were in Anais's room listening to music, the dense political rap she loved, which she was constantly pausing to explain the meaning of the lyrics to me. She turned off the music and pointed the end of a flaming blunt at me. "They're not superhuman, Javi. *We* are. You and me. We're magic. They're just in control. That's the difference."

"So we're magic? But they're, like, behind some curtain moving the levers? You really believe that?"

"Yes, Javi. Because it's the truth." She moved closer to me. Leaned in. I could smell that perfume of hers I'd come to love. The hint of lavender. "Javi, you're too important to become one of *those* POC," she said. "The ones who think that nothing is wrong. That everything is just fine. That all we have to do is pull ourselves up by our bootstraps. Those are the worst. They undermine the goal. They might be worse than white people. So don't be one of them." Anais passed the blunt to me. "It would be a shame. Because I actually like you a lot, Javi."

I had more questions—*What type of boots are we talking about? What goal? Revolution? Civil war? Genocide?*—but I kept them to myself. We made out instead.

And we kept making out whenever we were alone after that. But every time things started to get hot and heavy, Anais put her hand on mine to stop. She pulled away with a long kiss. She got up, fixed her clothes, and turned the television on to cable news. She pulled a book off the shelf that she wanted to tell me about. She bent my ear about something on campus that incensed her. And each time, I sat there, hard as a rock, wondering if I was doing something wrong.

This went on for a month or so before I decided to even tell Gio. In the letters we were sending each other, Anais surfaced little by little. She began as an unnamed "shorty I seen around" but progressed to a "shorty I been chilling with a bit" to being named:

"Her name is Anais. She's Dominican and Puerto Rican and a white girl, too. Bad."

Gio asked me to tell him what she was like, tell me about the things we did. As soon as I started mentioning Anais, he wanted to track my progress with her, just like he used to in school, when we'd shoot hoops and trade updates on the girls we were talking to, or trying to talk to, or coming to the realization that we'd never, ever have a chance with. I described Anais and me going to see concerts on campus; walking around the nearby lake; attending lectures by writers, "thinkers," and artists; or taking the bus to a small theater to watch the obscure independent movies Anais loved. "They're like regular movies as far as I can tell, just slower, longer, and with a lot less guns and explosions."

"Sounds wack," Gio wrote in response. "She don't like action flicks? What's wrong with homegirl?"

When I finally told Gio about my issue with Anais, the fact that I was getting nada despite all the time we'd spent together by that point, he responded in the way I expected him to. "I figured as much, with all those corny dates and hand-holding. That's no good. You my boy, so I'ma keep it a buck. If she ain't giving it up by now, you probably in the friend zone. She probably just waiting around for some other dude to come on by. You better hurry up and make a move. And if she don't go for it, drop homegirl. She sound kinda weird anyways. Don't waste your time, son. Trust me, time is everything."

GIO'S WORDS were on my mind as I walked Anais home after the next LTC meeting. It was the last one of the semester. The frigid wind nipped at the bits of skin that weren't covered by our gloves and coats. We passed what everyone on campus called the "downtown" section of our tiny college town. I could never bring myself to call it that because it was only four blocks.

I fiddled with Anais's hand as we entered her apartment and made our way to her room. Anais grabbed beer from her mini fridge. "Nightcap?" she said, waving the cans at me. I reminded myself that we wouldn't be seeing each other until after winter break. A month apart. A month for her to go to Albany and probably find that other dude that Gio was talking about. Probably come back with a boyfriend. Probably marry that dude.

For the first time in my life, I was jealous. I wasn't excited to go back to the city and put an end to my dry spell by running through the usual suspects. I wanted Anais. And only her.

Liquid courage already ran through my veins thanks to the stiff coquito one of the girls had brought to the LTC that night. Anais and I drank a quarter of our beers on her couch before I leaned over and started to kiss her. Slowly, like she liked. I moved my hands through her curls. Our tongues danced. I moved my hand lower and began to unzip her sweater, exposing a bit of her T-shirt, the hint of a black bra underneath. She did not stop me when I began to slip her T-shirt off. I cupped her breasts, then removed one from her bra for the first time. Anais gave me a long kiss, then pulled her mouth away from mine.

"Hey, hey." She smiled and pushed my hands away. She leaned back against the cushion of her couch, adjusted her bra, and grabbed her beer.

"How's that final paper coming? Did you go to the tutor?"

I sucked my teeth. "You really want to talk about my writing seminar right now?"

"Why is that such a problem?"

She knew I'd gotten another C on my last paper. I'd complained about it to her and the whole LTC during a meeting. According to my professor, I'd gotten a C because I'd failed twice to cobble together a thesis statement about Foucault's panopticon that was "rigorous" enough for his liking. He said my thoughts on the issue of discipline, while "engaging and entertaining," were "too surface level and too emotional in scope" compared to those of my peers. Over large chunks of my essay, the professor crossed out what I'd written about the things Gio told me about prison in his letters. Unlike Ms. Rivas, who used to write encouraging notes to me, my professor wrote things like "Okay, but we need facts above anecdotes," "Refer to the text," "Complicate your thinking here," and "Let's bring in some research." He, like the other professors at Donlon, always seemed to want me to "back up" what I had to say. A process I began to abhor because it required far more work and effort than I wanted to put in.

According to people at the LTC, the reason I got a C on my paper wasn't because I couldn't back up my thinking but simply because my professor was a racist. This felt comforting, just like when Diego offered to start a petition on Facebook to get my professor fired, or when Alexandra said there were reams of research about how white professors saw minority students as having inferior ideas. But even so, I knew none of that would actually change my grade. Anais, who also called my professor racist, seemed to instinctually know that, too. Which was why she quietly suggested to me when we were alone that I go to the writing center on campus.

"I'm working on it," I told Anais.

She loaded up a bowl of weed. "Good."

"Satisfied?"

She smiled.

Her room had old wood paneling on the walls—which was about the only thing that lent itself to the truth about this room being a college apartment. The furniture was modern. There was a flat-screen television near her bed, and her mini fridge was one of the nicer models—not one of the cheap ones that muttered to itself at night. Whenever I was in the room, I wondered what Anais's house in Albany looked like. What her life was like before she got here.

She passed the bowl my way, but I put it aside. I pulled her onto my lap, and we continued kissing. She pushed forward into me. I reached around behind her and fiddled with her bra clasp until it was open and both of her breasts were suspended there before me for a moment before she crossed her arms over them.

"Stop," she said softly.

I thought about Gio. I reached to pull her closer. But she stiffened up.

"Javi."

"What? What's wrong?"

"Not yet."

"Seriously?"

She got off of my lap. "Excuse you?" She reached for her shirt and quickly put it on.

"I don't get you," I said. "I've been a good guy. We've been hanging out. I've been, like, fucking faithful to you, haven't been messing with *nobody* else, and we're not even official like that. You're just playing me, aren't you?"

"Wow, Javi. So, what, because you're being a nice guy, being fucking decent, I'm just supposed to throw pussy at you? Men like you *deserve* it for doing the basics?" Anais shook her head, nostrils in full flare. "That's what you're telling me?"

"I wasn't saying that . . ."

"Get out of my room, Javi. Please leave."

"Are you serious?"

Anais stood and walked over to her door. She opened it. "Very."

I DIDN'T SEE OR HEAR from Anais again until the morning of our sociology final, three days later. All my texts and phone calls had gone unanswered. When I showed up at the LTC, she wasn't there. "She's studying" was what people kept telling me. I showed up early to the lecture hall where our exam was being held and waited outside for her. When I finally saw her crossing the lawn, I prepared myself to apologize. But she didn't give me a chance. She looked me in the eye and walked right past me. "Don't even," she said.

She finished before me, handed in her test, and left the lecture hall. After I finished my exam, I looked for her outside, but she was nowhere to be found. I went to a store just off campus and overpaid for flowers. I'd never bought flowers for a girl before. But I figured from watching those movies that Anais liked that this was the sort of thing you did to win over a girl like her.

When I got to Anais's house, the lights were off in her room. After some knocking, one of her roommates opened up and said Anais had made plans to leave for winter break right after the test. "I'm pretty sure she's gone by now," the girl said, frowning at my flowers.

The next day, I hopped on a coach back to the city. I stared out the window as the grimy bus wound through a handful of small upstate towns. One of the stops was near a prison. I could tell because of the men who got on lugging trash bags of their belongings and wearing the same release uniform. Their faces conveyed a mixture of bewilderment and perhaps annoyance that no one was there to pick them up in a nice car like in the movies.

I didn't blame Gio for the way things had gone with Anais. But I figured I'd messed up by listening to him. I decided I wouldn't mention Anais much at all in our letters moving forward. I'd excise her like I'd largely excised the LTC. There were just certain things he couldn't understand. Certain worlds he just didn't know how to navigate.

I watched one of the men from the prison stuff his bag into the small compartment above our seats. He sat next to a girl wearing a Donlon sweat suit. The girl turned toward the window, averting her eyes from his presence.

I tried to imagine Gio at Donlon. Tried to imagine him turning in papers and getting back comments. Would he respond the way I was used to him responding in class? Talking back, grabbing his nuts, and eventually walking out altogether? What would he think about the LTC? Would he bother going or "showing support" at rallies for things he didn't really know about or, truthfully, care about? Would he also start to realize he was suddenly becoming attuned to things he'd never paid attention to before? Small moments, like a pair of girls at the café leaving behind a mountain of crumbs and shrugging, saying that cleaning them up was what the Latina bus girl nearby "gets paid for." I'd left a mess at restaurants before. But suddenly, seeing the same scene played out in the world of Donlon, I thought of Titi Nilda. Would people here just see her as a "bus girl"? And if so, what did that mean? Was it racist?

I couldn't imagine Gio asking himself these things. And I certainly couldn't imagine him going to a meeting and sharing what he'd witnessed, coloring in some of the scenes as I did—"For fun, I think, one of the girls just flicked her plate on the ground, spilling the leftovers everywhere, and laughed on her way out."

I couldn't see any of that for Gio. There was a chasm between his world and mine. And when I really thought back, really tried to reflect on things, I realized that maybe there always had been.

SOPHOMORE YEAR. I remember the day clearly. The chunky, fur-laced coats everyone wore made the mass of students exiting the high school that afternoon look like ice fishermen. A scowl hung on Gio's face, but it had nothing to do with the temperature.

"Who does she think she is?" he said.

The "she" in question was Ms. Rivas. In class, she'd chewed Gio out for not completing a reading report on *Down These Mean Streets* that would've given him ten free points on the midterm. Free points he needed. "I'm trying to give you a break," she'd told him, in front of everyone. "But you don't seem to care about your grades at all. That's a problem I can't fix."

"What you can fix is deez nuts," he'd retorted, resulting in a swift ejection from the room.

The two of them butted heads more than Gio butted heads with any other teacher during his brief stay in high school—which is saying a lot. He'd never been a great student. But in high school, all of his effort went out the window. The further he became enmeshed with Manny, the more obnoxious he became. Clowning teachers for sport. But Ms. Rivas never rolled over. I think that frustrated him the most.

"Have you studied at all for the midterm?" I asked as Gio and I walked to the bus stop.

He just laughed. "But you did, right, *Schoolboy*?"

"Don't fucking call me that."

"It's kind of catchy."

"It's juvenile. A third grader could come up with a better nickname."

"Whatever. I *know* you studied for that test. Which is why you really need to keep that paper to the left-hand side tomorrow, son."

I had in fact studied. Studied more than I had for any other test in my life up to that point. I wanted to impress Ms. Rivas. I felt joy hunching over the big computer in my bedroom and trying to arrange words in a way that would stand out to her. It was because of the way she'd talked about me at my first parent-teacher conference when I was a freshman. When she'd sat across from Mom and said, "Your son is talented. If he'd like to, he could be a writer someday." In response, Mom pretended to smile. "That's cute. But I was thinking more like engineering or science. Something that makes money." Mom and Ms. Rivas spent the rest of the conference in a discussion about whether money or happiness is more important. I didn't pay attention. I thought about what Ms. Rivas had said. That I was talented. I never forgot it.

"That bitch ain't worth impressing," Gio said, already set in his belief that Ms. Rivas was Satan's spawn. "Deadass, fuck her."

We passed the last remaining cuchifrito vendor on the block, valiantly frying pinchos on a grill as he boxed the cold wind. When we hit the corner, Gio didn't turn toward the bus stop. He said he had to make a stop in the park to meet Manny.

"For what? Won't you see him on the block? It's cold as fuck."

"Nah. We moving a little different right now."

I thought of all the times Pops would suddenly do drastic things, like hop on flights or drag me to storage containers out in the fields in Puerto Rico with duffel bags and an anxious look on his face. "Why do you suddenly need to change things up?"

"Seriously, Javi. With all the questions you ask, you should go work for the FBI." He sucked his teeth. "Just come with me, man. It'll be quick."

We crossed the street. The grass in the park was brown and dry and looked like the sage people burned when they were trying to be all spiritual. A homeless man was splayed out on a bench as if it were a bed at a four-star hotel. Gio spotted Manny sitting near the empty swing set. He wore a baggy sweat suit and black shades, even though the sky was gray.

"Welcome, gents," he said. "How was school? What did *you* learn today, Schoolboy?"

"I learned stupidity is a trait that, unfortunately for you, Manny, cannot be cured."

Manny placed a hand on his chest. "Damn, that's too bad. Guess I'll just have to make *stupid* money instead."

"You're a fucking idiot."

Gio shuffled. "It's cold as fuck, man. Hurry up. Let's do this already." He took his empty book bag off and placed it at his feet.

"Aight. You remember what I told you?" Manny asked.

"Yeah, yeah, man. I ain't dumb."

"I don't know. Sometimes I'm not so sure." Manny looked up at me. He screened me like the metal detector that greeted us at school every morning. "You cool, right, Schoolboy? I don't have to worry about you talking to anybody, do I?"

"I'm cold."

Manny dug into his sweatshirt and unveiled a brick of something wrapped in plastic baggies. With a magician's grace, he stuffed it into Gio's book bag and zipped it up.

Manny leaned back on the bench. "In and out. No detours. And if you get stopped—"

"Yeah. I know."

We walked out of the park in silence. Gio's step lost its bounce. He kept his head on a swivel. For the first time in a long time, his book bag had some heft to it. Real heft. Not the little dime bags he was pushing to kids here and there from his locker or when school let out. We crossed back onto the avenue. Cars inched forward at the red light until they were halfway into the crosswalk by the time the light turned green.

"So what's up with that?" I asked as we waited at the bus stop.

Gio held the straps of his book bag tight, looking left, then right. "With what?"

"You're holding like ten pounds of what, weed? Coke? Crack?"

He punched me in the arm. "Why don't you say it louder, dickface." He walked up to the curb and looked down the street for the bus. A patrol car drove by, and he backed up.

I stared at the two cops in the car. At their faces. If not for their blue uniforms, they would have looked just like us. Like family. They made a left and disappeared. "So you're like a real drug dealer now? You're really moving shit."

"You say it like I murder babies and eat their intestines."

"I'm just a little concerned. Like you know where that leads, right? You know my Pops—"

"Yes, Javi. I know about your damn Pops, okay?" Gio shook his head. "I just help Manny. It ain't no big thing."

"That looks like a lot more than help to me."

He leaned against the wall of the bodega. It was painted in a mural commemorating someone named Fly Guzman. It depicted the man wearing a white bucket hat and a white shirt with angel wings sprouting out of his back and a thick rope chain hugging his neck. On the ground, near the icebox, was a shrine of red and white candles and some old, wilted flowers. I never knew who this Guzman was or what he'd done to earn such real estate. But I often would stare at the mural and do the math on the twenty-two years it said he'd walked the earth. I'd think about Pops and his funeral in Puerto Rico. He also wasn't very old when he was killed, even though he carried himself like he'd been on this planet forever, like he knew the answer to everything.

"You do know you could go to jail for this, right? Or worse."

Gio rolled his eyes. "I'm not doing all the risky shit. I'm just making some cash pulling it out and weighing it. Stuffing baggies. Delivering. Easy shit. Low-key. Under the radar. No guns, no action, no heavy weight." More phrases that had been fed to him. More phrases meant to give him a sense of security.

"And if you get caught?"

Gio shrugged. "I'm a minor with no priors. I say I don't know how it got there. Play dumb. Don't snitch. They'll let me go eventually. It's all good."

"All good, huh? So you and Manny got it all planned out."

Gio pushed himself off the wall and looked for the bus. "Listen, Javi, don't worry. It's all under control." He patted me on the shoulder. "Soon I'm gonna have enough for that whip. A nice one. Tints, booming system. You'll get off my back once we're riding around in it and all the bitches want you."

"You know you need to get a license to drive, right?"

"You sure about that?" Gio said, grinning.

I nodded and forced a smile. We were both quiet again. I racked my brain for a way to get through to him. "What about school?"

Gio waved his hand like I had laid a nasty fart. "Fuck school. I'm tryna be my own boss. Entrepreneur mentality. Big pimpin' like Jay. School is for squares. For *schoolboys* like you," he ribbed me.

"You should at least graduate. The shit really isn't hard. That book Ms. Rivas assigned was actually good."

Gio nodded. "I know. I read it. Piri Thomas was a G. Mad respect."

I was taken aback, more so than by the drugs in his book bag.

"Why are you so surprised? I know how to read."

"So why didn't you do the report?"

"Because there's no point. You see how that bitch talks to me. It wouldn't matter either way. It's the same thing with all these teachers. They don't care. So why should I?" Gio shimmied and did a little dance. "I rather make this moneyyy."

Maybe I should have said more. Prodded harder. Provided encouragement. But the bus came. We were barely sixteen years old. So I laughed at his little dance, and I hopped through the back doors with him. I never bothered bringing up school again.

Seven

GETTING BACK in Anais's good graces was a process. Eventually, not long after I got back to the Bronx, she finally responded to one of my many "I'm sorry, please, please speak to me" texts.

"You have a lot of toxic-masculinity issues to work through," she wrote.

I agreed that I did. I made it clear that I needed her to help me do that, in the hopes that it would salvage something between us. "Obviously, I just need some guidance from someone who knows better."

Over Skype that winter, she in Albany and I in the Bronx, we discussed some of the hip-hop songs I'd been raised on like they were lullabies. We discussed their videos, the majority of which included busty, half-naked women. We discussed the examples of older men I'd seen before me: people like Pops, Manny. The words they used to refer to women, the way they described interactions with them as if they were objects to be controlled.

Anais shook her head often during our conversations. She'd say things like "It's almost like the world was trying to make you into this hypersexualized beast, right? I wonder who would want to do that?"

I'd go along. "The people running things, of course." I cringed on the inside. But for the time being, I ignored the little things. I didn't ask questions. Didn't try to challenge her. I missed her. So I took the path of least resistance.

Eventually, my strategy paid off. Eventually, we were talking about things besides toxic masculinity and the influence of poverty on a man's life. And eventually, at the end of our frequent video chat sessions that lasted late into the night, the two of us would undress, keep an eye out for our sleeping parents, and quietly touch ourselves on our grainy cameras until we came in small, measured shudders.

It was pretty easy at first to focus on the good parts of Anais. There were many things about her I admired. For one, she was well-read. And being back in the Bronx reminded me of how odd I'd often felt carrying a book around while growing up. It reminded me of my Schoolboy moniker. Of how much like an outsider I felt around girls who always found my reading "cute," which always seemed to be code for "I'm not going to fuck you."

It was different with Anais. I didn't have to hide my intellectual curiosity. I could, instead, imagine a life with her. And I did.

I imagined the two of us having a cozy home, with a comfy couch, reading together, discussing what we read. I imagined the two of us going to events and book fairs like we did on campus. Even though she had such myopic taste in books, I appreciated the recommendations she gave me, passing me nonfiction books about unrest, protest movements, and activism from back in the day that put me on to harrowing shit. Murders, coups, assassinations, hangings, castration, so much racism. And the forces fighting against those things. Activists with berets and 'fros and stylish clothes, cigarettes between their fingers, yelling into loudspeakers, throwing fists. It was all fascinating. But it also felt so far away. So removed from the realities of our time, where the slights seemed smaller, and the supposed forces for good seemed far less gangsta. Nonetheless, I still felt like I was getting an education. I was learning how to deploy new terminology—*the cause, liberation, reparations, empowerment, solidarity*. Words that would soon come in handy.

Then there was also the fact that Anais actually seemed interested in what I wanted to do with my life. More than that, she seemed like someone who could help guide me. When I told her I wanted to be a writer, she didn't smile and look at me like I was delusional. Her mother was a professor of English at a local university. In the way that I'd grown up mixing with the occasional drug dealer or hit man at house parties, she'd grown up attending smaller, quieter gatherings with novelists, journalists, and historians. Therefore, she asked me questions that made me think: Why did I want to be a writer? What did I want to write about? What audience did I want to write for?

"The things you've been through. The journey you've had from your home to Donlon. Your voice is important," she said.

As should be clear by now, I was, and always have been, a sucker for praise.

WHEN I WASN'T speaking with Anais during winter break, I was busy noticing things in my neighborhood, in my other life back in the Bronx, which felt increasingly more distinct from the world of Donlon. They were the sorts of things I'd never cared to notice or pay attention to before. Things that made me realize my mind was changing.

For instance, while picking up Chinese food on one of my first nights home, I watched a girl who was probably twelve years old douse chicken and broccoli in sauce so heavy the container sagged. I'd eaten this countless times before, but now it made me think about the trays of salad and veggies at the dining halls on campus, the assortment of fruit to grab on the way out. I thought about fucking sodium and high blood pressure, about the research I'd read in Professor Gleeson's class, about why people in the hood die so young. I shook my head on the way out of the restaurant, trying, desperately, to cast the thoughts from my mind and enjoy the food in my hands. But I couldn't. As Mom and I ate at home, I felt I had to bring it up. Perhaps, I thought, these were the sorts of insights people had and I was simply learning about them for the first time.

"Don't you ever wonder why there aren't any *real* vegetables in our neighborhood, Ma? Why we have to settle for greasy stuff like this?"

Mom stared at the lottery numbers on her fortune cookie, trying to decide, it seemed, if they were worth playing. "Since when do you care about vegetables? You know how much I had to force you to eat them as a kid?" she said without looking up.

I sensed an argument. So I conceded, eating my food quietly but not enjoying it as much as I used to.

A few mornings later, I went to the corner bodega for fresh bread. I'd been going to this yellow store with a bright awning my entire life. I'd seen two generations of cats born and raised there, lounging on all the items, hissing at me in the aisles like the little pricks they were. But for perhaps the first time ever, I noticed the icebox out front plastered with advertisements for events in the area. They featured pictures of big bottles of liquor, scantily clad women, and men with shades fanning out hundred-dollar bills. I thought about one of the last lectures I'd gone to before leaving campus, featuring the recent winner of the Pulitzer Prize for Fiction. It took place the same night that a Sundance Award–winning independent filmmaker was in town screening her latest film, which left Anais and me torn about which to attend.

Was Anais right? I suddenly wondered, staring at the icebox. Were our "overseers" really just creating conditions for us to fall into certain traps? But how? Were there groups of white guys in vans coming like thieves in the night to our neighborhoods to plaster these images around for us to see?

I couldn't shake the idea from my mind. But it sounded too implausible to bring up to Mom. So I wrote it down in a notebook and brought it up to Anais during our next Skype session. She seemed pleased by my newfound awareness. "Javi. You're opening your eyes. You're seeing the world for what it really is. I'm so proud of you."

A couple of weeks later, as I read in my room and waited for dinner to be served, I heard several police cruisers in a row and looked outside through the bars of my bedroom window. I watched the cars speed away. Again, a normal sight. As normal for me, throughout my childhood, as looking outside and seeing the sky. But for some reason, I thought about how rarely I ever saw police on campus, or security guards in general. I wondered why there were so many cops around me to begin with. Who put them there? And for what purpose? Was it really, like Anais suggested, to keep us in check? To make sure a healthy percentage of us ended up in the prisons that they thought we belonged in?

"My campus is so safe," I told Mom, inching into the conversation, as I helped her wash the dishes that night. She was pouring leftover oil from a frying pan into a plastic container, watching carefully to make sure none spilled.

"I'm glad, Javi. But don't drop your guard, entiendes? You never know when shit could go down."

I thought about the way Anais referred to the police, calling them "agents of the state" and "vestiges of our racist past." I liked the word *vestiges* a lot. But I asked her how she could think that when her dad was a police captain in her little town. "I love my dad," she said. "But that doesn't change the fact that he's chosen to be on the wrong side of history. It's not my fault that he doesn't realize the harm he contributes to. Sadly," she said, "too many of our parents have been brainwashed."

I cut the water off. What did Mom think about the police?

"You know," I said to her, "at school, some friends of mine have talked about what it might be like if there were no police in neighborhoods like ours. Since, you know, they tend to lock so many of us up. Like, what if communities could police themselves, like they did back in the day. Before Western society was imposed on us. Before we had to deal with all of these racist structures." It was probably the first time I'd ever deployed some of what I'd learned at school back at home, outside of the nice, tall gates of Donlon's campus.

Mom raised an eyebrow. "De qué hablas, nene?"

"I'm just saying. Maybe it's not a bad idea. I never noticed before, but there are a lot of cops around here."

"Yeah, Javi. Because there are a lot of locos out here. You know that." Mom finished pouring the oil and snapped a lid on the container. She held the oil up to the light, and I stared at the little particles of tostones floating around in it. Pleased, she stuck the container in the fridge.

"If you don't want to get locked up, don't do no stupid shit," she said. "That's all you have to know about the police."

ON NEW YEAR'S EVE, we went to Titi Nilda's place in El Barrio. Family was there, neighbors. Little kids ran through the rooms. Styrofoam cups were filled with coquito, Hennessy. There were numerous flans to choose from. Despite the protests of everyone under thirty, nothing but salsa was played. At one point, Mom and Titi were drinking, red-faced, in the kitchen. I came in to deposit my empty paper plate in a garbage can that had long been stuffed to capacity.

"Hi, handsome," Titi said, pulling me close for a hug. "Aren't you lucky to have such a smart boy," she told Mom.

Mom twisted her lips and downed the contents of her cup. "Hmm. Very smart. Este tipo came from school with these big ideas all of a sudden. Thinking he knows it all."

"What's that supposed to mean?" I said.

Titi Nilda put her arm around my shoulders. "Oh please. So what? That's the point of going to college to learn, right?"

"Yeah, but he could be learning real things. Like how to run a big company and make a lot of money so his pretty mama doesn't have to work anymore. You should feel lucky Luis never was a big reader," she said, referring to my older cousin, a truck driver, who was in the other room, belching and drinking his seventh beer.

Titi Nilda pinched my cheek, like I was a little kid, until I pushed her away. "Don't complain, Sonia. He could have a felony and two kids by now. Let him have his little ideas."

I fumed for the rest of the night.

On the car ride home, Mom lowered the music at a red light. "So I know you only have another couple of weeks before you leave," she said, "but I was wondering if maybe you want to meet this guy I'm seeing now. He wants to meet you."

I was tired of meeting the guys she'd been seeing since Pops got killed. They were all the same, and we'd all go through the same motions. They'd ask me about school, what I wanted to be when I grew up, what my favorite sports team was. All these questions, as if they really were there to get to know me, not just appease Mom enough for her to sleep with them.

"His name is Jared," she said. "He's friends with one of the doctors at my job. The doctor introduced us." She pulled the car forward. "There's no rush. But I thought it would be nice."

I zeroed in on the man's name. I thought about Anais's parents. How she'd described their union. How critical she seemed to be of them, which, even by my own standards, seemed harsh. "My dad basically married into whiteness," she told me once. "Then he took a job to uphold its values. It's sadly the progression that too many of us find ourselves in. Falling in love with an American dream that is really just a fantasy."

Was Mom living in the same fantasy?

"Is he white? This Jared?"

Mom seemed confused. "Yeah. So?"

I put two and two together. Why Mom always got excited about receiving attention from the doctors at her job. Why she sometimes talked about them the way teen girls talked about heartthrob actors or lead singers. Why she never brought up Pops, and why when she did, it was only to talk about all the bad things he'd done. "So you only date white guys now? Why? Do you think there is something inherently better about them?"

Mom scoffed. "See. This is what I was talking about. Esta mierda."

I decided to try to channel Anais. To channel the LTC. "You obviously can't see it for yourself, but you have internalized issues, Mom. Maybe we should talk about them. Maybe I can help you educate yourself."

Mom hit the brakes, forcing me to fly forward. She ignored the honking car behind her. "Internalized qué? Listen, nene. Don't let that fancy school of yours fuck you up in the head, okay? I like Jared because he's a nice man. He's a professional with goals. He's not a bum. And he treats me with respect. So what if he's white? That doesn't make *me* any less Puerto Rican. Don't come around here talking about what I am and am not, and what I need to learn, entiendes? I'm the one who brought *you* into this world, not the other way around. Don't get it twisted."

I'd gotten under her skin. I felt it. The power. It was like I was a lawyer. Like I was putting her on trial. Oh, it felt good. "You don't have to be so defensive, Ma." I understood how Anais must have felt. I repeated one of her favorite phrases. "It's okay," I told Mom. "The truth can be uncomfortable."

Mom did a double take, as if she was wondering if I was still her son or if I had been body-snatched. "The only thing that is going to be uncomfortable is my foot up your ass. No me jodas más."

She drove the rest of the way in silence.

I didn't mind. I reveled in my victory.

Eight

BY THE FALL of my junior year, Anais and I were a serious, thriving couple. A goals couple, in fact. King and queen of the LTC. We were young, but we'd already discussed a life together. Not marriage per se, as Anais believed it was an "archaic" institution "created to enslave women as the property of men." These conclusions were fine by me. Instead, we discussed a "life partnership," being "co-conspirators" working toward progress in the world. What exactly that progress was, and what specific changes we were seeking, was unclear, but for our purposes, we didn't feel it was all that important to define it.

Anais decided that after she graduated that year, she would get a job nearby and wait for me to graduate the following year. She had it all planned out. Get work experience as a community organizer locally, save money, then move to the city with me to make a "real impact somewhere." I loved many things about her, but one of the biggest was her clear-eyed vision. I'd never met anyone who lined up their steps like she did. She seemed to know what would happen each year of her future: *Forbes* 30 Under 30 (for "leadership," not "capitalism") by twenty-eight or twenty-nine. Two kids by thirty-five. A run for office around age fifty, "once the kids are old enough that they can tend to themselves." She also seemed to know what her strengths were, and she was happy to tell you about them, as if she were a walking résumé: "I'm assertive, I'm bold, I'm a leader, I'm an organizer, I'm an agent of change."

The closer we became, the more her approach started to rub off on me. It was only natural that she would help me solidify my own goals, the same ones that would one day lead to my downfall. I'm sure she wouldn't be happy to hear me say this, but the truth is, were it not for her, my brilliant—albeit brief—hustle likely wouldn't have reached the heights that it did.

The first time I spun a tragic tale, it was to get into college. Early on at Donlon, the storytelling returned as a way to get attention from others, namely Anais, but also to walk around campus feeling like I was someone. To make certain I wasn't one of those nameless students who shuttled from class to class and could disappear off the face of the earth without anyone noticing. But as I neared the end of my college tenure, Anais helped me realize, unbeknownst to her, that telling stories people wanted to hear, making them sound good, making them sound "authentic," could be my golden ticket, not just to a fancy degree but to a thriving career.

I was in Albany when this realization really sank in. Anais and I had decided, given our plans to build a life together, that I should finally meet her parents. One weekend, I took a drive with her to her home upstate. We drove through the early evening to make it in time for a late dinner. But instead of going straight to her house once we got off the highway, Anais took me to a park with no lights illuminating the lot.

"Is this where you murder me?"

She unhooked her seat belt, moved over to my side, straddled me, and began to undo my belt. "No. Not yet."

When we finished having sex, she let out a long, yoga-like sigh. "I figured we should get that out of the way, since there'll be none of that at my house."

I grinned. "We can keep quiet when your parents go to sleep. Or at least we can try."

Anais hitched her bra up and turned the car's engine back on. "My dad would literally shoot you."

I was struck by how my carefree, confident tigress suddenly seemed so serious. In our relationship, there had been few rules or boundaries as to how or where we'd make love. "Don't try anything in my house. For both our sakes," she said.

Anais drove until we reached a tree-lined street. The large houses had nice porches, with doormats, lights, and wind chimes. They looked like the houses on those streets in the opening credits of Disney shows. Where the camera pans around the neighborhood and everyone waves at each other from their cars or smiles while picking up the newspaper on the driveway. Anais pulled up in front of a white house with a red door.

"You ready?"

I was here because I was serious about her. Because I had a vision of us together, living in a house perhaps not all that different from the one before me. Maybe even in Riverdale. I saw myself, a famous writer. Her, a famous activist or political figure. Little brown babies on the lawn. Maybe even one of those magazine spreads about our life, showcasing our interior decor and our pithy thoughts on morning routines.

"Yeah," I said. "Are you? You seem off."

"I'm fine."

When she opened the door, I noticed pictures on an entranceway table. One was of a young Anais in a yellow cheerleader outfit, smiling, holding pom-poms, and standing next to a bunch of little white girls. The Anais in the picture seemed so alien to the one standing before me, frowning.

"Maybe you could show me some moves?"

"Shush." She pushed me through the hall, past a wide staircase and into the dining room. There was a long wooden table set with silverware and cloth napkins. In the center was a roasted chicken, a pie, rice, potatoes, and an abundant salad. Not even the slightest whiff of adobo in the air.

"This is all for me?"

"Don't let it go to your head. My mom loves a reason to cook."

She led me into the large, modern kitchen—marble countertops, subway tile backsplash, stainless steel appliances—where her mother, Samantha, was stirring a big jar of iced tea, stopping to taste it. Upon seeing Anais, she widened her eyes. "My little girl is home," she said, hugging her tight as Anais remained limp.

"Hi, Mom," Anais said in return.

When she noticed me, Samantha smiled and stretched out her hand. "Oh, you must be Javier. It is so nice to meet you. Welcome to our home. I hope you came hungry."

She wore red glasses, a colorful scarf around her neck, and a yellow dress. She had a bright, cheery air about her—in stark opposition to the rebelliousness Anais always seemed to display on campus, always ready to march, to stand up and shout.

"Nice to meet you too, Ms. Delgado."

She flicked my arm and shook her head of thick, gray hair. "Please. Samantha is fine. Or Sam." She winked. "Eddie," she called out. "Come here."

From another room, I heard a grunt, and moments later, Anais's dad appeared with a folded-up newspaper. He was a large, pear-shaped man. Bald head, but skin the same color as mine. There was a gruff look about him, and despite the golf shirt and khaki pants, I could tell he was from around my way. He forced a smile. He stuck out his large hand and nearly ground mine into dust. "Hello, young man. I'm Edwin. You can call me Mr. Delgado, at least for now." He looked me up and down.

I smiled uneasily. "Of course, Mr. Delgado."

"Be nice, Daddy," Anais said, in a soft, mousy voice I'd never heard before.

Mr. Delgado smiled. "I'm always nice." He extended his arms, and I watched as Anais melted into them. He kissed the top of her head. "How's my princess doing?"

Princess?

"Tired. It was a long drive."

Mr. Delgado peered at me. "Your boyfriend here didn't drive you?"

"He doesn't have a license."

"Tsk. Tsk. What kind of man doesn't drive?"

I forced my lips to form a smile. "I grew up near the trains. Never had a reason to learn."

"The Bronx, right? My princess here told me a little about you. I grew up in the city too, even spent some time in the Bronx. But I learned how to drive. Stick shift. I guess we're just different types of men, aren't we?"

Anais clapped her hands. "Okay, I'm going to give Javi a tour of the house." She tugged me away by the arm.

Mr. Delgado grinned. "Why don't you start with the living room? And the couch, where Javier will be sleeping while he's here."

Samantha slapped Mr. Delgado's arm.

"Nice to meet you both," I said.

"Dinner will be ready in ten," Samantha said.

Anais showed me into the living room, where a large sectional couch with built-in cup holders sat in front of a television with a fireplace underneath. "At least it looks comfy," I whispered.

"It is. Sorry. He's always tough the first time around. He'll grow to like you."

She led me to an adjacent room that she said was her mother's study. I'd only heard the term *study* in books I'd read, usually old books describing old writers sucking on pipes and writing in longhand with a feather quill and shit. I didn't realize people still had them. Three of the walls were lined with shelves filled from top to bottom with books. Many of them were thick academic-looking tomes, but there was also, I saw as I scanned the shelves, poetry, fiction, and general nonfiction. In the center of the room was a wide desk with a beautiful curved lamp on it. Behind the desk, there was an old typewriter on a credenza, and her mother's degrees hung on the wall above. "This is incredible," I said. "Your mom seems so cool."

"She's okay."

Anais led me upstairs to her bedroom. I expected it to be similar to her room off campus, filled with posters of figures like Angela Davis and Che Guevara and books whose titles all seemed to be about revolutionizing this and decolonizing that. But her room in her house almost seemed like it belonged to another girl. Clean white walls, a shaggy silver carpet, a bed full of little fluffy pillows. On one wall was a bulletin board with pictures tacked up. Anais on camping trips; Anais posing with white boys in football jackets; Anais doing karate; Anais on prom night, standing on her front lawn wearing a tiara.

I stared at them closely. "So you were really a cheerleader?"

She crossed her arms over her chest. "Yeah. Why do you say it like that?"

"Like what?"

"Like you're surprised or something."

"Because I am. A little bit."

"Why?"

"I just didn't see you being a cheerleader."

Anais sat on her bed. "It was just a phase."

I looked around the room. The large computer monitor on her clean desk, the reading chair near the window. And outside her window, the view of the backyard, the grass, a tree in the distance with a little tire swing hanging from it. I tried to imagine what it would be like to grow up in a place like this.

"Your house is real nice. It feels peaceful. Quiet. I'm used to chaos and noise. I'd probably be worried about getting murdered if I lived up here."

"Well. That is what privilege buys you, Javi. Peace and quiet. A way to look past the real struggles that most people face. It's delusional."

I chuckled. "It's okay to have a nice house, *princess*. I'm not judging you. I'm just saying. It's nice."

Anais narrowed her eyes at me. From downstairs, we heard her mother call us for dinner.

At the table, I tried my best to mimic her family. They ate delicately, cutting chicken into little pieces, chewing slowly, resting their utensils between bites. They used their thick napkins—miniature blankets, basically—to wipe the corners of their mouths. It made me realize how I tended to eat, bunching my elbows up on the table, never dropping my fork and knife until the food was gone.

"So the Bronx, right?" Samantha said. "What a vibrant culture. Eddie here spent some time there in his youth. Oh, maybe you're from the same neighborhood, Eddie?"

Mr. Delgado asked me what neighborhood I was from. When

I told him, he nodded and cleared his throat. "That was all Irish and Jewish back in my day. We didn't go up that way. Things had a certain order to them, you see, despite the dysfunction. There were just certain streets you didn't go down, certain neighborhoods you didn't bother to set foot into."

"It's sort of like that now, too," I said, excited to bond over something. But I didn't get very far.

"No. It's very different than when I was growing up. It's not the same at all, trust me."

"When was the last time you were back?"

"Never," Anais said. "He won't take me to see where he grew up."

Mr. Delgado shrugged. "There's nothing to see. No reason to go back. No hope for that place, far as I'm concerned. The best thing you can do is run far, far away from it."

I looked at Anais. I figured she hadn't told her parents about her plans to move to New York just yet.

"Anyway," Samantha said. "What do your parents do, Javier?"

I told her Mom worked at a hospital, which made her brighten up, even made Mr. Delgado pay attention. "A doctor?" she asked. "Oh, how wonderful."

"No. Not exactly. Sort of like their assistant."

"Oh, okay. A nurse?"

"No. Not that either."

I didn't know whether to go on, so I stopped myself and reached over for more chicken. "This is really good," I said. "Delicious."

Samantha smiled.

Mr. Delgado sipped his soda. "And your dad? What does he do?"

I looked at Anais again. I hadn't told her the entirety of what had happened. I had only told her he was tragically gunned down and that I'd seen it. That he was a businessman who "did what he needed to do" to support his family, which I'd picked up as a vague, offhand way of describing the exploits of a career criminal and drug dealer. All the other details seemed like a lot to get into. Besides, Pops had drilled into me as a young boy that less was more. "If someone asks what I do," he'd tell me, "say I run my own company." That's how he always saw himself. As an entrepreneur.

Anais put her hand on top of mine. "Javi's father died tragically when he was young. He was an entrepreneur who was gunned down. So full of potential. Very sad."

Samantha sighed and looked at me like I was a depressed elephant at the Bronx Zoo.

Mr. Delgado arched an eyebrow. "Very, very sad, indeed." He shifted his weight to one side. "What kind of business did you say he was in?"

I had asked Pops that myself once. "What should I say when people ask what kind of business?" His reply wasn't useful. "Tell them it's my business, not theirs."

Samantha, ever thoughtful, noticed my discomfort and tapped Mr. Delgado on the hand. "Enough, Eddie. He's not a witness to interrogate." She turned to me. "Don't mind him. He can't turn off his cop brain sometimes."

I wondered how the two of them got along. In a way, the fact that they did was reassuring. I figured it was proof that whatever differences there were between Anais and me—in our manners, the way we thought, or the way we grew up—could be overcome in the end.

Mr. Delgado took another sip of soda. "Sorry. Very sorry to hear about your dad."

"Thanks," I said.

We continued eating, and eventually, Samantha gestured toward the pie. As we ate it with ice cream and coffee, I complimented her on her study. "I want a room just like that one day."

Samantha beamed. "Yes. Anais tells me you want to be a writer? That's wonderful."

I sat up. I figured this would be my chance to impress them. An academic with a room full of books. A man who read the newspaper. "Yes," I said. "That's my dream."

"So what kind of writer do you want to be?" Samantha asked. "What genre? What type of stories interest you the most?"

The questions sounded like the ones Anais would periodically ask me. So I gave her mom the same answer I'd given her. The answer I'd give anyone if they asked me, which wasn't all that many people. "I'm still figuring that out."

It was the truth. At that point, I hadn't written anything substantial. No essays, or stories, or anything I could publish. I had yet to even really grasp the media landscape and how it could be shaped to my liking. All I had were little journal entries to myself. Noting the differences between Donlon and the Bronx, recounting exploits on campus with Anais. Then, of course, there were my letters to Gio—at least one or two every semester.

Samantha seemed disappointed. She looked at Anais and gave her a tight smile.

"So no plan, then?" Mr. Delgado quipped. "I'm guessing my princess here hasn't told you the motto yet." He looked at Anais. "Why you holding out on this boy? Tell him how it goes."

Anais sighed. "Do I really have to do this right now?"

Mr. Delgado tilted his head. "He obviously needs to hear it."

" 'By failing to prepare, you are preparing to fail,' " Anais said, rattling off the words through gritted teeth.

"Words to live by, Javier. Do you know who said them?"

"No."

"Benjamin Franklin. One of our founding fathers. A brilliant, brilliant man."

I looked at Anais. I expected her to say something about Franklin owning slaves or being an architect of systemic oppression or creating the "system" we were caught in or something like what I could count on her saying at school. But she remained quiet.

"Remember that saying," Mr. Delgado said to me. "I made Anais repeat it every night before bed. That's part of why she's the wonderful young woman you see before you today. Right, princess?"

"Yes, Daddy," she said.

THE NEXT AFTERNOON, Anais and I had uncomfortable sex in her car as it was parked in the farthest corner of a mall parking lot. "If only your *daddy* could see what his little princess was up to," I said as Anais and I put our clothes back on.

She didn't laugh or try to hit me, which was how I knew something was on her mind. We went to the mall food court and stared at the various options for watered-down ethnic food. As I weighed the pros and cons of Sbarro and Panda Express, Anais asked me something she'd never asked me before. "Where do you see yourself going?"

"I'm leaning toward Sbarro, because that Panda Express shit looks stale. But at the same time, it's not *real* pizza, you know?"

"I'm not talking about food. I'm wondering, like, for real. Where do you see yourself going? Like in your future? In life?"

I knew this had to do with the previous night.

"I'm not saying it's all that important," Anais said as we paid for the Panda Express. "It's okay not to have everything planned out. But what do you think? You always say you want to be a writer but never really mention more. You can't just say you want to be a writer but not write anything or even have real goals."

"Ouch," I said.

"I'm not coming at you. But you are going to graduate soon. And then what? My dad is annoying, but he's right."

"So I should just be like good old Ben Franklin, huh?"

"It's just a saying."

Anais led us to a table. She removed her fork and knife from the plastic wrapping. I'd always noticed how formally she tended to eat, finding it cute, but now that I realized where it came from, I saw the contradiction in it.

"How about the newspaper?" she said.

I'd thought about it, and even gone to one of the information sessions my freshman year. But I'd checked out when they'd mentioned that for me to write anything interesting, like an opinion column, I'd have to first start out as a beat writer covering something on campus. I knew enough to know I didn't want to be a real journalist. I didn't want to have to do any of the hard work of researching or interviewing or getting things like facts and dates straight. I didn't want to "back up" my work like all my professors droned on about. That seemed boring, tedious, and not at all glamorous.

"We can get you on the opinion page," Anais said, confidently.

"And the requirements? It's a little late in the game for me as it is." Aside from the barrier of having to actually report first, coming up with something every few weeks seemed like a lot of extra work on top of my studies, which were already hard enough. It was easy to talk myself out of the proposition. It was just a campus newspaper, after all. But as we sat there eating our shitty Chinese food, Anais gave me a reason to try that I hadn't considered before.

"Do you know they've never had a Latino columnist in their entire hundred-year history? Isn't that fucked up? You could be the first. In fact," she said, pausing to think, "you could use that in your pitch. At this point, with everyone all of a sudden caring about diversity, you could basically demand that they print you."

Now, that seemed worthwhile. My name somewhere in a history book. Maybe even up on a wall somewhere. I'd be remembered as a boundary breaker.

"You really think the paper would go for a column like that?"

She removed her phone from her pocket and furiously typed. "Let's find out."

THANKS TO ANAIS'S pressure on the editor in chief of the paper—an email she sent him, on LTC letterhead, that promised "sustained, frequent protests and negative attention" if my application was not given its proper consideration and the "unreasonable, not to mention harmful and classist barriers" were not removed to allow me to write a column in the first place—my proposed column sailed through an initial screening. Anais and I workshopped the title of it, Brown Boy Observes, and came up with a short description: "A minority student making his way through a white supremacist campus and world shares his valuable insight on day-to-day campus life, challenging the status quo, bearing witness, and speaking truth to power." I thought it was a little silly and didn't really know what I was "bearing witness" to, but it worked.

To actually get the job, however, the editor in chief said I still had to submit a sample column to the rest of the editors. "This is something we make everyone do," he assured me in an email, cc'ing Anais, who had taken on the role of my manager—or enforcer, depending on how you looked at it.

The ball was in my court. The chance to be the first Latino columnist at Donlon was right there at my fingertips. I was cognizant enough to know this could be the first step to better things, to the things I really wanted. But first I had to put something down on paper.

A columnist is someone who a publication decides has a perspective interesting enough to share with its audience. So what does it tell you, my dear readers, if in the 100-plus-year history of this fine, independent publication, not one Latino columnist has ever graced these pages? Not one brown person has had a perspective deemed worthy of sharing with the rest of the student body?

I guess you could argue that 100 years ago, this made sense. Latinos, just like Black people and other marginalized groups, were seen as inferior, less than human. But I really thought that had changed. I thought we were all "progressive" now. I thought we were all "colorblind." Apparently not on Donlon's campus. Apparently not even among the current stewardship of this esteemed publication.

Or perhaps there has just never been someone good enough to meet your standards. Perhaps those who came before me spoke a little too much Spanish. Perhaps they had a little too much kink in their hair. Perhaps you just didn't realize the harm that has been waged on our community.

So here I am. Giving you the benefit of the doubt. Taking up the mantle. Attempting to showcase what makes me different. What makes me the first Latino to rise to the top?

Since I was old enough to walk in the Bronx, I've been dodging bullets and a societal structure that automatically pushed me toward drugs and street crime rather than books. My teachers always said I was "one of the special ones."

I thought I was saved because of this. It landed me here, at this gorgeous place supposedly committed to so many ideals: diversity, inclusion and all of those other nice-sounding words in our mission statement.

Finally, I thought, I'm safe. Finally, I thought, I can live without the fear of constant forces of oppression looking to take me out or lock me up. But the truth is, this place is no safe haven for people like me.

Here I got stuck. I knew I needed something heavy and serious as an example. Not just some run-of-the-mill injustice. I thought long and hard about anything I could realistically consider racist or fucked up that had happened to me since I'd arrived on campus. I thought about the books Anais had given me, about the political dissidents who'd been tortured, beaten, spat at, and murdered in cold blood. The only things I could come up with seemed so small in comparison: being asked if I'd been shot while growing up, being asked if I was Mexican because it was clear that that was the one type of Latino some white people knew existed, being asked if I spoke Puerto Rican. Shit, that, when I wasn't talking about it at the LTC with a whole lot of gravity, made me laugh more than anything else.

I called Anais. I told her my dilemma. Her response proved pivotal.

"If you're looking for something timely, check Twitter, Javi. I keep telling you to create an account. That's where all the conversations are happening these days. All the media people are there. See what people are talking about, what's trending. With all that you've seen and experienced, I'm sure there's something you would be able to add to the conversation."

So I created a Twitter account. I added a profile photo of myself looking serious with my arms crossed, my little desk in the background, all my books on a shelf above it. I put "A brown boy observing and writing about injustice everywhere" in my bio. I looked up #racist and saw that the majority of the tweets were related to people's experiences with the cops—random stops, beatdowns, interrogations.

I'd had a few of my own interactions with the police, but they were benign. Almost all of them had to do with police looking for my Pops, probably for good reason, if I'm being honest. I didn't have any stories like the ones I was seeing on Twitter. Did I not look dangerous enough? Did everyone, including the cops, just automatically know I was a moist-ass bitch?

Then I remembered one night when I was a freshman on campus. A night that I'd long ago forgotten because it was so seemingly innocuous. I had walked Anais home from an LTC party. This was before we were even making out or smoking or doing any of the things we'd later do. I decided not to wait for the campus bus, which always took its sweet-ass time, and walk the twenty or so minutes to my dorm on the other side of campus. Even though it was two in the morning, I felt fine and at ease. I felt that way walking all over Donlon. The only thing I ever really feared were wild animals. Deer; even nasty squirrels that had popped out of the bushes and scared the shit out of me on a few occasions.

I had been walking for a bit through a particularly dark stretch of off-campus houses when I saw a campus police officer pull up beside me. I'd never cared about these people until I'd realized one day that they actually had guns on their hips. The car slowed to meet my pace, and the cop rolled down the window.

"Hey, buddy," he said. He was white, with an unusually large head. He wore reflective sunglasses even though it was late at night. "You lost?"

"Just walking home," I said.

"You go to school here?" he asked.

"I do," I said.

"Freshman, I'm guessing?"

"Yeah."

The cop stopped the car, and I instinctually stopped, too.

"Mind showing me your campus ID real quick?"

I took the ID out of my pocket and handed it over. I thought maybe he'd study it. Look at it, then look at me, then hold it up to my face to make sure. But he didn't do any of that.

"Okay. You live on north campus," he said, pointing to the bottom left-hand corner of my ID, which displayed my address. He nodded and handed me back the ID. "Why are you going this way, buddy? This is kind of a dark deserted path. Things are better lit over on Main Street. You could cut right up here and it'd be a whole lot easier."

"Oh," I said.

He pointed to a path on the corner. "That path right there. Looks creepy, but it's very short, and it'll shoot you right out onto Main Street. You really shouldn't walk in the dark like that. We keep this place safe, but you never know, right?"

"Right," I said. I thanked him. He smiled. And with that, he took off.

I never thought about this again. Never questioned if he'd stopped me because he was actually trying to help or because I was brown. I took his advice and realized he was right.

But that was then. Three years in, I had become a whole different Javi.

Now I looked at the interaction in a new light. I realized that in my search for something dramatic enough to get my column, I already had something that would slot nicely into the "conversation," as Anais said. All I needed to do was stretch the truth a bit.

Why not? I told myself. What would be the harm? I wouldn't mention the cop's name. No one had been around to see the interaction go down. I figured no one on campus knew me well enough to call bullshit. Not even Anais. I'd already lied to her in the past about being with Gio during a couple of his stops, about being slammed on the hood of a car while cops patted me down. It was an innocent stretch. To get the column. To put in motion the "plans" she so wanted me to have. It was just like my college essay, I reasoned. A means to an end. But that's how all addictions start. With one little hit. What will it hurt?

I learned that I was not safe on this campus on one of my very first nights here. I was walking home from a party, the same sort of party that all students here attend. But little did I know that I was not just any student. I was Brown Boy walking home in a predominantly white, protected space. Which is why I was stopped by the campus police.

The officer rolled down his window. He barked at me for my identification. I saw his hand inch toward his waistband. I thought about my dead father, who'd been shot and killed in Puerto Rico. I thought about my hometown of the Bronx, where I've been stopped by the police countless times, to the point that I know some of them by name. (Look at me now, Officer Moynihan!) There, the killing of Black and brown youth by cops is about as common as breathing. (Take one breath. There. One of us is dead.) If you're someone like me, you live in fear of the police every single day. It takes just one moment for them to blow you away, to end your life, destroy your family and get off the hook as if it were nothing.

But this wasn't the Bronx. This was Donlon. It was safe here. Or so I thought.

As the officer looked at my ID, I thought about who might find my dead body. What the police would tell my mom. Thankfully, the officer chose to spare my life.

Do you know why? Because he realized that I was not just a run-of-the-mill brown boy walking around a sacred place where I wasn't meant to be. I was one of the "special" brown boys who somehow managed to get in through these pearly gates of paradise. For now, and probably only for now, as long as my college ID is valid, he'll have to treat me differently than is his instinct to.

I watched him drive away that night and thought about how close I had been to losing my life. I've never shared this story publicly because I was scared. He'd won. He'd put me in my place. But no longer.

My story deserves to be shared. As do the stories of everyone else like me on this campus. Those of us lurking in the shadows. The question is: Are you ready to hear these stories? Are you ready to confront them? Or do you want to go on ignoring them just as they've been ignored for the past century?

The ball is in your court.

Hopefully, I've made my case. Hopefully, you'll find the perspective of this brown boy "interesting enough" to share.

THE COLUMN WAS ACCEPTED. At the time, I truly believed it was because of the power of my words. Sure, there was pressure on them, but in the end, my story had swayed the panel of editors. Like the admissions committee, they saw something in me worth admiring.

It was only later, much later, that I realized it was in their best interest to take my column. That I had done them a favor. Nearly every other columnist at the paper was a white man—something that others had pointed out but that had only recently gained traction as a real problem worth taking seriously. In other words, my timing was impeccable—a fact that, fortunately, or unfortunately, held true for the rest of my brief career. I was on the rise during yet another period when *diversity* was a buzzword. This wasn't the affirmative action days, though. There was Twitter now. And I was a trending topic. Even my shitty little college newspaper was not immune to realizing that they needed to cash in, needed to "join the conversation" if they wanted to survive.

I was too naive to understand any of this then. When the

editors decided to run my sample column as my actual first column and place it prominently on the front page alongside an editorial apologizing for their "dreadful history of exclusion" and promising to "do better," I took it as a sign of my talent. When I looked at the printed paper in my hands, I could quell all the little spats my faux story had created.

Anais, upon reading my final version, was hurt that I hadn't shared this incident with her before. For a moment, there was even a hint of skepticism; that is, until I explained that I'd kept it to myself out of fear.

"You should never be afraid to share something like that with me, ever," Anais said, nearly tearing up, and allowing me to breathe a sigh of relief.

Once the column was printed and word got out about the incident, the campus chief of police was forced to issue a statement apologizing for any "perceived offenses that may have occurred." He vowed to work with the university to undergo training to "ensure that these sorts of incidents" wouldn't "be repeated in the future." The LTC, however, was livid, and a whole meeting was devoted to how they might bring the whole department down after identifying the officer in question—I said I had never gotten his name, and his makeup, as I described it, just so happened to resemble that of about 90 percent of the officers on the force.

I tamped down the flames as best as I could, thanking the other students for their solidarity but pleading for peace. "I don't want to be a target. They might come for revenge, just like they've come for our brothers and sisters in the past. I'm not afraid, but I need to be smart." I thought that everyone had bought it. At the very least, the conversation, thankfully, moved on.

Once that was out of the way, I was able to enjoy what came next. The emails from other students on campus sharing their own stories with me, calling me "brave" and a "voice to champion." The professors who praised my words and said they'd be "reading closely" and cheering me on. The trickle of followers on Twitter, even a few retweets of my piece from people far away from campus. It felt good, felt like I'd accomplished something.

Little did I know that it was just a taste of what was to come.

Nine

WITH EACH SUCCESSIVE COLUMN, the fawning emails and tweets and followers kept coming. Little bumps of my drug of choice arrived as my phone buzzed with a new notification. I was hooked. Enough to keep me writing, to keep me fudging when I needed to. After all, it wasn't very hard.

A lot of what I wrote in my columns was based on anecdotes I'd heard at the LTC and retold, nodding to the person who'd brought it up, often making their day when their full name, or first name, or something vague like "my Chicana sister" (I gave them a choice) appeared in the paper. As far as I knew, they didn't think I was stealing or exploiting them. I was using my perch to "shine a light" on their stories, as they often liked to say upon sharing my columns with their followers.

When I really didn't have anything to write about, I inserted more made-up things that I figured no one could check me on. Little things that happened to align with the news cycle or with topics that I knew would resonate with readers and perhaps get me more of those followers and notifications I was starting to really enjoy.

For instance, it just so happened that the same week the president gave a speech about immigration, I was leaving the library late at night when a car full of frat boys—whose faces I couldn't make out, because it was so dark—drove by and yelled, "Go back to your country!" So what if I had actually just left the library without any problems and devised the story on my walk home? Anais bought it hook, line, and sinker. She practically demanded that I write about it. So what if it hadn't actually happened to me? It had happened to other people on other campuses and in other places, right? What mattered, I told myself, was that it *could* have happened to me. As far as I was concerned, I wasn't harming anyone. I wasn't doing anything wrong.

MY FIRST SIX MONTHS as a columnist were smooth sailing. At least, I thought they were, until I learned that at least one person out there wasn't buying all of my stories.

You see, along with the nice emails and tweets and messages I got after each column, there were always a couple of dumb ones. People calling me a "race-baiter," people telling me, "Stop writing before I make you stop writing." I guess you could call the messages threats, even though I never took them that way. They were always so weak and juvenile. "Banana-eating monkey." "Spic." "Wetback." I'd heard more cutting things said about me by my own mother. The only thing those messages were good for was column fodder or posting screenshots of them on my Twitter feed to get sympathy.

But this time was different. It was a text, from Ricardo: "We need to talk."

Ricardo had never reached out to me directly before. We'd exchanged numbers when I was still a freshman and he was the elder statesman at the LTC. But we'd never hung out alone. We only ever saw each other at the parties attended by mostly LTC people. Then Anais and I became a thing and, rather quickly, began to take the center stage he'd once held. He stayed on campus to go to graduate school and stopped coming to the LTC as much. His presence didn't seem to be missed. It had been a couple of months since I'd even seen him, much less talked to him. Which was why I found it so weird that he wanted me to meet him at his apartment.

I went because I thought he might have a story to share with me. I had another column due in a few days, after all. But when I got to his place, Ricardo opened the door and wordlessly led me inside.

I'd been in his living room a number of times for house parties. I sat down on the beat-up leather couch, which sagged and smelled like stale chips. The same spot where Anais and I had made out on too many occasions to count; the same spot where I'd caught Ricardo watching us do so, much to my enjoyment and his dismay.

"What's this about, man? I feel like I'm about to get detention. You alright?"

Ricardo nodded. "Oh yeah, I'm cool."

He sounded not at all cool. He turned to his desk and gestured to a copy of the school paper on top. The most recent edition, with my latest column on the front page. "You have yourself a nice little platform, don't you?"

"Yeah. It's been fun."

"Fun." Ricardo grimaced. "You know, I did a few months of reporting my first semester as a freshman. I applied for a column each semester after. But I never got one. They always said my ideas and my writing were too dense. They didn't think they'd get a wide enough readership. They said I would bore people."

Perhaps he's just jealous, I thought. One of those people who don't deal well with the success of others. He'd already lost out on Anais. And now this? Rough. I tried to cheer him up. "I'm sure they found your voice too radical. Probably made them too uncomfortable. After all, it's been a hundred years that they were trying to stifle us, right?"

"Maybe. But not you. Not your voice. They like you. They really like you." He pointed to the newspaper. "They put you on the front page. Every single time, it seems."

"I guess I got lucky."

"Maybe." Ricardo stood and began to pace around his living room, making the old floor creak. "I wonder something, though, Javi: Are you really as serious about being a voice for this community as you like to say you are? Are you really serious about doing what's best for us? Or is this column just about doing what's best for Javi?"

I felt myself grow warm. Felt almost like I was back on the block, being pressed. "What's that supposed to mean?"

Ricardo smiled. "Come on. I see you. I know what you're doing. Writing your little cookie-cutter articles. Talking about all the big injustices on campus. Talking about your background, your personal history. You had it so hard, right? So, so hard. That's what we hear. Then, of course, we also get these crazy scenes from campus. Cops berating you. Frat boys telling you to go back to your country. But, oddly, no one is ever around to hear any of this. No one else sees it. Isn't that weird? On this big campus? You really do have a special perspective, don't you?"

I sat back, trying to assess where Ricardo was going with this. Was he trying to out me? Extort me? "Is there something wrong?"

"Yes!" Ricardo smacked the paper. "What's wrong is that this was supposed to be me, Javi. I was supposed to have a column like this.

This was supposed to be written by someone who cares. Someone who really wants to be a representative for our community. Someone who wants to lead. Not a poser looking for fucking clout."

"Poser?"

"Yes, poser. Come on, Javi. Why did you even come to the LTC in the first place?"

"Does it matter? I thought it was supposed to be a welcoming environment for our 'hermanos and hermanas,' Ricardo."

"Sure. It is. But come on, why did you really show up? It wasn't about the community. It was about Anais. You were chasing ass, just like the regular street dude that you are. I could see it a mile away."

More than anything, I was surprised. I realized I'd pegged Ricardo all wrong. I didn't know all that much about his background. I figured he was like most of the others at the LTC. A third- or fourth-generation Latino who came from some money, at least relative to the rest of us, and who was using their time in college at the LTC to try to connect with their roots or something. To make up for some big, identity-shaped hole in their heart. That was the vibe I got from Anais, and one that I was fine with. Especially since it was clear that she was enamored with me and the way I'd grown up.

As far as I knew from the little he let on and the gossip that inevitably happened among other LTC members, Ricardo came from a good family out in California. Parents had a successful business of some sort. Had gone to college before him—good ones, too. He wasn't someone, in other words, I was going to let press me. He wasn't someone I was going to let take away the status that I had earned with my column. Not without a motherfucking fight, at least.

" 'Regular street dude,' " I repeated. "Wow, Ricardo. That isn't an uplifting way to refer to your 'hermano,' now is it?"

Ricardo looked like he wanted to curse me out. If he'd been from my block, from my world, he would have done worse by then. But I could see in that moment that he didn't have that instinct. It *was* foreign to him. He came from a world of big dramatic blowups. A world of stomping off to another room and slamming a door. A world of subtweets and long, written rants.

I breathed easier. "Seems like you might be the poser here. And if we're talking about things being clear, I gotta say, I noticed that things changed once Anais and I got together. All of a sudden you weren't so welcoming anymore, 'hermano.' "

"You're full of shit, Javi. And you know what? Yeah, I was trying to get with Anais for a while. Fine. She's not all that anyway. But this? You being the *first* Latino to get a column at the *Bulletin*? It's not right. That honor should have been reserved for someone of substance. Someone writing with real heart and soul about issues, about solutions. You've done nothing of substance since you got here. Your dramatic, self-indulgent little columns help no one but you."

I smiled. He was right. I wasn't delusional. I knew what I was writing was formulaic. My editors, after the first two columns, had even said as much. Had tried to get me to "go deeper" in my writing and "crystallize salient points" readers could take away. But it was easy for me to get around that bullshit. After all, I had come through the door of the newspaper due to pressure. All I had to do was apply some more, to complain about them trying to colonize my voice and make me write to their European standards, in order to get away with how I really wanted to write. Little pop songs crafted quickly and with little effort to make the crowd bop along in unison and feel like all the right notes were being hit. And it was clear, from the emails, the social media followers, and the messages, that I was hitting the notes.

I was fine with that. My columns didn't need to be literary masterpieces. They were on trend, increasing my influence, and getting me on the radar of editors and publications I could write for outside of school.

"Okay, Ricardo. So what about you?"

"What about me?"

"Do *you* mean any of the shit you spout? Do *you* actually care about anyone but yourself? Be honest."

I wondered if he'd ever been in a real fistfight. Even though I'd lost every one I'd ever been in, I had entered the arena. I knew what it was like. I figured I could probably take someone who didn't even know what it felt like to get punched in the face. I crossed my legs and sat back on his couch like I was in a fancy hotel lobby. "I find it interesting that you preach all this shit about community and uplifting and supporting each other, and yet when someone else gets some recognition, you throw a fit. Seems kind of hypocritical, doesn't it?"

"I care about this community," Ricardo said, almost pleading. "I helped start the Dentro de la Familia meetings. That shit was *my* idea. I organized LTC events. I organized protests. I've spent nights making flyers and writing to administrators. I'm the real representative. I was supposed to get the recognition. I was supposed to get the column. That was part of the plan."

"Ah, the plan. Recognition. So at the end of the day, you just want the same thing I want, Ricardo."

"No. That's not true."

"It sure sounds like it."

"Well, you're wrong." Ricardo sat down, deflated. "We're not the same!"

He was right, again. I had something he didn't have. Something I figured I got from Pops. A killer instinct.

"Why are you in grad school?" I asked.

"To study philosophy. To get my PhD. To become a professor. To break boundaries in a field dominated by white men. A noble fucking goal."

"That sounds nice. And I really would like to see you end up there. I would really like to see you graduate from this place without any problems, Ricardo."

"What's that supposed to mean?"

"I'm just saying, it would be a shame if you didn't, you know? It would be a shame if you were, I don't know, chased out of here. Or worse." I stood and picked up the copy of the newspaper on his desk. "These stories are online, you know. I've actually gotten a lot of responses to them. You'd be surprised at just how many people who don't even go to this school love my 'cookie-cutter' articles. When you google my name, they all come up. Right at the very top. What comes up when you google your name, Ricardo?"

"What are you getting at?"

"It would be *such* a shame if what came up when you got googled was an article in the campus newspaper. An article about you, written by the first Latino columnist in this pasty-ass elite school's history. An article about how you threatened him and called him a dirty ghetto kid just because you're more privileged and think you deserve more than he does."

"Are you serious?" Ricardo stood. "You know that's not what I said."

I smiled. "Honestly, that's pretty weak. I'm better than that. I could make it much more dramatic." I stroked my chin. "Hmm. Maybe you said something about my brown skin? You're a lot lighter than me, you know. Maybe you said I was just a dirty Puerto Rican with African blood and you're better than me because you have that good Spanish blood. That might get more attention, don't you think?"

Ricardo shook his head. "No. They wouldn't believe you."

"Are you sure about that?"

Ricardo crossed his bony arms. I felt like if I wanted to, I could crush him. As if he were an ant. "What do you want from me? Money? Weed?"

"Ricardo! What do you think I am, a rapper? A mobster? You're more racist than I thought."

"Fuck you."

I pressed the newspaper against his chest. I felt like Pops. I felt I was channeling him. His blood was my blood, after all. I, too, had that same power inside me. That same authority. I thought about that chicken back in Puerto Rico. I thought that if Pops could see me now, maybe he would finally be proud of me.

"You're the one who called me here," I told Ricardo. "I don't want anything from you. The only thing I want is for you to remember what's going on here. Remember who holds the cards. If I don't hear anything about me, you won't hear anything about you. Entiendes, hermano?"

Ricardo looked outside.

"We have a deal or what?"

"Yes," he said. "I got it."

I patted him on the shoulder. I walked out of his living room. I strolled down the sidewalk feeling a new kind of high. The sort of high I assumed would last forever.

Ten

I HAD ENTERED DONLON as a kid who was only just beginning to grasp that he had an identity that was "in," so to speak. But I left as a young man who was clear on how he could pimp that identity to his liking. By the time I walked down the runway at our football stadium the day I graduated, I was a noted columnist on campus who had leveraged his platform and respectable number of followers into a few freelance writing gigs at bigger publications. To top it all off, I had Anais by my side.

The plan, on leaving college, was that Anais and I would move to New York City. She'd only been to the city a handful of times. Making trips down with her girlfriends for concerts while in high school and taking the train back, going with her family to visit the Museum of Natural History or the Statue of Liberty. Basic tourist shit. But she yearned for more. She wanted to experience the grind, the hustle, and see what kind of person an environment like that might turn her into.

Knowing that, I figured we would be on the same page about where to live. Her ideal location, she told me, was somewhere "clean and cute" but also somewhere that would allow her to feel like she was "part of a community." In other words, she said, she wanted to make sure we would not be gentrifiers. "I couldn't live with that on my conscience."

The concept of gentrification was being written about everywhere. *Beware! White people are flooding out of Manhattan and invading the outer boroughs. They bring with them nice coffee shops, salons, restaurants, and noise ordinances. Watch your backs!* I read this from afar while I was at school but never experienced it when I went back to the Bronx. My neighborhood was too far uptown, well past 125th Street, which seemed, as far as I could tell from what I read, to be the unofficial dividing line between "a hip, *authentic* locale" and "a savage wasteland where you will still 1,000 percent get robbed." Since my neighborhood had yet to be touched by white hipsters, it was, I thought, the "community" Anais might be in search of.

Graduation came and went, and we began packing up our lives in Donlon to prepare to move to the Bronx and stay with Mom for a bit until we found our own place. It was during this period that I first saw some real red flags. Whenever Anais showed me listings of places in the city, they were always well over my price range and in boroughs I had no interest in being in, like Brooklyn or Queens. Unlike her father, I didn't want to run away from the Bronx. I loved it—warts and all. As far as I was concerned, the two of us would buy a house there one day, and when I was old, I'd fall over and die on a gum-stained sidewalk.

I broached the issue with Anais a couple of nights before our drive down to the city. She'd just shown me another apartment in Brooklyn and was going on and on about the community garden down the block. "Says here they grow tomatoes, basil, peppers. They even teach residents about composting. It's perfect, right?"

I thought about the patch of weeds outside my apartment building in the Bronx. The only thing it seemed to grow were beer bottles, dog shit, and crumpled bags of chips. "It's nice, I guess. But it's a little pricey. Most of the stuff in Brooklyn seems to be."

Anais squinted at the number on the listing. "Oh. That's not so bad. All you need to come up with is half. I'm always good for my half."

Before graduation, I'd accepted an offer to teach creative writing to high school students in the Bronx. I decided it was the best option for me. Although I was interested in the internships and entry-level positions I'd been offered at magazines and other publications, I had zero interest in being unpaid or, worse, being paid about the same as a McDonald's hamburger flipper but having even less job security. A stable government check that always came no matter what seemed nice. So did summers off. I figured I'd have plenty of time to write on the side. I also figured I might be good at teaching. My students, I thought, might even appreciate having someone like me come in and show them all that I'd learned. I could be their Ms. Rivas.

"Are you sure you're going to be able to afford your half of the rent?" I asked Anais.

She had yet to line up a job. And the titles she was interested in—community organizer, community leader, activist, person of the people, change agent—sounded nice, but they also sounded like some shit you don't really get paid for.

"Don't worry," she said. "My parents said they'd chip in until I get on my feet. My dad will probably even put in extra just because he's so concerned about me living somewhere 'safe.'" She continued scrolling through the description of the community garden, then followed their Instagram page.

BEFORE WE MOVED IN with Mom, she had only met Anais once, during graduation week. Mom told me later, while I was walking her back to the car, that she thought Anais was pretty and nice, but that she seemed a little "bobita" to her. "You sure she's Puerto Rican?"

"What does it matter?" I said. "Weren't *you* the one to tell me that?"

"I can't say anything to you, can I? Listen, she's nice, like I said."

Once Anais and I were living with her, Mom found more things to complain about, like the fact that Anais didn't ever cook for me ("You're going to starve to death with that girl. She can't fry an egg or something?") and the fact that she didn't make the bed ("She grew up with a maid or what?"). Anais seemed oblivious. Perhaps because Mom made an effort to smile (forced, I could tell) when Anais was around and because Mom always complimented her on her appearance. "At least I'll have cute grandchildren." She sighed as she picked up a wet towel Anais had left on the bathroom floor.

Anais acted genuinely grateful to be in my apartment those first few days. She complimented Mom's food, calling it "authentic" and putting down her own mother's more traditional American fare. She noted the fact that everyone in my building seemed to know who I was and liked to mention offhand how they'd once changed my diaper. "Now, this is a real community." In the bodega, she took a picture of the latest cat and awkwardly danced to the merengue playing on the speakers, enough to warrant a side-eyed look from Papo.

But it only took a week or so for issues to pop up. After she went to the kitchen one night for a glass of water, I heard her shriek and thought maybe someone had broken into the apartment, was holding her up at gunpoint. But when I ran over, I saw the cabinet door open and her aghast at a few roaches crawling out from the shelves. "I think you have an infestation," she said. She looked confused when I told her that the roaches were basically tenants who didn't pay rent. "There's only two or three. That's not a big deal."

While we were having dinner later that week, the couple next door began to yell and scream at each other—just as they'd periodically done throughout my childhood. Mom and I didn't comment on it, continuing our conversation about the Powerball jackpot and what we'd do with all that money. Anais grew increasingly perturbed.

"Shouldn't we do something? Maybe the woman needs help."

Mom shook her head. "Oh no, don't worry, nena. They'll make up by bedtime."

"Yeah," I said. "They do this, then get high and have sex. You might hear some of that, too. But then it's all good. At least for a couple of months, until the cycle begins again."

Anais played with some grains of rice on her plate. "Seems a little violent, if you ask me. You sure we should just ignore that?"

"Mira, he's not your husband, right?" Mom said, waiting for Anais's response.

"I mean, obviously, no."

Mom rolled her eyes. "So *obviously,* it's none of our business, right?"

Anais looked down at her plate.

Mom gave me a look before standing. "Anyone want more?"

IT DIDN'T TAKE LONG for Anais to make appointments for us to see apartments in Brooklyn. Before we went to the first one, I took her to the most "communal" place I could think of in my neighborhood: the diner. "This place has been serving the community for decades," I said as we walked inside. I saw a little glint in her eye and thought maybe, just maybe, I might have her.

We sat in a booth and looked at the plastic menus. I talked up the omelets as Anais flipped through the pages. She smirked. "They have pictures next to all the food."

"Isn't it great? You know exactly what you're getting."

"It's cute, I guess." She put the menu down. "So what do you usually get? What's a traditional Bronx breakfast?"

The waiter appeared. He coughed and scratched his belly. He too had seen me grow up. Seen me come into this place and eat there with my mom and Pops, seen us have dinners here, breakfast, coffee, cigarettes. "Papo. Qué quieres?"

"Let me get two bacon, egg, and cheeses. And two coffees."

The waiter made three marks on the paper, as he always did, to pretend, for those interested, that he actually wrote something down. "Cream, sugar?"

"Yes."

"Actually, almond milk for me, please," Anais said.

The waiter squinted. "Qué?"

"Almond milk."

The waiter looked at me, as if asking me to translate for him.

"Cream and sugar is fine," I said.

He turned and left.

"What?" Anais said.

"They don't serve almond milk," I said.

"That's weird. Most places have it."

I thought about the campus café, where we'd often met between classes to study and read. It had all these special milks I'd never heard of, from shit that I didn't even know made milk. We'd been to a few cafés like that during our excursions into Manhattan since coming back to the city. They were all the same, as far as I was concerned. Plants. Chalkboard menus above the counter. Jazz or bossa nova softly humming in the air. The sound of a coffee machine grinding fresh beans from some tropical locale.

At the diner, our coffees were deposited by the waiter. He threw some packets of sugar and little plastic cups of half-and-half on the table, too. There was no foam or intricate drawing of a leaf. Moments later, our bacon, egg, and cheese sandwiches arrived, wrapped in foil. I opened mine like it was a Christmas present, marveling at the steam rising from the bread, the cheese spilling over. I bit into it ferociously.

Anais tried to grip her sandwich with her hands but put it down when some cheese dripped over the side. She looked around on the table. "Utensils?"

"For what? Use your hands, girl. Be a local."

When the waiter walked by, Anais asked for a knife and a fork, which he provided along with another side-eyed look. She finally took a bite. "Not bad," she said. "But a bit greasy, no? I also don't know if I can finish this. It's kind of a lot."

I thought about the plates she would order at cafés. The way they were presented. Fresh fruit and yogurt drizzled with honey, delicately cut pieces of bread. All of it looked like art. All of it prompted her to pull out her phone and take pictures. Like it was almost bought to be photographed and shown off rather than eaten. Anais took a sip of the coffee and winced. She pushed her plate forward. "I think I'll take it to go. I don't want us to be late."

THE APARTMENT WAS DEEP in Brooklyn. Over an hour on three different train lines deep. On the ride over, Anais said that if I would have let her bring her car to the city instead of convincing her to leave it in Albany, the whole trip would have been faster. I had to re-explain how much trouble having a car in New York City is, and how we would have spent more time in traffic and circling the block looking for parking than just riding the train like normal people.

After our tortuous journey, we ended up in a neighborhood in Brooklyn I'd never heard of before. When we got off the train, I looked up and saw a street sign that made me freeze. I didn't know shit about Brooklyn, but I remembered the names of streets and projects and blocks that had been dropped by all the rappers I grew up listening to. This street was one of them.

"You sure this is a good neighborhood?"

"Yes. I have a couple of friends who live near here," Anais said.

We passed one of Anais's signature coffee shops, then a cycling studio. But there were other things I noticed that made my ghetto senses tingle. A liquor store with thick, bulletproof glass shielding the attendant and all the bottles. A Chinese restaurant with faded pictures of food in the window. A pair of sneakers dangling from a light pole. Suddenly, though, we found ourselves in front of a gleaming new building that looked like it'd been airlifted there from SoHo.

Inside, the lobby was white marble and well lit. A man at the front desk asked for our names and licenses, checking us in, doing his actual job. The elevator smelled like lavender, not piss. On the eighth floor, we met a real estate agent Anais had been in contact with named James. He wore a silver sport coat, fashionably tight jeans, and suede loafers. He told us the neighborhood was "up and coming" as he led us into the apartment. He talked up the open-concept kitchen, the wraparound windows, the granite countertops, even the cabinet pulls. I admired his sales pitch.

The place was nice. I won't front. It had the sort of finishes I imagined our home might have one day. The sort of luxuries I thought I maybe even wanted. But all I could think about was how tiny and expensive it was. A box that cost double what we would pay in the Bronx for a one- or two-bedroom that was basically a mansion in comparison. James knew he had Anais in the bag, but he could sense my apprehension.

"You have to see the rooftop garden," he said.

Anais turned to me. "We really must, Javi."

I thought about the cheerleader in that photo in her house. Had that version of Anais ever really been extinguished?

When we got to the roof of the building, there were blooming flowers, a grill, and lounge chairs. James nudged me. "Nice, huh?" He put his arm around my shoulders. "Let me show you the best part." He led me over to the edge of the roof. I saw a beautiful, expansive view of not only Brooklyn but the whole city. Down below it all, though, I noticed something nobody else seemed to see—the projects, the basketball court in the center, the boys standing around in strategic locations. I thought of Gio. The last time I'd heard from him was at the beginning of my senior year. After I became a columnist, the response time between letters grew longer and longer, until they eventually sputtered out and he never answered my last one. What would he say about this place, I wondered. My trance was broken.

"Wow," Anais said, her eyes glittering. She nearly signed the lease right then and there.

I WAS SILENT as we took the train back uptown. Anais thought out loud about how she'd decorate the apartment. "An L-shaped couch would work best for that corner near the kitchen," she said. "Maybe a cute little coffee table with storage."

I saw my plans slipping away. My cheap apartment. My easy

commute to work. Compromises I didn't want to make. Compromises I hadn't expected to have to make, given who I thought Anais was.

"I can't believe you like that place," I finally said.

"It was gorgeous, Javi. What's not to like?"

"But it doesn't seem to have much of a 'community.' I thought that's what you cared about."

"I do. Which is why I like it. It's a nice place in a working-class area." She talked up the coffee shop, the renovated community center a few blocks away, a bar she'd read about that held poetry readings every week.

"What about gentrification? That building looks like it was built yesterday."

Anais fidgeted. "Yeah. But we're not gentrifiers. We're brown. It's complicated, but, I don't know, I don't see the harm in us living in a nice place if we're not going to come and try to change things."

Who was this girl? I wondered.

"But it's not real. It's so obviously out of place. Don't you see that? You came here saying you wanted to live in New York City and really help those in need. The ones at the bottom."

"I still do, Javi. I'm not selling out. I just don't want to live in a place with roaches, that's all."

"So the Bronx isn't good enough for you?"

Anais sighed. "I'm not saying that, Javi. The Bronx is great. I just—I don't know—I see myself living in Brooklyn more."

IT TOOK SOME CONVINCING, but I finally got Anais to see an apartment a few train stops south from my own neighborhood, walking distance from the world I knew so well and from my job. But that wasn't even why I chose the listing. It was because of the window looking out onto the street, the half wall right next to it. It was perfect for a desk, a nice desk that I'd be able to afford because of the cheap rent. It wouldn't be a study like the one Anais's mom had, but it'd be something close to it. My own version of it.

We got off the train and passed an old flower shop, a couple of 99-cent stores, and a Dominican barbershop. A pair of dudes out front whistled when Anais walked by.

She stopped in her tracks. "Excuse you. Who do you think you are?"

"Oye," they said, slapping each other on the chest. "She's a feisty one."

"Are you serious right now? What year do you think it is?"

The men looked at each other and broke out into belly laughs.

I knew there was no winning this sort of thing the way that Anais was used to winning things: through debates, spiels, and shaming.

"Chill out," I said to the guys.

"Él dijo, chill," one man said to the other, removing his hands from his pockets.

I didn't want to get my ass beat in front of Anais, so I quickly pulled her away.

"What the fuck was that?" she said at the end of the block.

"I understand it's fucked up. I do."

She squinted at me. "But?"

"But, Anais, you can't start an argument with everyone. This isn't Donlon. Sometimes you're better off moving along. Cutting your losses on some shit."

"Cutting my losses? I don't know who you think I am, but I don't compromise for no—"

"You seemed about ready to compromise to live in a Brooklyn high-rise, though, right?"

Anais huffed. "Whatever, Javi."

I kissed her. "Just give this a chance. That's all I'm asking."

I hoped that would be the end of it, but when we reached the apartment building, there was a group of four men parked out front. I could tell they were as permanent to the building as the light fixtures. It was three in the afternoon, and not one of them looked like they'd seen a minute of work that day.

These men reminded me of Gio, or Pops. There was this idleness to them, this existence in an alternate reality. People like that had a certain swagger. I saw it in Gio before he was arrested, and I saw it in these men in front of the building. I knew, judging by the number 179 tattooed on each of their arms, that there were likely more of them.

They hushed up and looked Anais and me over as we entered the building.

"Sketch," she said once we were in the cavernous lobby with faded tiles.

"They're just building community," I said.

She rolled her eyes. "*Okay,* you don't have to hit me over the head. I get it. You were right to call me out the other day. I was tripping." She grabbed my hand. "That's why I'm happy to be with someone like you. Thank you for keeping it real with me, Javi."

I smiled. "Just reminding you what you're looking for."

We waited three minutes for the elevator before I told her it likely wasn't working. "I'm sure it's just for today, though." We climbed the four flights of stairs. Sitting on the top landing was a hairy super, picking dust off his work boots. He sniffed when he saw us. "5A?" He made a lot of effort to stand, grunting like he was ninety years old, and eventually fished out a jangling ring of what seemed like a hundred keys.

When he opened the door, the place seemed to cough. The smell of fresh cheap paint stung our noses. The living room had scratched old wood floors. The windows were not floor-to-ceiling and had bars over them. The countertops were Formica, and the stove was plain old gas, not electric. But the apartment was enormous.

I walked into the living room and saw the corner where I wanted my desk to be. It looked even better in person. "So? What do you think?"

Anais strolled from room to room. She looked up at the low popcorn ceilings. Then she stood for a while and looked out the living room windows. "The finishes are pretty old. But I guess it's not bad. The price is definitely great." She looked down to the sidewalk, where the men we'd passed were howling with laughter at something. "I am a little worried about those guys, though. They give me a bad vibe."

I was impressed that Anais had the capabilities to feel a vibe. Then I remembered that she was, at the end of the day, a cop's daughter—no matter how much she didn't want to admit it.

"Babe. Wow. I mean, you're kind of judging them right now, aren't you? What if they're just hardworking men with a day off?"

Anais looked back down at the guys. "What? No, I'm not judging them at all. I have no problem living here." She leaned against the windowsill. "It's just. You really don't think they're up to anything bad? I mean, you would know, right?"

"Psh. No. They're harmless, babe. Trust me."

The super coughed. "Mira, you want the place or not? Yo tengo basura pa' sacar."

Anais looked at me. I waited with bated breath. She nodded and hugged me.

"Yes," she said, "we'll take it."

She had the loveliest smile on her face. So genuine that it made me feel just a tiny bit sick. It was for the best, I told myself.

DESPITE THE PROTESTS of Anais's parents—more vociferously Mr. Delgado, who tried to persuade Anais to leave me altogether for even being willing to "risk her life" by living in the Bronx—we signed the lease.

The crew of guys were still outside as we moved our stuff in. Anais even went out of her way to introduce herself, stopping to shake hands with one of the men. "I'm your new neighbor," she said. The man looked at her, confused. "Oh, aight. Cool."

As we slept on an air mattress surrounded by boxes that night, we were awakened abruptly at two in the morning by a thumping bass. We looked out the window to see that the gathering out front had suddenly ballooned to more than twenty men. They sipped from cups, joked, and spoke as if they wanted the whole world to hear them. A black SUV parked in front of them functioned as a massive MP3 player. The scene was as normal to me as crickets in the suburbs.

"It won't be like this every night," I lied to Anais.

We got back in bed. I spooned her. She tried to go back to sleep.

Then outside, we heard a man with a voice that sounded like a pickup truck driving through gravel tell the others about a date he'd had at Dallas BBQ. "When the waiter came back, I looked at shorty and was like, 'We going home together or what?' She gave me a stank face. So I told the waiter, 'Aight, split that check.' " The laughter sounded like a gathering of wily hyenas. I chuckled but stopped when Anais turned and shot me a fatal look.

I tried to think of something to say to smooth things over. But I was tired. The lease was signed. She'd get used to it eventually, I told myself.

I rolled over and went to sleep.

Eleven

THE DAY EVERYTHING CHANGED—for me, for Anais, and, eventually, for everyone close to me—began like any other at that point in my life. I flicked on the lights in my classroom and dumped my bag on the desk. I walked up and down the aisles and straightened out my students' wooden desks carved up with dicks and hearts. I sipped cold, shitty black coffee. I opened my email and saw a new message from Rebecca, the editor I'd been working with at *The Rag*.

Most of you reading this probably know *The Rag*. But for those of you who don't, here's what you need to know: *The Rag* was the MLB of writing as far as I was concerned. Everywhere else I'd written up until then was the minors. Online-only outlets whose links would often stop working within a year or two of my piece's publication. *The Rag*, in comparison, had been going for decades and had launched the careers of some of the biggest American writers. In any era before mine, it would have been almost impossible to write for them. But thanks to the collapsing media industry, the reign of clicks, and the urgent need for "new" and "unheard" voices, I stood a chance.

Still, it took me months to even get through to Rebecca that first year back in the Bronx. All of my initial pitches were rejected—and often her rejections contained the same language used by my college professors and my editor at the *Daily Bulletin* (before I had enough sway to shut him up): "not nuanced enough," "too preachy," and "too personal." The latter criticism was particularly hard to hear, as it made me think that to get to the next rung that I wanted to be at, I might actually have to do some hard work, might actually have to report things, back them up, find sources, and all the other shit I didn't want to bother with.

Luckily, I persevered, and through some luck of the news cycle, enough events in my wheelhouse—poverty, men of color getting killed for various reasons, incarceration—took place and garnered enough nationwide interest that all of a sudden, *The Rag,* which employed an impressive stable of writers, *needed* my pithy personal essays.

My initial success was quite small in comparison to what would come later. I published a few short essays for *The Rag* that they stuck in the back of their magazine. This in itself was an accomplishment for me. But I was no longer some naive and complacent fool. I wanted more than just my words printed on some paper. I had goals. I wanted to be on staff. I wanted to write a cover story. I wanted prizes and awards. I wanted to be a star. And I wanted to do all of that without really having to break a sweat.

The email that morning was similar to the rest of my correspondence with Rebecca up until then: a quickly fired-off query to see if I'd be interested in writing about the latest traumatic incident. After getting in the door, I peeped game. I knew that I was, unofficially, and perhaps begrudgingly, the underprivileged minority correspondent who was tapped to write sentimentally about tragic things that happened to me or to other people with melanin whenever they happened to align with the news cycle. It was a natural outgrowth from my position as a columnist at Donlon. Now the whole country was my campus.

The "conversation" could still be found on Twitter and other social media outlets. But things online no longer stayed online; they were remarked upon by world leaders, they changed policies, they got people fired and condemned. Whenever there was a new swell of a story, an issue, a trending topic, my job was to try to hop on the wave and provide some personal context that was in stark contrast to the nuts-and-bolts things that the real "reporters" at the publication focused on—my headlines were always something like "Why [Insert News Event] Matters to Me as a [Insert Relevant Identity Marker]" or "When [Insert News Event] Happened, It Triggered My [Insert Trauma/Past Harm That Is Sort of Relevant]"—and collect the followers, page likes, and clicks that *The Rag* prized above all else.

Rebecca wanted me to write about teaching Black and brown teens during "this time." By that she meant in the aftermath of yet another murder of a young man who looked like my students by police for reasons that were still unclear but were also unimportant. What was important to Rebecca, a dry white woman from Brooklyn who I sensed from her curt responses to my emails didn't think very much of me, and other editors like her—as well as seemingly the entire media apparatus—was that the man who was killed was killed on video. What was important was that his name and picture had been trending all over social media, signaling that his murder was one of the ones to pay attention to instead of the countless others that happened every single day. It goes without saying that the cop who killed the man was white.

"I imagine it must be hard for your students to focus, to just go about life right now," Rebecca wrote in her email, providing me with my ready-made angle. *How hard? How painful? Tears? Tears would be nice.* She did this every time. Not that I needed these cues anymore. My Brooklynese was spot-on by now. Nonetheless, I found the premise she suggested—the idea that the death of one man, who my students didn't even know, and who didn't even live in the same state as them, would trouble them, when, as far as I could tell, they had their own fucking problems and mostly cared about sex, video games, and dancing—hilarious.

Although I consciously made them my bread and butter, I admit that stories like these were starting to feel a little rote to me at the time. To tell the truth, I was beginning to long to write more ambitious things—the long, unwieldy essays the "literary artists" wrote. Why didn't I try to write them? Maybe I was scared. Maybe I was starting to believe the criticism my writing often received from editors before they realized it was in their best interest to just go ahead and publish it. But at the time, I didn't think about all of that. I told myself that each saccharine story I wrote was a step in the right direction. Another notch on my belt. Another credit with a place like *The Rag*.

As my first-period students trickled in that morning, I quickly responded to accept the assignment: "Of course. I'd love to. They've been thinking about this all week." Miguel gave me a halfhearted nod and slouched in his chair. Tyrell came in after, and I dapped him up even though the principal had told me I should stop talking to the kids like they were my friends. "That's probably why they don't respect you," he'd said.

Despite this, I returned Jessenia's stank face when she walked into the room that morning. "It's too early for you, Mr. P," she said.

She was correct. It was eight-thirty in the morning, to be exact. And I knew full well that nobody really wanted to be in my classroom. I didn't take it personally. I didn't really want to be there myself.

By my third year as a teacher, I accepted that in my class of twenty-seven, about twenty would show up each day. Of those, maybe eight really cared. Another eight or so I could grasp on a good day, if I really had my shit together and had really planned my lesson out to a T. But those days were few and far between. Then there were four students who just couldn't be bothered to give two fucks about what I said. Students like Gio, who would, no matter what methods I tried, continue to call me names, sleep, or text. Three years in, I had stopped trying to change this. I accepted that these odds were just mathematical certainties.

When my class was assembled, I decided to bypass the lesson plan for the morning and bring up the shooting. Although it had occurred a week ago and attracted some local coverage, the body camera footage had just been released, which elevated the man from a run-of-the-mill person killed by police or killed in general to one of those victims whose name people in states all over the country suddenly knew. As with the other victims, there were video clips of the man dying all over the internet. Stills of him bleeding out on a sidewalk were on the cover of newspapers and the first image on news sites, alongside pictures of the man smiling in a graduation photo. His anguished mother standing alongside solemn family members wearing cheap T-shirts with his name and picture emblazoned on them filled television screens. At night, cameras ran around with angry protesters in the streets. They captured the fires. The tear gas. The rubber bullets.

I knew my students had to be aware of it all. Everyone was. "We're living in a crazy time. Especially for people like *us,*" I told them. I hoped for nods. Even better, those tears Rebecca desperately wanted. But Xavier yawned. Nia popped her bubble gum.

"Have you been paying attention? Have you seen what happened to that poor kid?"

A couple of kids lifted themselves up out of their slumber. Keith, a lanky boy who liked to doze off by leaning his head against the window, raised his hand. "They iced homie in the middle of the street, Mr. P. *Blam!* Cold-blooded."

Guadalupe, whose thick black hair fell from either side of her center part like a river, picked at her cuticles. "Yeah, but like, didn't he have a knife and like wasn't he wiling out?"

Miguel aimed the tip of his pencil in the air and slashed. "I saw it on YouTube. My son was out here like Jason before twelve showed up. He *was* kinda wilin'."

"What about the police?" I said. "What about how they handled the situation?"

Nia stared up at the ceiling, looking like she didn't want to be called on. "Nia?"

She sucked her teeth. "Why me? 'Cause I'm Black, Mr. P? What you think, he's my brother or something? I don't know him."

"Damn, you mad racist, Mr. P," Miguel said.

"I'm not," I said. "I'm trying to get you guys to discuss what's going on in the world."

Charles, in the front row, adjusted his glasses. "I thought we were going to talk about creating compelling characters today."

Miguel untied the hoodie on his face and finally revealed his mug. "Word. We already talked about this shit in history class last week. And in homeroom today, the counselor came in and gave some speech about it, too. Talking about a safe space in his office. That shit sound *wild* sus."

"Ayo!" yelled a voice in the back.

"Pause," another voice said as a rejoinder.

"I understand. But this *is* about writing," I said, attempting to pivot like I had planned this lesson all along. "Thinking critically about the world, about things happening, about race, is all part of being a writer. Especially for us writers of color."

The classroom groaned. Tyrell laid his face on the desk. "Dead-ass, I'm tired of talking about race, Mr. P. We had Spanish history month, the day Rosa Parks sat on that damn bus, MLK's b-day, Black History Month, Malcolm X's b-day. Like, shout-out to all them, power to the people and shit, but I'm tired of always talking about all that stuff, bro." He turned over his notebook to show a drawing of a character he'd created wearing a hoodie, headphones, and a thick rope chain. "I'm really tryna talk about the adventures of Super G."

"That's a corny-ass character name," Jessenia said.

"Ya face is corny," Tyrell shot back.

Charles inspected Tyrell's drawing. "What kind of music is he listening to?"

Tyrell grinned. "Jazz. You see, my son is sophisticated. He don't mess with basic bitches." Tyrell looked at Jessenia.

Charles nodded. "Respect."

Jessenia stuck up a middle finger at Tyrell.

I sighed and grabbed my chalk. "Fine. Describe Super G's characteristics, Tyrell."

I WAS HIGH in my "study" later that evening when Anais got home. I was trying to come up with compelling ways to describe my students' imagined tears for the opening paragraph of my article when she entered the apartment with wet hair. I'd gotten so lost in my own narrative that I hadn't even realized it had started to rain.

"No umbrella?"

"Obviously not, Javi."

Anais had that end-of-a-long-day, dead-eyed, staring-vacuously-a-hundred-yards-past-the-etched-windows-of-the-subway-car look. She was finally becoming a real New Yorker. And she'd earned it.

After trying to get funds from the city council for a community garden in the neighborhood but only ending up with empty promises and a selfie with a local councilman who was later arrested for bribery, she'd decided she needed to join the existing local infrastructure to effect real change.

She became a part of La Gente, a community organization in operation since the times when people in the Bronx had to fight just to get their trash picked up. But during a campaign for free job training and English language instruction for recently arrived immigrants in the area, Anais caused a stir when she kept interrupting meetings to argue that the organization was wrong to be "imposing Western values and language" on people of color. "We're acting just like our colonizers in the past. Don't you see that?" When she practiced these arguments on me, I told her they were convincing. But they didn't land very well at La Gente. The president of the organization asked her to leave and come back after she'd "spent some time in the real world," Anais told me.

Disappointed, and feeling the pressure from her dad, who had never gotten over her choice to live with me in the Bronx and was threatening to cut her off, Anais took a new job her mother arranged for her. It was at a nonprofit, Zero Waste, that collected donations from large for-profit companies and corporations and distributed them to smaller, "on the ground" organizations making an impact in the realm of social and racial justice.

They had a nice office in Lower Manhattan, regular happy hours and retreats, and a mission statement that sounded great: "We take pride in being the noble stewards. The takers from our most fortunate and the givers to our most unfortunate." But it didn't take Anais long to realize that despite all this talk, all she really did was launder taxable money for the rich. "I looked through the books, and do you know that the majority of the money goes toward funding these big events and paying our salaries?"

Of course it did, I told her. "Everyone is always in everything for the money, even when they say they aren't." I thought Zero Waste was the kind of place that might wise up my naive Anais. In the grand scheme of things, I figured, there were a lot worse places she could work and make a lot of money. Why not this one? But she didn't see it that way. It was clear from the look on her face that the soullessness of the job was getting to her.

"There's one good thing about the rain," I said. "At least the homies won't be hanging out tonight. You might actually sleep."

She forced a smile. "One can only hope."

She went into the bedroom without giving me a kiss. I didn't make any effort to change that. This was how things had gotten between us. Once, we were stars on the rise with big plans. She dreamed of starting a nonprofit. Organizing for a higher minimum wage. Changing laws. I dreamed of teaching kids to unlock their writing superpowers, writing for the biggest publications, and banging out the world's best book one day. But instead she was kissing the asses of overpaid nonprofit executives and I was teaching kids who didn't really respect me and telling ghetto tales to hipsters for three hundred dollars a pop.

At the very least, I saw there was a purpose in what I was doing. I knew it would eventually lead to something bigger. But what really troubled me about Anais, what made her go from the girl I loved, the confident girl with a plan, to a girl I didn't even recognize, was that for the first time, she was lost and without a purpose. Whenever I brought up simply quitting Zero Waste and taking some other job, even working for a spell as a barista at one of her "to die for" coffee shops in Brooklyn, she dithered and made excuses. "I can't just quit my job, Javi. And besides, I don't see myself serving coffee. Come on. I graduated from Donlon."

We ate dinner on the couch that night and watched the news coverage of the police shooting in silence. Jackie Knox on NNN broadcasted from the scene, marching with a throng of young people on a dark street as they moved toward a line of police. People with bandannas and scarves wrapped around their faces held signs. Tear gas floated through the air. A chyron read, "Protesters continue their battle for justice."

It felt like a scene from an old movie. Each day it seemed I woke up with a new name to chant. A new face to look at and say, Damn, so young. A new criminal record to pick apart. A new police chief to hate. A new officer who "feared for their life." A new item mistaken for a gun. A new movement mistaken for an attack. A new set of body camera videos that made us all wonder, deep down, who was right and who was wrong.

In better times, back when we'd first moved in, Anais and I would have our laptop screens open to Twitter as we watched. We'd tweet our outrage and pray for someone to hop in our replies with something like "Well, you have to look at both sides" or "You can't blame racism on everything." These people always appeared. And when they did, we reveled in barraging them with witty retorts and links to articles from the sites that confirmed everything we believed in. After taking every Latino Studies and Africana Studies course there was to take at Donlon, learning about the Black Panthers, the Brown Berets, and the Young Lords, I sometimes imagined Anais and myself as modern-day versions of them, fighting for what was right against ignoramuses. We tweeted and tweeted. But eventually, it would come time to wheel out the bomb Anais and I had in our back pocket. The be-all and end-all to every such conversation: "You're just a racist who wants to preserve a white supremacist world!" *Click. Boom.*

Jackie Knox adjusted her microphone and stood before a blaze. It was only right that she was there on the screen. Her show, *Night-time with Knox,* had become the go-to for people like Anais and me, people in our tribe, people who tuned in every night as if it were some binge-worthy television series. Jackie Knox had established herself prominently as one of the "good ones," the white woman who "got it."

"We have here a new, exclusive statement from the chief of police." The statement appeared on the screen. "As you can see, yet again, a 'thorough' investigation is said to be underway," Jackie said. "And yet again, a promise has been made that 'justice will be served.'" Jackie paused, took a deep breath, then motioned to the fire behind her. "Something tells me, however, that these valiant young people out here on the streets won't be happy with this. And truthfully, why should they be? Why should they believe the powers that be this time around when they've been let down every time before? Think about it. While you do, I'll be here. Bringing you the real stories from the ground. Until tomorrow. Signing off."

"I'm going to write something about this. *The Rag* reached out to me today," I said.

Anais's eyes were vacant and turned to the window. Usually, she would inquire more about the angle, maybe even make suggestions about context to include, about what lede sounded better. Back at Donlon, she'd been the sounding board for my pieces. Oftentimes, my first reader. And even though I could tell she'd sometimes be surprised to hear for the first time anecdotes from my life that miraculously fit the storyline I was working on, she never pressed me about it, never really questioned me. Since moving to the Bronx, though, she'd taken less of an interest in my work. If she read the pieces at all, it would be a few days after they'd been published, and her feedback would be generic—"I liked it"—instead of the detailed praise I'd once received from her, which I now relied on my respectable number of Twitter followers for.

The rain had cleared. I changed the channel. Over the sound of the television, we heard the familiar thump of the SUV, the cackle of laughter, clinking bottles.

"I hate this," Anais said.

"Me too. I just wish the cops would own up to what they've done."

"I'm not talking about the fucking shooting, Javi. I'm talking about this. My life, this apartment, those fucking assholes outside."

I could tell by the look in her eyes that we were in for one of those *serious* conversations. The ones that were happening far too often for my liking. "Is this about your job again? If so, I'm really not in the mood."

She scowled at me, staring for a long time, as if coming to some realization. She stood and paced. I tried to remember how I'd felt when I first met her. Tried to rekindle those feelings. But without a campus where we were on top, when it was just us, in a five-story walk-up (the elevator never had come back online), going to the supermarket and trying to pay the rent and electric bill on time and figure out who does the dishes and who makes the bed, the sexiness of it all quickly vanished and we were left with who we really were.

The SUV's bass reverberated outside. "What is it?" I asked.

"I just told you. Aren't you listening to me?" She moved to the window and peered through the blinds, down at the street. "It's your fault I'm even here. It's your fault I have to deal with all of this."

"Oh, so I'm the one to blame for everything? How convenient, Anais. Will you grow up already?"

"Why did I listen to you? You tricked me. You made me feel all guilty. I could have been in Brooklyn or Queens. Doing the work

I'm supposed to be doing. Living the life I'm supposed to be living, Javi."

I shook my head. I stood and started walking to the kitchen for a beer.

She followed me, standing in the kitchen doorway as I opened a cold one and sipped.

"Do you know that I feel trapped? I feel unsafe walking in my own neighborhood sometimes. Why should I live like that when I don't have to? Just 'cause my boyfriend has some dumb complex about living somewhere nicer? My dad is right. You should care enough about me to change things."

I brushed past her and went back to the couch. I picked up the remote.

She stood over me. "Nothing? Nothing to say?"

"What do you want me to say, *princess*? Sorry your daddy thinks I'm such a bad boyfriend? What *you* want is to live with hipsters in some la-la land fantasy world where I'd have to scrape by just to pay for overpriced rent and my eight-dollar morning fucking coffee. You want to sell out, Anais. I ain't gonna do that."

Anais rolled her eyes. "Oh, right. Because you're so authentic, Javi. You're just *keeping it real*." She moved over to the television and unplugged it from the wall, making the screen go black. She stood in front of it. "You're so full of shit, you know that? You claim to hate hipsters so much, and yet who do you think reads *The Rag*, Javi? If hipsters are so terrible, then why do you always talk about how many of them follow you or how often they retweet you? Why do you constantly look at your phone, waiting around for their attention?"

"So I'm the hypocrite? You know, Anais, for someone who used to care about POC, it seems all you want to do is be as far away from them as you can be."

"Oh please. Prospect Park doesn't have people of color?"

"You know what I mean. The *real* POC."

Anais put a hand on her chest. "So I'm fake?"

I sipped my beer. "Yeah, Anais. Maybe you are." I felt backed into a corner. It was time, I thought, to boss up. It had worked every time before. But Anais didn't crumble now like she had the other times.

"Okay, Javi. Well, since we're finally being honest, you're one to talk. You write your little essays and tweets and make it seem like you're so real and genuine because you've stuck to your roots and you're *sooo* tough. But you know what? I think a lot of what you write is just a front."

"Are you calling me a liar?"

Anais crossed her arms. She hitched her hip to the side, glared. "I don't know, Javi. Maybe I am. All I know is that some things just don't add up. There's the way you talk about your childhood versus the way your mom talks about it. You told me, and I think even put it in a story once, that your first language was Spanish, which is bullshit. Your mom always complains about how you *never* learned Spanish, about how you resisted it and now your kids, or *our* kids, will be little whitewashed gringos."

"That was just one little stretch," I said. "So what?"

"Okay. What about the way you write about teaching and the way you talk about it? According to your tweets, you're 'shaping minds' and learning more from your students than they learn from you. But please. You want to talk about real? You don't give a damn about those kids. All you do is complain about how they don't respect you and how they make fun of your clothes. Well, maybe you're just a shitty teacher. Did you ever stop to think about that?"

I put down my beer. *Deflect, subvert, throw it back at her.* "This isn't about me. This is about you, Anais. This is about—"

Anais got closer to my face. "Yes. Yes, it is about you. You pretend to be this real, authentic guy, but it's all a game. So do I want better for myself? Yeah. Do I think I deserve better after putting up with this for three fucking years? Yes. But you know what? At least I'm ready to be honest about who I am and what I want. Unlike you."

Anger welled up in me in a way that was surprising. Anais had hit a raw nerve. She had pierced through some layer she was never meant to get through.

"Did Benjamin Franklin teach you about that, too?" I noticed a slight softening in Anais's posture. I smelled blood. "I used to think you were so interesting, Anais. You kicked all this radical shit at school, but now that you're here, you want to run. You want to be the little privileged white girl you've always really been. Well, you know what, Anais? If you hate it here so bad, if these people repulse you so much, then maybe you *should* leave."

A glass bottle smashed outside. A car alarm blared. The hyena laughter shot into the air. Anais blinked slowly. I thought I saw her lip quiver. Perhaps I'd gone too far. I thought about Pops, about the day he'd slapped that man and thrown rice and beans on his porch. What would have happened if he'd just called him a pendejo like he usually did?

Anais snatched her phone from the table. She started dialing. "You know what, Javi? I *am* going to leave. But first, I'm going to do something. Something I should have done a long fucking time ago." Anais put the phone to her ear and stared out the window. "Hi, hello? Yes, I want to report gang activity outside my apartment building. Yes. A gang. They sell drugs every day. They are probably a cartel. What's that?" Anais paused. "Yes. Yes, I am in danger. Everyone in this neighborhood is in danger. Especially women." She paused again. "Weapons? Guns. I'm pretty sure they have guns. They are dangerous and need to be taken care of." She waited on the line for a few more moments. "Anonymous. Thank you."

She hung up. We stared at each other in silence.

You should know this: I really did care about her. I really did, at some point, imagine a future for us together. I could see it all at one point, until I couldn't anymore. The dissolution of that takes time. It doesn't happen overnight. It's hard to even pinpoint exactly where it goes bad. To dissect, like a losing baseball game, which errors, which pitches ultimately made the difference in the final outcome. I don't have that kind of scorecard for you. All I have is this moment. This moment when it was clear to me and clear to her that there was no going back.

I slept on the couch that night. A squad car came by an hour after Anais's call. The cop didn't even get out of his car. Through his loudspeaker, he told the men to disperse and go home. He sounded annoyed that he had to do it. Like he'd rather have been at home playing Xbox. The men cursed at the cop and told *him* to go home. "I really wish I could," he said. After about a half hour of back-and-forth, the men disbanded. Despite what was on the television screen, no one was shot. No one was arrested. There would be no protests or burned buildings. At least not that night.

I SHOWED UP at Mom's the next day to give Anais space to move out. Mom's reaction to the breakup was feigned sympathy, until I told her I had initiated it. "Oh, bueno," she said. "I had a feeling things might not be going well when you guys invited me for dinner y esa niña finally cocinó. How do you call the terrible thing she made? Kin-i-wa?"

"Quinoa."

"Whatever. When I asked her why she made that instead of rice and beans, she said something about calories and less risk of diabetes, no sé qué." Mom shook her head. "That's when I knew." She rubbed my back. "Date a normal girl next time."

Back in my childhood bedroom, I tried and failed to write my piece for *The Rag* after teaching class, but after pushing the deadline back twice, Rebecca became annoyed. "This sort of story has a shelf life," she wrote, meaning that eventually everyone would forget this dead boy's name—if they hadn't already. I knew this. But every time I opened up the draft, I kept coming back to Anais's words. Her doubts about what I was up to. It had been years since I'd felt any concern that people might figure out what I was doing, might catch me. I was writing about my feelings, my memories, my alleged aches and pains—things they couldn't fact-check.

I hadn't ever had a reason to worry about Anais. She'd always been on my side. But now I worried about what she'd say about me out there in the world. Who would she say it to?

Yet again, my back was against the wall. I considered all the gangster movies I'd watched with Pops, how often, at some point, people who seemed to be friends would turn on each other, how one of them would set the other up, knock them out to ensure their own survival. "Dog-eat-dog world, papo," Pops always liked to say.

I needed to make a preemptive strike.

I wrote to my upset editor. I pitched her a better story than the one I was working on. I told her about the phone call to the cops. That moment in our living room. The breakdown of a relationship. Realizing someone you'd thought was on your team really wasn't.

She wrote back first thing the next morning. The boy who'd been killed, the pain of my students, and the pain of young people of color were now afterthoughts. "Forget previous story, we've likely missed moment. Pivot to this. Sounds juicy," she wrote. But instead of giving me a precise word count to hit, she added something she'd never said to me before, something I'd been waiting for her to say: "Don't be afraid to go long."

I WROTE IN A FLURRY over the next few days, mapping the story out in a way I'd never tried to before. Creating a narrative mountain, leading my reader by the hand through exaggerated and outright manufactured moments that, looking back, made clear to me Anais's disdain toward communities like mine. Like the time when we were seeing that brand-new building in Brooklyn and I pointed out that we'd likely be displacing lower-income residents and Anais simply shrugged and said, "Oh, so what, Javi. Poor people will always find somewhere to live eventually." Or the time I suggested we attend a (made-up) block party but Anais dismissed me, saying, "Why? So I can get shot? No thanks."

I wrote that when she called the cops the night of our breakup, several cars arrived, and officers with bulletproof vests and drawn guns swarmed the block. I wrote that they'd thrown the homies—who, I added, were not actually a gang, but in fact just a group of neighborhood boys hanging out—against the hoods of their cars. I wrote that Anais watched from the window, while my stomach turned as I thought about the prison sentences that might result from her actions, about my best friend—who I hadn't actually thought of in a long time, hadn't actually bothered to give my new address upon moving back to the Bronx—locked up behind bars. "That could have been him," I said, to which Anais shrugged and said, "Not my problem." I wrote that afterward, we had a big fight, and I expelled her from my life despite the fact that I had once planned for her to be my life partner, because I couldn't live with the idea of being with someone capable of such malice. I also couldn't live with the idea of her not facing any consequences.

What my ex did when she called the cops on those young men is not just wrong. It's an example of the many things people do that lead to systemic, generational harm. The sort of thing that leads to men who look just like her rotting in prison cells.

So what if I care about her? So what if we have a history? Things like that need to be called out. If we have any hope for a future, we cannot be silent about the injustices all around us—no matter who's committing them.

I'm ashamed, now, that I didn't feel all that guilty about sending the piece off. I even felt a little proud of it. I'd actually tried this time around, actually taken the time to read it over and over, tinker with things, and make sure the lies stung as much as possible. Perhaps that's how delusional I was. Perhaps that's how heartbroken I was. I didn't consider Anais getting hurt. I even thought I was looking out for her. I didn't use her real name. Our friends would know, sure. But how many of them would even read the piece? Sure, it would be a longer one. A six-hundred-dollar check instead of a three-hundred-dollar check. But in the end, I figured it'd be a sidebar like all my other pieces. Enough to brag about on Twitter; get some retweets, followers, and applause; and feel good about myself for a couple of days, before realizing I'd have to pump something else out, hop on another wave and do it all again.

As I waited for Rebecca to get back to me about the draft, I went through the motions at school and then at Mom's. It was nice to be back, in a sense. Nice to get home-cooked meals again that I actually enjoyed—quinoa is pretty trash, after all. What I didn't like about being around Mom were the questions about my future. The constant jabs from her about how I could be doing more.

As we ate dinner one night, she brought up a friend of hers whose daughter taught at a fancy private school in Manhattan.

"From what Theresa tells me, her daughter makes great money and has a nice schedule." She chomped on the corner of a perfectly soft maduro. "Why don't you do something like that? Why bother making so little money at your school?"

"Because I want to make a difference," I said. "Because I'm more valuable teaching people of color than teaching privileged white kids in Manhattan, Mom. But sorry if that is something you don't get."

Mom rolled her eyes. "Okay, ya con eso, Dios mío. Making a difference sounds nice. But don't you want to have a nice life? I came here, busted my ass, you go to this fancy school and learn all this stuff, for what? To make forty grand a year? Be smart, Javi. That's all I'm saying."

ANAIS TEXTED the next morning to say that her stuff was out of the apartment. The text was short: "I'm done."

I read it over and over and looked for more underneath the words, as if I were back in college and it was some centuries-old piece written by a dead white guy that I had to "contextualize." When I opened the door to the apartment later that day, I felt like I was walking into the wrong place. The main items were still there: couch, bed, even the television she'd left behind. But it was the absence of little things that made me realize she was really gone. Missing from the kitchen counter was the blender we'd use to make bad margaritas. So was the flyswatter she wielded like a gladiator in the summer. The bookshelf was cleared out by more than half. The plants that had decorated the shelves and that I thought gave the apartment a luscious feel, vanished. The shelves, and everything else, looked cold.

I looked through the bathroom cabinets and suddenly missed the tangle of cords from her various devices for straightening, curling, and combing her hair. I missed all the little earrings and thin necklaces that would find their way into places they shouldn't be.

I wondered how her new place, a sublet room in Brooklyn, looked. I pulled out my phone and had it in mind to say something to her. *Sorry. Let's talk. I miss you. You're right about me. Let me explain.* But I thought better of it. I thought about Gio instead. It'd been so long. Why hadn't I tried to contact him since leaving Donlon? I guess, I realized, somewhere along the way, Anais had supplanted him. Had become my go-to ear. But maybe this was the moment to reestablish a connection. To get back in touch. I went to my computer.

> *Gio, my bad for not writing in a while. I know it's been a minute. I know part of that is on me, too. But I wanted to—*

I didn't get far before I saw an email notification from Rebecca at *The Rag*. She'd finally responded to my draft. I clicked out of the letter and opened her message.

Instead of the standard "Thanks for this" before she launched into cold directions for me to change things on an extremely tight timeline or a suggestion to "cut back on the sentimentality," there was an apology. "I'm so sorry for the delay," she wrote. "It's just that we were talking about this piece a lot. I ran it up the chain because it blew us all away. Your bravery and commitment to your ideals, to your community. The details and description. The tension. In fact, the top editors liked this so much, we've decided to reorder the print edition and have it run more prominently in there. With a mention on the cover! This is a big deal!"

I forgot all about that letter to Gio.

The email might seem inconsequential to you, especially if you're not in the world of media (congrats, by the way; you're one of the smart ones). But for me, it was a moment I'll never forget. It wasn't just about the cover mention, which was great in and of itself. I was experienced enough to read through the lines. The "top editors"—three of whom, including the editor in chief, Nic Ossof, were cc'd on the email—talking about my piece. I knew what this meant. It was the opening of a door. A clear sign that I was being moved up in the ranks. Evolving, in their eyes, from the lowly freelancer being used for trauma clicks to someone with a voice. Someone who, eventually, could write about whatever the hell they wanted to.

Delight washed over me, but fear soon followed as I read the rest of the email.

"Because this will be a substantially longer—and more prominent—piece than we've ever run from you in the past, we will need to do some homework on our end," Rebecca wrote. She said Anais could remain anonymous in the piece, which was "great legal cover, anyway," but "internally," they wanted to make sure she was aware of the story and didn't refute some of the central claims. "Of course, she might have her own feelings about them, which is fine. We just need to dot the *i*'s and cross the *t*'s and make sure everything checks out. I'll do a quick reach out just to be sure, and then we should be set." She asked me to pass along any contact information I had for Anais before ending things cheerily once more. "We're all very excited!"

I read the email over and over, feeling a dull ache develop in the pit of my stomach. Feeling, I imagined, like Gio must have felt the moment police barged through his door the day he was arrested. The moment he realized the jig was up. I imagined what Anais might say if I actually gave Rebecca her real contact information. Imagined how she might tear me down, might ruin everything, and knew immediately that this was precisely what I would not do.

Instead, I came up with a plan. I started writing back to Rebecca, attempting to be as casual as possible. "Of course! It only makes sense that you would do your due diligence." I told her that, naturally, Anais had stopped responding to my phone calls and text messages, and lied that I'd tried to give her multiple opportunities to say her piece before sending the story in. "I don't think she's very happy about the whole thing." However, I said, Rebecca was free to give it a shot herself. I thought long and hard about which fake phone number to include in the email. An obviously fake one, like for a pizza shop, was not the right play. Then I remembered Gio's old number, his Motorola that always annoyed me because he only took calls on speaker instead of up to his ear like a normal person. I dialed the number and found it had been disconnected. A plausible event, I figured. Anais, so distraught, so upset, *would* change her phone number just to move forward, right?

I was cooking with fire. All I needed was an email address. I created a Gmail for Anais that was only slightly different from her actual email address—which, thankfully, was nowhere to be found online. I nearly sent the email, but stopped.

I considered Pops once more. As cocky as he was, he had always underestimated the people who might be out to get him. Sure, he had guns, but he still walked around like he was untouchable, like no one would have the balls to really go after him—until they did.

I looked at the email Rebecca had sent again. I wondered how much of this "homework" stuff was her idea. It was she, after all, who'd always been less than enthusiastic about working with me. Always discreetly, and passive-aggressively, negging my copy, making it clear that she thought my writing wasn't up to snuff. I looked her up online. She didn't have much in the way of a social media presence: a Twitter with a handful of scattered tweets and less than three hundred measly followers, a private Instagram with another couple hundred followers. But I knew she was smart. Smart enough to be on top of all the trends happening online, especially all the ones concerning POC, and assign them to me.

So before I hit Send on my response, I took one last precaution. I'd long stored Anais's Twitter password on my phone after she'd given it to me absentmindedly one day, back at Donlon, when she had more followers than I did and I asked if she could please retweet one of my early *Bulletin* columns on her page. We were in my room, doing homework, and she casually told me the password and said I could do it myself. "Just log out when you're done." Looking back, she had such trust in me. But even then, something told me, after I typed in the password, to hit the Save button when I was prompted to.

I logged in to her Twitter account. I saw that she'd already tweeted about the breakup, indirectly, as was her custom, saying that she was "inhaling the future, and exhaling the shit out of the past." I went to her settings and added Rebecca's account to her blocked list, ensuring that Rebecca wouldn't be able to DM her. Then I quickly went over to Instagram, thanked the heavens that Anais used the same password there, and repeated the process.

When my sleuthing was done, I looked at the email once more, double-checked my work, and hit Send.

I got a quick response from Rebecca, who said she would be back in touch soon. I didn't leave my apartment and tried to fight off the doubts racking my brain: What if *The Rag* was already on to me? What if Anais had already been contacted? Were they just giving me more rope to hang myself with? I kept a tab open and monitored the fake email account I'd set up for Anais until I saw the email from Rebecca come through with the subject line "Some Questions Regarding Javier Perez."

> *Hi, Anais. I'm an editor at* The Rag, *a publication your ex (it seems) boyfriend, Javier Perez, has been writing for for a little while*

now. As you may be aware, at least according to what Javier has told me, he is writing a story that centers on your relationship—and in particular some very damning claims about things you've said and done during that time. The story as it stands now suggests that your actions don't always match up to your avowed progressive beliefs. You are not named in the story. But because it is sensitive and because I have some of my own concerns about Javier's thoroughness in writing it, I wanted to reach out to you to see if you'd be willing to talk through some of the claims. The story has garnered a lot of attention internally and we will likely be running it prominently in our next edition, which closes for editing tomorrow evening. Would really love to speak to you beforehand.

I breathed a sigh of relief upon reading the email. I was thrilled to see that my suspicions about Rebecca were correct. My instincts impeccable. Yet more proof that I was built for this game. Rebecca was smart, but not smart enough. I took great joy in composing a response to her from Anais's account.

Rebecca, respectfully, I have no interest in talking to you or Javi or anyone. I'm moving on with my life. He already sent me a draft of the story. I'm not proud of what I've done, and I hate that Javi is writing about it. At least he isn't using my name. I hope that you won't either. Please, please leave me alone.

Any remaining doubts I had that Rebecca might still be working behind the scenes to bring me down vanished when she emailed me a link to the online version of the piece, which was published ahead of the print edition's release a few days later. I was in my classroom during my lunch break. Immediately, I was captivated by the cover art. Instead of a stock photo, there was a big splashy animation attached to the piece. A couple, the man standing on one side of a room, backed by protesters with signs, and the woman on the other, backed by police officers in riot gear, staring each other down intensely. I scrolled through the piece, admiring how official my words seemed against the white background, in *The Rag*'s characteristic font, with the magazine's imprimatur. Like a stamp of approval on my words. On me.

I went to my Twitter page, which normally might have one or two new notifications upon my opening it. But there were over a hundred. The little number shrouded in blue felt like a prize. I refreshed and saw the number rise and rise. New followers, people I'd never met, quoting my words, retweeting the piece, applauding me. Unknown faces on the other side of a screen calling me a "brave soul fighting for justice." They said that what I'd done, or said I'd done, was "what a real stand against racism and classism looks like"; they said the way I'd handled Anais, or at least the version of her in my story, was "the type of energy we all need to move through our life with." I refreshed and refreshed, ignoring the ringing of the bell and not even looking up to acknowledge the kids streaming into my room.

I went through the motions of teaching. I kept my eye on the clock in the corner of the room. I took a peek back at my phone sitting on my desk, at the screen that kept flashing with every new ping.

It was in my apartment that evening that I realized that, for the very first time, I had gone viral. The posts kept pouring in. My follower count had nearly doubled in the short time since the story had been published. I scrolled down to find negative comments, anything that might worry me. But all I found were the same meaningless sorts of things I was used to: snide remarks, a handful of people upset that I had aired a seemingly private matter. "Do we not have any more decency?" one man tweeted.

What was new, however, were the benefits of going viral. These little messages didn't just hang there for me to ignore. They were almost immediately handled by dozens of responses from faceless warriors who'd suddenly pledged allegiance to me and taken up arms. "Fuck your decency, especially when it only serves to protect privilege," one replied.

I was no longer an infantryman. I had been promoted. I was a general, admiring the work of my seemingly loyal subordinates.

IT WAS LATER that night that I got the first of many calls from Anais. I stared at her picture on my screen, a photo of her from college, sophomore year, back when all I wanted was to be lying next to her. That time seemed so far away now. Never did I think we'd get here. I watched the phone ring and ring without responding. Texts poured in after.

Javi. What the fuck?

Answer the fucking phone, Javi.

What the hell is wrong with you? Why would you do this???

I CAN'T BELIEVE YOU!!!

I see you retweeting shit, Javi. I know you can see this, you coward.

There was silence after this. No calls. No texts. Midnight came and went. I opened Anais's Twitter account again, double-checked to see if there'd been any communication between her and *The Rag*. But all I saw were some messages exchanged with Ricardo's account. He'd sent her the link to the story and wrote, "I told you he was a fraud. You should have listened to me."

I went back to my account, relieved. I kept reading responses to the story in the dark, kept looking at the profiles of people who'd responded to me, kept imagining them thinking about me, kept focusing on their praise. I compulsively opened up every new notification as it arrived. I hoped that one of the tweets, or the totality of them, would help push away the guilt that was beginning to creep into my head. I hoped I could shovel all the praise and applause over that guilt and bury it like a dead body I didn't want anyone to find.

At four in the morning, I was awakened by another text from Anais alerting me to an email she'd sent. I jumped out of bed and grabbed my laptop, worried she might have gotten in touch with *The Rag,* might have gotten an attorney, might be threatening legal action. Her parents were professionals, after all. The type of people who have those connections. But after opening the email, I breathed a sigh of relief. It was just the sort of thing that people like Ricardo, people like Anais, did when they faced some adversity. They weren't warriors like me. They didn't fight. No, they complained.

> *I've been trying to figure out what to even say to you. I have so many questions. But there is just one big one: Did you ever love me? I really don't know. I really don't know you. Or, I thought I did. But now I know the truth. You're a self-centered asshole, a manipulative fraud. Sick in the head. A fucking liar. Yeah, maybe I am privileged. Maybe I don't have your street smarts. Maybe I did have it easy growing up. And maybe something about that gives me anxiety. But I don't deserve this. What you've done to me is evil, Javi. I'll never forget it. And no matter what you say, I'll never forgive you. You fucking coward.*

There is a chance that Anais's anger, her hurt, could have eventually saved me. After the buzz of the story, there is a chance that during the comedown, when I looked around and saw nobody, I might have arrived at a much-needed realization. Perhaps I would have even turned everything around before imploding my life.

But that didn't happen. There was no self-reflection. Because just a few hours later, I got another email as I sipped my morning coffee.

This one was from Nic Ossof, editor in chief of *The Rag*. It was short, sweet, and life-changing: "I read your essay with great interest. Let's chat about making your writing a more regular thing here."

Twelve

THE TRAIN RIDE to *The Rag*'s offices in Brooklyn that morning took me well over an hour from the Bronx. I refreshed my Twitter notifications like a cratering junkie scraping to pass the time. Even days after the story was circulated, it was clear that it had blown up. It was also clear, at least to me, that I had transformed from an aspiring writer trying to break his way into the game into *somebody*. A blue check mark appeared next to my name on Twitter. The number of followers I had crossed the threshold from respectable to enviable. A hashtag based on the piece's title, "Why She Had to Go," had even been spawned after others online read the piece and were inspired to share stories about their own exes who proudly espoused progressive ideals online that proved empty in real life.

I felt like I was in the center of a big room with a massive audience of people clapping for me. It was, basically, a legal drug. A high so good and strong that it allowed me to box out, like a blue chip center, any doubts, any reflection on Anais's words. In my mind, I wasn't a fraud.

I was making moves up the food chain. And, clearly, my moves were working.

By 59th Street, my train car had filled with the sharp suits and skirts crowd. Coffee cups encased in fancy sleeves with ridges. Glossy leather briefcases and purses. Carefully folded copies of *The New York Times*. As the train crossed over into Brooklyn, the suits were replaced by hipsters. Their jeans black and stuck to their bodies like skin. Their shirts bright and the sleeves rolled up to the elbows. Canvas bags on their shoulders. Fragile-looking bicycles with curved handlebars. They clutched worn novels, books of essays, and, in the case of a white woman in a loose purple dress standing up in front of me, the latest issue of *The Rag*. I saw my story's title in small letters in a corner of the cover. A reader, a real reader, out in the wild. I was thrilled. But I was also grateful that she had no idea who I was, because I had no interest in actually talking to her. No interest in making it even clearer that Anais was right after all. I was writing for people like this. Was that a good thing? I didn't want to answer that. I focused on what *was* the good thing: the place I was heading, the meeting scheduled, the opportunity in front of me.

The Rag had recently relocated its offices from Midtown Manhattan to Brooklyn in an effort to "refresh" their brand and better connect with their new core audience. The offices were now housed in a large warehouse, right next to a wooden pier that overlooked the water and downtown Manhattan. *The Rag*'s logo was spray-painted on the door of the building. In the center of the lobby was a large desk that looked like it had been cut right out of a tree. A man with a gold earring and a colorful paisley shirt asked for my name.

While I waited for Nic, I looked up at the unusually high ceiling.

The air ducts, vents, and wires were exposed, as if the construction workers had just walked off the job. On the far wall was a line of framed issues of *The Rag*. On closer inspection, I saw they spanned fifty years, back to when the magazine was first started. I walked down the row until I got to the very last issue. The one with my story in it. And now it was here, on a wall, just like the platinum plaques hanging in record labels.

"A fantastic piece," said a voice behind me.

I turned to face a slender white man wearing a shark-blue blazer, a gray T-shirt with Biggie Smalls's face plastered on it, tight jeans, and crisp white sneakers. Nic Ossof. The head of the magazine—the man who'd saved it from shuttering like so many other publications and figured out a way to build a profitable online operation in addition to keeping the print edition afloat. His face had graced the covers of several magazines profiling his rise, his foresight, and his ability—in spite of the critics who suggested that he was, at the same time, watering down the magazine's legacy—to mine value out of viral stories and turn clicks into online subscribers.

"Really," he said. "We were so moved by it. Especially me."

I smiled.

Nic took me up in an elevator. The doors opened to a mammoth space with desks all along the walls. Sitting at them seemed to be the same sort of people I'd noticed on my train, down to the canvas bags and bicycles. In the center of the room was a theater-like setup with chairs and a stage. "For our big meetings," Nic said. He took me through the kitchen, where a long table boasted a bevy of snacks: peanuts, popcorn, M&M's, granola, dried fruit. He pointed to four shiny spouts next to an Italian espresso machine. "Kombucha, locally sourced craft beers. You're free to take as much as you like. We find that it only helps the copy around here."

I detected a rasp in his voice and was reminded for a second of the frat boys I'd come across at Donlon. The ones who wore shades every day of the week to hide eyes weakened by late nights of formal dinners, boat parties, and other private hook-up sessions with sororities masked as events. We continued down the center of the space, which buzzed with conversations and clicking sounds, the shutter of a camera somewhere far off. A Tribe Called Quest song played softly on the speakers.

Nic led me to a desk where a woman sat. Her look—tight ponytail, sophisticated glasses, white blouse, dark skirt—seemed distinctly at odds with the casual dress of everyone else in the place. As if, perhaps, she was a holdover from the publication's previous iterations, despite the fact that she seemed to be in her early thirties at most.

"Rebecca," Nic said. "Look who's here."

She glanced up and squinted. I looked at her silver nameplate on the desk, and everything crystallized for me. We'd never met. Never so much as spoken on the phone. But seeing her in person, the pointedness of her stare, made me understand just who I was dealing with.

When it became obvious that she had no clue who I was, Nic cleared his throat.

"It's Javier Perez."

Rebecca's eyes widened. She stood quickly. "Javier. So nice to meet you." She shook my hand.

I felt like being petty and reminding Rebecca of all the times she'd ignored my emails. All the times I'd "circled back" on late payments for stories but heard nothing for weeks. I had the power in my favor. Nic, her boss, was impressed by me. But in spite of her clear reservations about me, I felt that I still needed her. Better to deal with the devil you know, I figured. So I told Nic that working with Rebecca had always been a joy.

She forced a smile. "Likewise," she said.

Nic led me to the only office in the space. A large room surrounded by glass walls. A table was plunked in the center facing a big screen on the wall. I watched as titles of *Rag* stories jumped up and down on the screen. I was reminded of the times Pops would take me to horse races in Puerto Rico in a decrepit stadium that smelled like cigarette ash. The horses on the dirt track galloped and passed each other until one came out the winner. Afterward, most people let out a groan while a few smiled and headed to the cashier. I looked for my story, which still, after five days of being out in the world, held the number one spot.

"Like I said, it was a fantastic piece," Nic said. "And it's obviously the sort of thing our online audience is looking for. Take a seat."

He directed me to a leather chair. I wanted to take a picture of the screen. I'd had a feeling that many people were reading my story, but now there were concrete metrics to put next to that feeling. A way to judge just how good it had been. "So those are real-time readers?"

Nic was eager to explain. "Yes. The system tracks every eyeball on our website and spits out the data. We keep a pretty close watch on it. It's the future of our industry—which is not something everyone gets. But I do. Print will soon be dead, sadly. Online is king. We need to make sure we're getting as many people looking and clicking and sharing as possible."

I was spellbound watching the numbers churning on the screen. I wanted nothing more than to take the screen home. To sit in my apartment and watch the numbers go up and down. To see in real time just how many people were spending time with my words.

Nick sat. Behind him, the streets teemed with people walking with a purpose. Cars zipping in and out of lanes. Cranes swiveling in the sky. I thought about Anais. About what it must have been like for her to see this view at work every day and then come home to the one we had together. I shook off the thought before it could pull me in any deeper.

"That is where you come in," Nic said. "We're always on the hunt for people who can drive traffic to our site. Voices that readers feel compelled to click on. People with the kind of stories that make it hard to resist. Stories that touch on the pulse of our culture." He gestured up at the screen. "You seem to have that ability. It is also true, I'll admit, that we've been looking to diversify this place a bit more. We don't just want our team to be a bunch of white people from well-to-do families. That's so, like, twentieth-century media, isn't it?"

He looked at me pointedly. I knew he was trying to earn points. Trying to signal that he was hip and down with the beloved *d*-word. By then it had spread from colleges and radical circles into corporate America, into seemingly every institution there was. Like the "conversation" online, it had become a wave. A wave that coincided so perfectly with my rise, you would have thought I'd planned it. "Diversity" was no longer just some activist chant. It was a full-throated demand. A necessity accepted by everyone. Too many industries, including the media, were too white, and everyone had suddenly come to an agreement on this. Everyone suddenly had to show their commitment to change in order to stay relevant. Everyone in the writing world had also agreed that hiring a token writer or editor of color and fast-tracking them to stardom was a perfectly fine solution.

I wonder sometimes: If Nic had met me in the dead of winter—when my skin was paler and I looked more Brazilian or sort of vaguely European—would he still have been enamored with me?

We'll never know. Because the fact is, sitting there before him in his office, I was blessed. It was summer. I was very, very brown, and Nic was very, very desperate.

I saw my window. All of my training and experience, the lessons from Mr. Martin, the college essays, the LTC, the column for the *Bulletin,* the takedown of Anais, all of it was to prepare for this.

"It *is* so twentieth century," I said to Nic. "I'm glad to hear that *The Rag* is willing to do the work of changing that. Take action instead of just talking about it. There's just too much talk out there."

Nic nodded like a puppy. "Yes, exactly. Too much talk. We gotta do the work, right?"

"Well. Not me. *You* have to do the work. It's not up to us."

I felt like a dominatrix. I felt as if my ancestors, who had cleaned buildings and chopped sugarcane, were cheering me on from the afterlife. *Pa'lante, niño! Pa'que tú lo sepas.*

Nic sat back in his chair and smiled—a happy customer. "Javier. My man." He clasped his hands. "Listen. Why beat around the bush? We want you to join us as a full-time staff writer. How does that sound to you?"

I wanted to jump up, to exalt like I'd just scored a touchdown. But I thought about Pops. I kept it cool. "It sounds enticing. I'd like to know more."

Nic seemed concerned that I wasn't smiling from ear to ear, that I wasn't shaking his hand, or perhaps kissing his expensive tennis shoes. "Well, sure. What else would you like to know?"

I crossed one leg on top of the other. "Money is important. But also, what sort of stories would I be expected to write? I'd only really be interested if I had free rein to write what I'd like."

Nic adjusted his jacket. "That sort of roving latitude is usually reserved for more senior folks, but we can work something out down the road. For the time being, we'd really like you to continue focusing on diversity issues. Race, social justice, police interactions. The hot-button things. We think it would be excellent to have someone like you who not only writes well but also represents some of the minority, underprivileged communities at the center of these stories, sharing your perspective on them."

I got a kick out of the thought of one man trying to write about the entirety of the minority experience in the United States. Trying to capture all there was to capture. While everyone else on staff, ostensibly, wrote about the experiences of white people. It was an inherently dumb job. But also, for me, a perfect one.

"You'd continue to work with Rebecca," Nic continued. "You like her, right?"

I smiled. "I do."

"Good. She can be a stickler. But she's got a good head on her shoulders. And a sharp eye for what a piece is missing."

"Oh yes," I said. "I can see that."

"Great. Well, we'll get into numbers, but I imagine you'll find the salary quite comfortable. Also, I should mention that we have generous bonuses for our writers who drive the biggest readership. I'd bet you'll rack up a couple of those a year, too." Nic smiled. "Then, of course, you'd be able to work from here. Everyone loves this space. We have regular happy hours. And I'm a sucker for treating people to drinks and food at the end of long days. There's a Michelin-starred Korean barbecue place right down the street."

I thought about that woman on the train. About the very real prospect of running into readers. Of having to chat with them, or even people like Rebecca, every day. Having to live up to who they thought I was. The Bronx was, ironically, safer. *The Rag* wasn't sold there. No one cared about what I did or what I wrote. I was still just

Schoolboy. Weird Javi, writing his insignificant little stories. The Bronx is where I needed to be. I glanced at the story leaderboard, at my brown hands, and remembered who the fuck I was.

"As nice as that all sounds, I live in the Bronx, Nic."

"Of course. But like I said, we pay well. You could move somewhere closer. We could even help you find something nice around here. This neighborhood is really—"

I cleared my throat. "The thing is, I have no intention of leaving my community behind like that, of abandoning them. After reading my latest piece, I would think you'd understand, right? I refuse to be just another gentrifier, taking up the space of some other person of color who can't afford to be here anymore. Some people are comfortable with that," I said, looking him up and down. "But I'm not."

Nic pulled at his collar. I loved to see him sweat.

"Absolutely. Gentrification is just terrible. My doorman is a great Dominican guy. His family used to live in the neighborhood, and he told me they all eventually got pushed out. Moved upstate. He misses them. It's sad." Nic sighed. "Of course, I give him an extra-big tip during the holidays every year. Feels like you need to do *something* in that situation, right?"

I smiled inside. *This fucking guy.* But on the surface, I remained cold. My face did not flinch.

Nic picked up a pen and bounced it off the desk a few times. "You know what? Don't worry about it," he said. "Forget I even asked. Where you work from is not important at all. As long as you're writing for us, we're all good."

AFTER I SIGNED my contract, I wanted to celebrate. But I didn't really have anyone to celebrate with. Anais was gone. Mom wouldn't care about my new job. Worse, she'd ask too many questions. I could write to Gio, finally. Update him. He'd be happy, right? But would he want to know more about what I was writing? Would he want to read it? Did I want to deal with all that? He wouldn't understand, I told myself. He was a whole world away from all of this. Why bother?

I ordered takeout. I drank beer on my couch. I tweeted about my new job title and comforted myself with the "Congrats!" and "You deserve it!" and "I can't wait to read you" messages I got from strangers online.

Thirteen

I DECIDED THAT my first story would be about how conflicted I was about leaving teaching to accept a privileged position as a staff writer at a lauded publication. The material was right there, and I was so high on confidence that I figured whatever I wrote would turn into gold.

Rebecca, however, was not thrilled about the pitch. She said it seemed a little "cheesy" and thought perhaps I might dive into something more hard-hitting. "I'm not sure there is a huge appetite for this sort of piece," she wrote. I rolled my eyes upon reading her reply, but I was no longer just a lowly freelancer she could push around. I was a staff writer. With a devoted audience.

I disregarded her orders to look for another story and instead scoured Twitter until I stumbled upon a popular and growing storm of tweets in the education space related to the lack of male teachers of color and the research showing how much it hurt students. In my response to Rebecca, I linked to a few of the tweets (only from POC accounts, of course) and a couple of studies. "Not sure what communities you are looking at online, or have access to, but I can safely tell you that in my community, this is a big deal."

Her trademark one-word response made me feel like I had her right where I wanted her. "Fine."

> *Silence hung over the room after I announced the decision to my students. The silence was eventually broken by a girl I'll call J. "Why are you leaving?" she asked. But I knew what she really meant. "Why are you abandoning us?"*
>
> *After all, she was right. In a sense,* I was *abandoning her. I was abandoning all of them. Setting them up for an uncertain, potentially disastrous future. And that is something I'll always have to live with. The weight of my decision. Not just on me, but on so many others.*

In real life, Jessenia *was* the first student to say something when I told my class I'd be gone by the end of the week. "Honestly, you lasted longer than I thought you would," she said.

Of course, my decision to leave was easy. I enjoyed hanging out with my kids, but the job was harder than I wanted it to be. There was grading, report cards, conferences, forms, trainings, emails. If I'm honest with myself—and that is the point of this book, isn't it?—the only reason I kept the job as long as I did was because it gave me a degree of street cred. What I liked most about being a public school teacher in the Bronx was being able to tell others that I was a public school teacher in the Bronx and watch them sit back and think of me as such a good, noble person. But that had no place in my story.

Instead, I layered it with my thoughts on the tough choices people of color have to make in their lives. The "agony" of deciding whether I wanted to "make money and use my voice for a privileged institution" or "stick to my roots and make a difference in my community." I wrote that I'd chosen the former not because I didn't care about the latter, but because I was forced to.

> *It is our capitalistic society that has forced my hand in this dilemma. Which is why you are reading these words today. I don't love the economic system this country is built around. But, unfortunately, I cannot deny its existence.*

I ended by meditating on a fabricated quote from Miguel.

> *"Mr. P, I just want you to know that you inspired me. I'll miss having someone who looks like me up there at the front of the room," he said. "I don't know if I'll ever have that again."*
>
> *That broke my heart. Statistically speaking, the chances are slim. I know that he's probably right. So while I'm excited about this new opportunity to fight new battles on new fronts, I'm not naive. I know I'll never truly be able to enjoy this new position of privilege. In the back of my mind, I'll always be thinking about my classroom. I'll always be thinking about students like M.*

In real life, Miguel asked me in front of everyone if my new job would pay me more money. When I said that it would—a lot more money, in fact—he seemed genuinely relieved.

"Thank God," he said. "Now you really have no excuse not to buy some fly kicks and throw out those dusty rags on your feet."

IT WAS UPON PUBLICATION of my first story as a staff writer that I learned that the metrics on *The Rag*'s site could be checked in an instant from an app on my phone. A gift and a curse.

In the days after the story was published, I found myself constantly returning to the app, refreshing and refreshing.

After the Anais piece, I was really feeling myself. I thought I was Jay-Z. I expected my new story to do numbers like my last one. To soar above all the other pieces *The Rag* had published, gain me thousands more followers, and continue to inch me up the ladder of success I so desperately wanted to climb. Can you blame me? It had happened the first time, so I figured it would just continue happening, over and over. The roller coaster would just keep on climbing up.

But the story never pushed past number thirteen on the site. By the third day of publication, it had crashed somewhere below the top fifty, replaced by stories published weeks and months before. My Twitter notifications became uncharacteristically dry.

At the end of the week, Nic sent a round-up email to everyone on staff shouting out the best we'd published over the previous seven days. I read intently and felt myself sink a little when my story wasn't mentioned. I sank even further when, minutes after the email went out to everyone, Nic wrote to me personally.

> *Nice try this week. Numbers not great. Maybe huddle with Rebecca to adjust game plan for next story? Moving forward, let's focus on the juicier race/social justice issues, per Rebecca's feedback. Thx.*

My heart sank. I realized I really wasn't Jay-Z. I was J-Kwon. I'd just had a hit single. And if I didn't get my shit together, that might be all I had. I'd be dropped from the label. Have to go back to teaching. Grovel to my administrator. Stand up in front of my kids and get flamed even harder than before.

Needless to say, I searched for my next idea with an added sense of pressure that I hadn't ever felt before. Pressure to please Nic and *The Rag*. But also pressure to please my new army of Twitter followers. Every time I refreshed the app, there were other writers sharing links to things they'd written, those links being retweeted and talked about thousands of times over—just like with my piece on Anais. And each time I saw this, all I could think about was how swiftly I'd fallen in the rankings.

I asked for more time before my next pitch was due. Rebecca gave it to me, but not without a jab. "I'll grant you an extension this time, but do keep in mind that our standards for staff writers are much higher than for freelancers. Looking forward to seeing what you come up with—I'm sure it'll be stronger than the last piece."

As I racked my brain for what that could be, I started having dreams of waking up and checking Twitter to find zero followers. In real life, I'd sign in and become deflated when I didn't see a big blue number next to the little bell on the screen.

For days, I stayed home. Smoked weed. Scrolled around online in search of something "juicy" like a madman. My confidence was zapped. Stories I'd normally just go for and pump out quickly in one evening, I questioned. Is this enough? Will this stand out among the pack? I was in this feverish state when I received a call from my mother.

"Have you had any chest pains recently?" she asked urgently.

"Uh. No?"

"Well, you should check yourself out. Just in case."

"Why would I do that?"

"Because I read this really sad story about a twenty-five-year-old who just had a heart attack and died. You could be next."

I switched the phone from one ear to the other. I thought about how easy Mom had it. She didn't have the sort of existential worries I had. She didn't have a shrewd editor to deceive or Twitter followers to please. There was no leaderboard of hospital secretaries she was ranking herself against. No platform with metrics showing who answered phones better. She could just go through life. Clock in and clock out.

"My chest is fine," I said. "Thanks for asking."

Mom said I sounded sad. "Are you dating again? Maybe you should go on a date with a nice girl. Don't go around wasting your time with bimbos."

"You can't say 'bimbos' anymore, Ma. It's derogatory."

She sucked her teeth. "Ay. Don't start. I didn't call you to get another lecture." She said she'd seen that Anais had uploaded a new picture on Facebook. Her first one in a while. "She looks good. Happy. Flaca. You need to upload one, too. You can't be acting all sad, Javi."

I'd seen the picture, too. Noticed that the brightness had returned to Anais's eyes and tried not to think about it. "Don't you ever think that maybe you spend too much time on Facebook?"

"Oh, please. You're the one always looking at your phone. Don't get mad at me because you're depressed, okay?"

"I'm not mad. Listen, is that everything, Ma? I'm really busy. Anything else you saw on Facebook that I should know about?"

"No, that was it for Facebook."

Just as I was about to hang up, she said one last thing, offhand, like it was nothing of consequence. "By the way, do you know who I saw the other day?"

"Who, Mom?"

"Giovanni. He looks really good. You know, everyone I know who goes to prison gets fat and loses their hair. But Giovanni looks good. He has a new tattoo that is un poco feo, pero otherwise he's good. You know what? Maybe you could ask him to teach you some workouts. Get in shape. Stop being depressed. Find yourself a nice young lady, not a sucia. There, is that better?"

My first inclination was to defend the sub on my weight. But before I could, my brain processed what she'd said. "Wait, Gio? He's out? Right now?"

"Yeah. He's either out or he ran away from prison. No sé. Either way, I saw him outside with his grandma."

"You spoke to him? And he didn't say anything about me?"

"Not really, no. The whole world doesn't revolve around you, Javi."

Fourteen

As I walked to our old building, I decided Gio hadn't reached out yet because he was probably embarrassed. He probably thought I didn't care about him anymore. It had been, after all, years since we'd exchanged a letter. He probably thought I'd moved on. Maybe he'd gotten wind that I was some hotshot writer now. Maybe Mom had told him. What would someone like that need a down-and-out felon for, he probably wondered.

Although I had been upset when I started my walk, I straightened up as I neared the building. *Gio is probably having a hard time adjusting, finding a job,* I thought. *He probably needs help and guidance. He needs me.* As I opened the large door to the building, it finally hit me. The opportunity. The lifeline I was looking for. Gio back, unsure about his next steps in life, likely ignorant of the forces shaping it. In need of guidance. In need of a helping hand.

My next story. My greatest story yet. A story I already knew that Nic, Rebecca, and Twitter would eat up. They had to. It was the perfect cocktail of poverty, strife, racism, and injustice that they loved. A tale of two boys from opposite sides of a beat-up building in the ghetto. Two paths that diverged in a cinematic way, only to reunite so the more successful of the two (me, obviously) could teach the other his ways. The best part, I thought, was that I wouldn't even have to make it up. It would be my transitory piece, my first experiment in telling something like the truth.

I RANG THE DOORBELL, and Gio appeared looking sleepy. He *was* in great shape. His chest was inflated like there was a balloon stashed inside. His biceps and neck resembled tree trunks. I suddenly became self-conscious about the beer paunch resting over my belt, the extra skin under my neck. I felt a little better when I saw the new tattoo Mom had mentioned. It ran across his neck like ticker tape. His mother's name, in fourth-grade cursive.

"Oh shit. Javi," he said, sounding surprised, but only because I was there, standing in front of him. Not, it seemed, because he especially wanted to see me. He gave me a floppy pound, the kind Manny would give me when I first started getting to know him and he didn't really trust me. There were no tears, no hug. It was as if it'd been just yesterday since we'd last seen each other, not years.

"You're fat," he said after looking me over more closely. "And your hairline. Jesus."

"And you took . . . steroids?"

"I worked out. A lot. Something you clearly haven't done."

"What about that tattoo, though. Did a child draw it? A child with no future in art."

"I'd like to see you do better with a pen, duct tape, and a beard trimmer motor, motherfucker."

I felt something, something I hadn't felt in a long time. Good? Happy? At ease? I don't know. But I realized that underneath, Gio, with his new, rugged exterior, and I were the same people we'd always been. The same kids.

Gio accepted my invitation to the diner and got dressed. I waited in the hallway and thought about my approach. I wouldn't bring up the article right away. But also, time was of the essence. It was Saturday afternoon. Pitches were due by Monday at noon. "No more extensions," Rebecca had warned.

Gio and I walked for well over a block in silence. We were on the same sidewalks we had walked down countless times as kids, but still, there was something off. Gio didn't seem like the person I remembered. There was something more restrained about him. At the crosswalk, we caught each other staring briefly at the other, seemingly working out what to say, how to close the gap between us.

We sat in a booth at the back of the diner. The waiter brought us coffee.

"I'm so glad you didn't ask for almond milk," I said, breaking our silence.

"What?"

"My girlfriend. *Ex*-girlfriend. I took her here. She made a big scene about the milk. She was so bougie. Mad fake and delusional. Figures, given she was really just some white girl at heart. You remember her? The one I wrote to you about?"

I expected Gio to say something. Ask me about Anais. Ask me about other girls. Ask for the anecdotes and little stories he seemed to want when I got to Donlon. But he just sipped his coffee, just looked at the old man reading the paper at the counter, the waitress taking down a telephone order, the man behind the register ringing up bills with one finger.

"So what the hell, man. Why didn't you tell me you were out? I had to find out from Mom. I thought you'd call me or something, at least."

Gio rubbed his head. I'd never seen him with so little hair. All his life, his hair had been wild and rangy like a forest. Now, with his buzz cut, he looked like a soldier returning home from battle. "I was gonna get around to it."

"How long have you been out?"

"A couple of weeks."

"And you didn't think to reach out at all?"

"I said, I was gonna get around to it."

"But why did you wait? It's not because you're embarrassed, is it?"

A bread crumb. I expected Gio to solemnly stare into his coffee. This would be the moment his stoicism would break. In my story, I would bring context to the scene, and Gio's initial reluctance to show any emotion at all. I'd weave in the history of masculinity in places like the Bronx. How a man is never allowed to truly reveal how he feels. How a man can never cry.

But Gio looked insulted. "What am I supposed to be embarrassed about?"

"I mean, you were in prison. I just thought maybe you didn't reach out because you were down on yourself. You know, I recently read this article about how dejected or even worthless people can feel when they leave prison."

"I'm not worthless. I got hit with time, and I did it like a man. Now I'm trying to move on with my life. I didn't call you because I didn't want to yet, aight? I got shit to do."

"My bad. I didn't mean to get you upset."

Gio sipped his coffee.

The diner was half full. A long line of Mexicans cooked bacon and eggs with astonishing speed. I watched the man at the counter hit the buttons on the register again. I focused on the sound of each key he pressed. Gio didn't seem to have more to say. He seemed perfectly content sipping coffee in silence.

"So. You got out early? I thought you were supposed to do ten?"

"Sorry to disappoint you."

"I'm just asking, Gio, damn. I thought I was supposed to be the sensitive one."

He relaxed his shoulders. Picked his head up from his coffee cup. "I got out on good behavior, if you really want to know."

"If only Ms. Rivas could see you now."

"If only." He smirked.

The waiter returned. I took a bite of my French toast. Gio crowded his burly arms around his omelet and ate as if someone might come and rip the plate away.

"It's cliché. But I have to ask."

"What? 'How was it?'"

"Yeah."

"Oh, real fun. Very educational. You should go visit sometime. Just don't stay too long. I overdid it."

We laughed. I noticed a new scar on his hand. A worm between his thumb and index finger. I glanced into his eyes. They were deeper than I remembered, looking back at me from the other end of a tunnel. I wanted to know what he'd seen. To write those experiences down. To contrast them with my own, illustrate the flaws of the system. My great escape from the grips of death. A version of this had gotten me into college, started this whole merry-go-round. But I was so much more advanced now. The same story would please my editors, just like it had pleased the admissions committee. But it would also win prizes. Get turned into a movie. Be the sort of *serious* piece that would vault me into another stratosphere. I knew the material I needed was there.

"Well, Donlon wasn't jail. But it taught me a lot, too," I said.

Gio pushed his empty plate forward. "Some weird shit, if you ask me."

"What is that supposed to mean?"

"Your letters, they started getting dry as fuck. Always lecturing me about something or another. Using these big fucking words. *Carceral*? Sounds like wack, off-brand cereal."

I failed to recall the contents of the last letter I'd sent to him. It had been years.

"Is that why you stopped writing to me?" I asked.

"The letter-writing business is a two-way street. You could have picked up the pen too, you know."

"You right. Things just got busy."

Gio nodded. "You were outside. You had a life. I can't blame you." He leaned back into the booth and draped one of his big arms across the headrest. "So go ahead. Tell me more about college. I can tell you really want to."

"I don't remember what I already told you, to be honest. But the letters might have sounded 'weird' to you because Donlon changed the way I think about the world. It taught me how to look at things in a new way and really understand them."

"Prison did the same for me. I lived with society's butt crack. All the citizens of butt-crack land in one little space. People who've seen and done shit most people won't ever have the balls to do."

"I bet a lot of them were innocent, right? You know how the *system* is."

"Maybe. It's not so black-and-white. To be honest, some of them probably need to be locked up. Some of them are just monstrous motherfuckers. But some of them got dealt a bad fucking hand, too. Like this one guy, a cellie I had, he told me he broke into a laundromat every night for three weeks and slept in the bathroom because he was addicted and broke and had nowhere else to go. When the owner found him one morning and started freaking out, he freaked out and cracked homegirl's head against the sink one time, real hard. She died. Mans was nineteen. He's spent the last ten years locked up and has more to go. Sweet dude. If you saw him, you'd think he'd never hurt a fly."

I wished I had my recorder on me or a notepad. "Was he Black? Brown?"

"Nah. Frail white guy, actually. Telling you, you'd never think it was him."

"Huh," I said, disappointed.

Gio looked confused.

The waiter came around. I looked at Gio, who looked back at me.

"I'm buying," I said, to put him at ease.

"Bet," he said, turning to the waiter. "Let me get a cheeseburger deluxe, my boy, and a chocolate shake."

I worked on my second coffee. I wanted to drill down. Get into better, more usable material. "How do you feel to be out? What's going through your mind?"

Gio thought for a while. It'd been a long time since I'd seen him so pensive. Before he was arrested, his life always seemed to move so fast. Parties, cars, girls, late nights. No time, it seemed, for thinking big thoughts. "I guess I just look back at shit and see it all so clearly now. See where I went wrong. The mistakes. I think about what I could have done differently. And now that I'm out, I wanna try to do shit differently, but it ain't easy. I'm still just getting used to living again. Living for real. Not just being told what to do, when to eat, when to sleep, like some fucking robot."

"What mistakes do you think you've made?"

Gio laughed. "I was a dickhead, Javi. Somewhere along the way, all I cared about was money and bitches. Overlooked a lot of shit because of it. Thought I was invincible. Thought my boys would always ride for me, always protect me. I thought whatever we were doing was what we were doing, and besides, we'd never get caught. We'd just party forever and they'd always have my back." He wiped the corner of his mouth with a napkin. "Obviously, that didn't happen. I ain't even heard from Manny since we got split up. Probably never see him again with the kind of time he's doing. I just wish I would've been more focused on other things. I wasted a lot of time."

"I get that. But also, you do realize that what happened to you was by design, right? Don't blame yourself too much. You got caught in the system," I said. "You got trapped."

Gio rolled his eyes. "Here we go. See, this that shit you started spitting in your letters. About me being some poor victim."

Pieces of our last correspondence began to form in my mind. I remembered Gio saying something similar, blaming himself for everything, not reflecting at all on other conditions that led to things turning out the way they did. I remembered trying to give him a cribbed explanation of systemic racism, the school-to-prison pipeline. Maybe the concepts I was trying to get across were too sophisticated. But now that we were here, sitting in front of each other in the diner, having a real conversation, I figured Gio might be able to understand. This conversation, I thought, could be the linchpin to the story. His reeducation.

"It makes sense that this would sound foreign to you, sound like a different language. But it's the truth, son. Things are not just your fault. There are other forces at play you aren't thinking about that have held you back."

I waited for Gio to lean forward. Stare enraptured. Inquire further.

He groaned. "You're gonna hit me with that conspiracy shit, aren't you?"

"What conspiracy shit?"

" 'The Man is to blame for everything. We're just slaves caught up in a modern-day plantation. The revolution is coming.' You know how many people were spitting that shit in jail?"

"And you don't think any of it is true?"

"I don't know. Maybe some of it is. Some of it is interesting to think about. Kinda like when we used to spend all that time wondering if Jay-Z really was in the Illuminati. But, after a while, you know what I noticed about them conspiracy heads?"

"What?"

"That's all they talked about. They always found ways to insert it into conversations and shit. They made it their whole life. Soon as I realized that, it turned me off."

"Why?"

"Because it's another trap. Just like Manny, the crew. If I went down that hole, that's all I'd think about, too. I'd just be wasting more and more time." He waved the waiter over for the check, like he was planning on paying it. "I fucked up once, but I ain't about to do it again."

AFTER I PAID THE BILL, I suggested we take a walk around the reservoir. I wondered about the things Gio must have heard in prison. I'd listened to enough ex-cons babble nonsense on the bus and train. Their narrative bridge always crumbled because there wasn't anything to sustain it. They didn't have the good fortune of studying with the professors I'd studied with, reading the books and articles from academic journals that they assigned. Learning how to understand and use these big words and phrases—*hegemony, structural, institutional, furthermore, all things considered, elucidate*—to ensure that your arguments stood tall and sturdy like rich people's houses, instead of slums built on mud.

We passed by the train yard. Subway cars slumbered in a massive lot. They gleamed metallic and free of the graffiti that used to coat them when we were younger and our days were more carefree, when our problems could be fixed by a ball against the wall, a joke, and a sugary honey bun.

Gio and I stopped to stare at the trains. I watched a white man wearing a jean jacket and holding a tote bag walk swiftly by us, in the direction of the train station. What the fuck was he doing here? I must have scowled.

"You know him?" Gio said. "He steal your bike or something?"

"No. It's just that he's a hipster. I don't know what he thinks he's doing here."

"What's a hipster?"

"Oh, you missed out on them in prison. They're the worst. They move into your neighborhoods, increase property values and coffee prices, and kick our brothers and sisters to the curb. They say they love you, but really they'll call the cops on you and refuse to send their kids to your schools. Then they'll go and pretend they're all fucking edgy because they live in your damn neighborhood. Basically, they're frauds." I thought about Anais. On Twitter (I checked her page compulsively, at least four times a day), she had begun to post about her new place in Brooklyn, the little garden she'd made on the fire escape, and also, more concerningly, about letting go of her "toxic ex" and realizing how much "emotional manipulation" she'd been subjected to. Thankfully, she never used names, never @'d me. She knew, I thought, who had the upper hand here.

Gio mulled over my definition as a fat rat ran by us and quickly darted into the sewer grate, stumbling on its way in. "So are you a hipster?"

"Of course not. I'm a native. I'm authentic."

"Authentic," Gio repeated.

Despite the years, I still knew *that* face. It was the same face, when he was a free man, that he'd give me when he'd ask for updates about girls I was seeing and I'd tell him these elaborate tales of doing it so hard their back hurt and they couldn't walk straight.

"What?"

"I'm just saying. The stuff you've been writing lately is pretty, uh, inauthentic? That's a word, right?"

"You talking about my letters? I told you, I barely remember what I wrote in those. I was probably high."

"No. For that magazine."

I nearly tripped, missing the curb as we crossed onto the next street. "*The Rag*?"

"That one. Yeah. What's up with the no-pictures shit? Can you make a complaint?"

Disbelief isn't a strong enough word, dear reader. "You're telling me that you, Giovanni Ernesto Mejia, read the fucking *Rag*?"

Gio's face became stoic. "You know I know how to read, right? I'm not a fucking caveman."

I imagined Gio in his cell. Legs crossed at the knee, sipping a coffee. Reading an article in *The Rag* about the merits of sustainable vegetable gardens on people's roofs in Brooklyn.

"I'm not saying you're a caveman. I'm just surprised. Can you blame me? You weren't much of a reader before."

"I'm a surprising dude, what can I say. I'll also have you know, motherfucker, that I got my GED upstate. Among many other certificates—bitch. And, not for nothing, I've always liked reading.

Sometimes I was jealous you had all these books in your room, and that you and your moms would go to the bookstore. That sounded dope. I just made it seem like I didn't care. I thought people would call me corny. It was dumb. That's what I'm talking about right there. That's the sort of stuff I shouldn't have cared about."

I remembered Gio as a kid, sitting there on my bed, asking questions every now and then about my bookshelf. The memory had a whole new meaning. "So, what, you got to prison and just became a *Rag* subscriber? How'd you get it? You can't even buy it in the Bronx."

"When it finally sunk in that I was gonna be upstate for a while, when I realized those legal aid dudes couldn't even remember my name or my case, it hit me like a Tyson punch to the mouth. Time. Real time. So you cry. You get upset. You believe in the Man and shit. But then it's like, well, you still got more fucking time. So what you gonna do? I figured I might as well do something different, right? So I started fucking around with Harry Potter, a lil Dan Brown, you know what I'm saying. I hit the Bible eventually because it's like why not, lemme me see what the ol' boy gotta say. I tried the Quran a lil bit, chopped it up with the Black Hebrew Israelites. I did the spiritual shit. *The Four Agreements*. Light work. Eventually I hit up Gladwell and those ten thousand hours."

"That's great, Gio. But how the fuck did that lead to *The Rag*?"

"So this one dude apparently donates his old magazines to the joint every month. *The Rag* is one of them, but I barely looked at it, to be honest. No pictures. No shorties. I went straight for *Sports Illustrated*. *GQ*. Sometimes I peeped those home decor joints. It was nice to imagine myself somewhere different. Imagine a future apartment or something, you know? I only picked up *The Rag* because of my boy Squirrel. He liked to peep it for the cartoons and crosswords. Anyway. Me and him used to chop it up a lot, you know. And I told him about you . . ."

I wondered how Gio had described me. I thought about how I'd described him whenever I brought him up to Anais, at the LTC, and even a few times in my columns for the school paper and freelance pieces post-college. To anyone or in any medium where it seemed opportune to mention that I had a best friend in prison—albeit a best friend I rarely spoke to. At the end of the day, he was one of my ace cards whenever I was looking to one-up someone and get the self-esteem boost I got from the look of another that conveyed, "Wow, you've been through some real shit."

"Squirrel knew you was a writer and shit. I told him and my other boys that you'd probably write a book one day and maybe we'd get to read it. Then one day Squirrel came into the rec room with the magazine and pointed to your name. I was like, Oh shit, I get to read my boy. But then I read it, and . . ."

"And what?"

Gio gave me a sly look. "It was that one about the Bronx having the worst food or some shit. You was in there talking about how you used to eat Kennedy Fried Chicken every day. I was like, Come on, man, you know your moms was the bomb cook. And I remember how she used to get on your ass if she found out you was buying too much candy from the bodega. You used to come to *my* house to eat bad."

The story was about food deserts in the Bronx. It was from the before times, when I was a lowly freelancer. Not an established staff writer. It was a piece Rebecca had assigned to me after a big report came out concluding that the Bronx was basically on some third-world status when it came to the availability of healthy food. "Anything come to mind for you on this? Maybe something from your upbringing? Your own poor eating habits?" she wrote to me in an email. The rest was history.

Gio brought up another article, which he'd read after realizing I was being printed in *The Rag* somewhat regularly and started to look out for my name. "That one about the kid who got murked—from what I heard inside, on some retaliation shit, for talking out his mouth—and you was talking about how *you* nearly joined a gang."

The story in question had been written after the gang murder of a kind of nerdy-looking fifteen-year-old boy who was hacked to pieces by other boys armed with machetes outside a Rite Aid. It was the kind of uptown crime that, every now and then, makes people downtown and in Brooklyn care about Bronx victims for a news cycle or two. Rebecca wrote to me quickly after the story made it beyond the local news and the mom of the boy gave a teary interview to Jackie Knox on the Nightly News Network. "Any personal ties to this one?" the email read. "By chance knew the boy? Or are related? You're Dominican, too, right?"

Gio keeled over with laughter, recalling the story I wrote about how I empathized with the boy and mourned his death more than others because I could've been like him. Because, I wrote, I myself almost got caught up in a gang.

> *What stopped me from joining? Luck? The voice of God? I don't know. All I do know is that while I'm grateful I traded in the knives and guns for books and pens, I'm not silly enough to ignore the fact that too many boys like me presented with the same option choose differently. Too many of them end up like an alternate version of me, standing on corners, repping flags and streets and avenues and buildings owned by white people that don't give a shit about them. Too many, in other words, fall into the trap. I'm just lucky enough to have escaped it.*

Gio laughed so hard that he started to cough. "You were *this* close to getting down, but then you pulled out and had a moment of clarity because they said you had to buck fifty someone?" He stopped walking for a moment and grabbed onto a light pole to steady himself. "I read that shit and died, bro. I really tried to imagine your bitch ass in a gang, and I started dying even more. Then I remembered this one time I had to shut down Manny's dumbass idea to get one of my homie's kid sisters to fight you while we collected bets on who would win." Gio nodded, reinforcing the truth of the story. "You should thank me, son. Homegirl had hands. You would've been cooked. I saved your life."

I cleared my throat and tried to force a smile, or something like it. Some kind of facial expression that would not convey what I was actually feeling inside—a mixture of shame, fear, and, mostly, anger.

"Why you tight? You *know* your ass was lying, Javi. That shit wasn't even close to the truth. It wasn't even my story. I didn't have to buck fifty nobody. It was a cool made-up story, though. Could've been a movie. If I didn't know you, I just might have believed it."

You might think I was delusional, and you're right, I was. But in my mind, I was not lying. I was not a liar. What I was doing was a means to an end. A shortcut. A worthwhile shortcut given that it seemed I only attracted attention from a publication like *The Rag* precisely because of my half-truths. And so, I thought, what did that say about them? Wasn't *that* the bigger issue? I wasn't evil. I was a hustler. I was Pops reincarnated. Playing the game afforded to me.

"I'm not a liar," I told Gio. "It's called taking artistic liberties. Look it up."

Gio flapped his hand. "Call it what you want."

I looked around to see if anyone was listening. "What you read in those stories is just what I do to make them sound better."

"Sound better to who?"

"My editors. The readers. That's what they want."

Gio looked confused. I saw another window of opportunity. Maybe I was thinking about this all wrong. Gio was like me. He was a hustler, too. I didn't need to trick him. I needed to cut him in.

"You haven't been out here—literally and figuratively. Things have changed. It's hard to explain. But this is what I have to do to get put on. Imagine I'm on the Yankees. I'm in the minor leagues, right. And I'm trying to make it to the majors. And it's like that, but maybe in the nineties. Before steroids were illegal and everyone was just pumping that shit into their butt. What I'm doing, basically, is pumping steroids into my butt."

Gio looked at me, at my gut. "You definitely ain't taking steroids. Or even working out, are you?" He poked my stomach. "I could help you out with that. A few simple workouts a day. Your moms actually asked me the other—"

"Not the point," I said. "It's a metaphor. Listen. There are no steroids, just my stories. Let's call them exaggerations. 'Cause yeah, I haven't lived them, but I understand them. There are things I maybe have seen or heard about. Maybe a combination of the two. Maybe I made them up, but I understand them, you get it? The core truth is real."

"The 'core truth'? What the fuck is that?"

I was growing frustrated. Not by Gio, but by my efforts to communicate. "Look, I have this *lived experience* that my editors and the readers want. This knowledge of a world that they don't understand because they're hipsters who have never made it past 125th Street. It's something that, if I lean into it just a bit, transforms me from a bum-ass backup outfielder into, like, a .300 batter who goes 40–40 every year."

Gio mulled it over. "So, basically, you're slinging?"

I realized that was a far superior metaphor to the baseball one I was laboring over. But also not one that I wanted to cop to. Being a drug dealer brought on real-world problems. It led to death. Destruction. Pain. Imprisonment. "In a sense. Really, I'm just putting a little spin on things. Because if I was just one hundred percent honest, they probably wouldn't care. They probably wouldn't even publish me."

We'd been walking around the reservoir, and in our conversation, we'd been going in circles. We approached a set of benches that looked out over the water. We sat. I could see Gio growing bored.

"Anyway. None of that is important. What is important is that people like you and me, people of color, and especially people of color like us who've been through some shit, we have a little leverage right now. And we can use it if we want to."

Gio picked up a rock and tried to skip it on the water. He was clearly lost. I tried to think of something simpler. I wanted my story, and I wanted his participation, which would make it all easier. But I also wanted him to understand me. I wanted him to admit that I wasn't a liar but a genius. I was gaming the system. I wanted him to be proud of me.

"You know what the best thing is, Gio? They want to hear from you more than anyone else," I said. "Even more than me."

Gio grabbed a fistful of leaves and let each leaf fall to the ground one by one like petals. "Why the hell they wanna hear from me?"

I gripped his shoulder. I finally understood how Mr. Martin felt that day in his office. He saw in me something I couldn't see for myself. An opportunity to be great. "Because you were in prison. You were in a gang. You were failed by the system. Your mom died young. *And* you're brown *and* you're from the Bronx. Fuck. You have it all."

Gio started to say something but stopped. He stood up. "I should probably get going."

On our silent walk back to the building, I thought about how to ask for his cooperation with my story. Fine, he didn't understand what I was doing. But eventually, he would. He just needed time. I, on the other hand, didn't have any time to spare. When we reached the entrance, we gave each other a loose pound. Before Gio walked inside, I stopped him and looked him in the eye. "What is it that you really want?" I asked.

He looked down the block. A young girl walked her dog absent-mindedly, pretending to look away as it took a massive shit in the center of the sidewalk. "A job would be nice. My own place. Eventually a car. It don't even have to be a new one. A hoopty." He pointed at a dented Corolla parked along the sidewalk, the paint on the bumper bubbling up like acne. "Even that would be fine. Something to ride around in."

"I can help with all that."

"You sell cars, too?"

"I can't help specifically with getting a car. I mean I can help you in general. Which would, eventually, get you the car."

Gio this whole time had been holding open the front door to the lobby. He let it shut. "You gonna give me a job?"

"No. Well, sort of. You see, I'm thinking of writing something. I don't know if you know, but I'm a staff writer at *The Rag* now. And well, I really need a story. I want to write about us. About you being back. About reconnecting, maybe the different things we've learned. Something big. Something that I *know* will—"

Gio patted me on my shoulder. "Stop, stop. I'm good, Javi." He grabbed the handle of the door and pushed it open.

"You didn't even let me finish."

"I don't need to. I'm not interested."

"But trust me. This can help us both out. It can get you everything you want right now. It'll be a big deal, and then, I promise, there will be tons of people trying to help you. We can start a GoFundMe. You'll get tons of money. Free shit. I'll help you manage the whole thing."

Gio rubbed his head and looked up at the building. The dirty fire escapes were like a trail of Zs climbing up the wall. "I don't want to be a big deal. I don't want nobody feeling bad for me. I just want to get on with my life, Javi. That's all. I don't care about any of that stuff you were talking about. I guess I understand why you do it now. Who am I to judge, of all people? So whatever, bro, do you. But it ain't for me."

I parsed his words. "So you're saying I *can* write about you?"

Gio shrugged. "Do whatever you want, Javi. It's a free country. You're free. I'm free. Even she's free." He pointed at the girl with the dog, who'd just finished squatting and was smelling his own pile of shit. She looked at the two of us and dragged the dog away.

Fifteen

I FELT TORN. More torn than I'd ever felt writing anything else. If only I hadn't already been so far gone.

Part of what bugged me was Gio, and his unease about the whole endeavor. But I promised myself not to include too many identifying details. He wasn't really Gio on the page, and, as far as I was concerned, I wasn't really Javi. We were both just stand-ins for people who maybe could have been us, maybe were us in some alternate universe.

No, what was much harder about writing the story was that it touched on things I'd actually spent a lot of time wondering about. Even before I went off the deep end, before I started spouting stuff just because I knew it was what people wanted to hear, there were questions that would always linger when Gio came to mind. How *did* we end up on such different paths? Who was to blame? What was I supposed to make of the guilt I felt?

The questions always stumped me. Everything played a role and everything didn't at the same time. In the end, it felt like there was something cosmic to our outcomes. They were out of our hands. There was no clear villain. No way I could think of, if I was really honest with myself, to wrap it all up nice and neat in a bow.

I began my essay thinking perhaps this was the time to try to untie the knot. I had my perch, after all. I was in the building. Wasn't this what I'd always been working toward?

But to my surprise, I couldn't get a word down. Writing something true, writing something real, putting the "game" aside, felt like standing in the middle of the Cross Bronx, butt-ass naked. I realized quickly that I was afraid of many things: what people might say, how they might respond to how I actually felt, to what I actually thought. In hindsight, my mistake was that I did not dwell on this fear, did not interrogate it or push through.

Instead, I chose to stick to the script. I decided to give people the version of the story they wanted to hear. The version that made everything simple and easy. Doing that required some alterations.

I moved up Gio's release date by eight months. I knew that in the real world, it was technically too early for me to write this story. I hadn't even really had the chance to get to know my friend again. But who would know?

And since his full name wouldn't be used, I went light on the details of his alleged crimes. I left out the parts he'd mentioned in his letters, about how he'd never done any of the serious stuff—the shootings, the robberies, the shakedowns—but knew they were happening and pretended not to know whenever the police came around. None of that helped the image I wanted to paint of him.

> *He got in trouble once. At age 17. Remember what you were like at 17? Young and dumb, probably. Making mistakes. Well, that's how old he was when he made one vital mistake. He was in the wrong place at the wrong time. In an apartment, at a time when the police were doing their job: perpetually harassing people of color.*

He was one of many young men that look like him who get caught up. Who fall through a trapdoor that takes them from one realm to another. That makes them go from free to enslaved.

I changed Gio's attitude about the world. That stuff about him wanting to move on and not even grandstanding a little bit about the injustice inflicted upon him was not very useful to my cause. It created gray areas, and stories with gray areas weren't the ones Rebecca or Nic wanted. They weren't the stories that shot to the top of the leaderboard.

When I met G at a dismal bus station in upstate New York, he looked nothing like the version of himself that I remembered before he was imprisoned and tortured. That version of G was bright, optimistic, and lighthearted. This new version of G was downtrodden and broken.

He was silent as we made the journey back to our neighborhood. We ended up at the diner we went to as kids. The very same diner where he first revealed his boyish aspirations for life. We were young and enjoying a mountain of rich chocolate cake when he announced he wanted to be the first Puerto Rican in space one day.

Now things couldn't be more different. When I asked him what he was thinking, he replied, "I'm lost, Javi. That's what I'm thinking."

It was clear to me that despite all the talk of reform, the system was working just like it was supposed to. My friend had been pummeled by it.

I wrote that his release had stirred up my discomfort as a well-educated writer of color moving his way through oppressive white spaces in a colonial landscape. It had lit a fire under my feet.

I have written before about how fortunate I have been to escape the system's grasp. I just happened to slip under one closing door and through an opening, suddenly finding myself in places and rooms that I was not supposed to be in, mingling with people I was never supposed to be around.

I've never truly been at ease. I've always looked at the skills and knowledge I've gained and wondered if they really mean anything. Seeing G like this before me, I thought perhaps they might be useful.

Given my teaching background, I wrote, it was only natural for me to want to help Gio, to want to provide him with information and context that might lift his spirits and open his eyes in the way mine had been opened.

I wanted him to see what I had learned. I wanted him to understand the system. I wanted him to notice the gears churning under his feet. If I could do that, I thought, I just might be able to set him free.

Of course, Gio had to be on board. Over the following weeks and months, I wrote, we began to meet regularly. We went on walks, went to the diner, went to the movies, and tried to rebuild a friendship that had suffered from having a chunk of it removed by agents of the state.

Eventually, G began to open up to me again. And eventually, when the time seemed right, I began to gently prod him with questions.

When, for instance, we walked past several homeless men of color sleeping in the park, I asked why he thought so many people in our community struggled, why so many of us lived on the edges of poverty, why so many of us seemed to turn to crime as a means to an end. His answer was the sort of answer you would expect from someone who had—purposefully—not been taught how to think critically about the world around him. "Maybe they don't work hard enough. Maybe they don't know any better."

I pressed. What are they really after? Many of them already work hard and long hours, so why don't they have their basic needs met? And, more importantly, who or what is standing in their way?

The questions were, obviously, not easy to answer. G shrugged them off. "I don't know, man." In the days and weeks that followed, he continued to act defensive during moments like this.

He did what you might expect: He poked fun at my fancy education, called me a nerd, asked me what the purpose was of thinking about such ultimately useless things. Wasn't it more important, he said, to simply focus on what was in front of him? To try to get a job, to try to rebuild his life? Wasn't he better off, in other words, just moving through the world just as he was meant to? "What is trying to answer all of this stuff going to really give me at the end of the day, besides a headache?"

Eventually, I realized, I'd reached an inflection point. The point at which people like G, who have harsh realities to confront on a daily basis, must make a difficult choice. They must ask themselves: Do I really want to go down the hard road of deprogramming myself? Or do I just want to keep life simple? After all, the quest for truth is the furthest thing from simple.

I wrote that, after I kept getting pushback, I decided one afternoon over slices of pizza to confront him, issuing the sort of direct challenge that a man like him, from a place like the Bronx, would have to respond to.

> *I knew my friend. I knew deep down who he really was. A survivor. Just like me. Just like everyone we grew up with. Which is why I asked him what he was really made of. "Do you really want to go through life asleep, G? Being a sheep? Being held down like you're some coward in the schoolyard? Or do you want to wake up, see things for what they really are and fight back? The choice, at the end of the day, is yours."*
>
> *I walked away from the table. Left him there. And hoped, with each step, that I'd gotten his attention.*

It worked, I wrote. Gio stopped swatting away my questions. He started to try to formulate his own answers. He started to ask me for more context, which I gladly supplied him. In our conversations, I found myself referencing the books and films and lectures I'd been exposed to.

> *Soon enough, you could find us having wide-ranging discussions about the prison industrial complex, the socioeconomic dynamics of the neighborhood we'd grown up in, the uneven funding of the schools we'd gone to, and the real reasons why so many of us suffered from all the same sorts of health risks generation after generation.*
>
> *Even though the information was, at times, rudimentary, haphazard and not at all organized like on an elite college's course syllabus, I could tell G was learning.*
>
> *Slowly, I could see he was beginning to understand what I had come to grasp myself. Beginning to take an accounting of his past, and see how often the things he thought of as missteps, the things he*

thought of as shortcomings of his own doing, had in fact always been out of his hands. Had in fact been traps that he was unfortunate enough to walk right into.

With this newfound understanding, little by little, I wrote, Gio gained a bounce in his step.

It wasn't long before he had questions of his own. Questions I couldn't answer. Questions that required him to check books out from the library, watch YouTube videos and read articles. And it wasn't long after that that I watched G start to unscrew the training wheels and take charge of his own reeducation.

I ended the story by circling back to the diner, eight months later. Our breakfast is different this time. Gio is no longer defeated. He is empowered.

We sipped our coffee. G looked at me in a very serious manner. "Thank you," he said. I could tell he wasn't thanking me for the food I'd bought, but for something deeper.

"Thank you for making sure I didn't end up a sheep. That ain't me. And now I know that."

I appreciated the sentiment. But I demurred. "All I did was show you the right direction to walk in. You're the one who moved your feet."

I left proud that day. Proud about how far my friend had come, how much he'd grown, how he'd come to see himself not as a pawn to be moved around on a board but as a player prepared to outsmart a game whose odds are against him.

I realized through this process that perhaps I was meant to witness and unpack all this racism, classism, colonialism, and injustice to help people like G, people who don't have all the same tools that I do, grapple with their own versions of it. Perhaps I was meant to go through my own arduous journey of deprogramming.

The two of us were both born to poor families on opposite sides of a beat-up building who shared the same problems. We were born facing down the same oppressive forces. But despite these same factors, the trajectories of our lives couldn't have been farther from each other.

I was lucky. I've always known that. Always felt guilty about it. Always felt that the fact that I even had to be lucky to get to a place like this is so unjust. But I never knew what I could really do about it.

Now, however, I hold on to some hope. I look at G's new lease on life and think perhaps the balance has shifted, even just a tiny bit. That's something. That's progress.

I felt good about the story. Not because I thought it was good. But because I knew others would be impressed by it.

I considered sending it to Gio. I thought maybe he'd understand how cinematic we could be, maybe he'd understand his role in the movie and want to get involved. But on the off chance that he wouldn't get it or, more importantly, would protest, I never hit Send.

I sent it to Rebecca instead.

"This is a very compelling story, Javier," she wrote back. "The transformation you detail here is quite the turnaround for your friend. This piece is certainly far more up our alley. I am curious, though, is there a reason why your friend doesn't want his full name in the piece? I think that would really help add to the legitimacy of it. Keeping these sorts of things anonymous is fine occasionally, of course, but we don't want to overdo it. You've already had quite a run of those kinds of stories. After all, this is such a positive piece, I can't imagine why your friend would decline to participate."

I was no longer surprised that Rebecca found something to take issue with. But this was a chess game, and I was a far more skilled player. So instead of just giving her another fake number or email, or even giving her Gio's real number and convincing him to say the right things or just ignore her as he likely would have, I decided to play things differently.

"Of course, I, too, would love that, Rebecca," I wrote. "However, my friend is wary of including his name. You probably don't fully understand, given that you are a white woman, but people of color who have been targeted by the authorities in the past are very reluctant to speak on the record—and for good reason. So, you see, what I'm doing by keeping his name out of the story is protecting him. I hope you can appreciate that? I'm looping Nic in here, too, so that we're all on the same page before moving forward. Nic, it was you who charged me with bringing more authentic stories to the table. Well, this is part of the territory."

I smirked as I hit Send. I imagined Rebecca reading the email, the sour look on her face as she spotted Nic's email address cc'd, the understanding, finally, perhaps, that I was not one to fuck with.

Nic's response, which came in less than an hour, was just what I expected. "Javier. Thanks for bringing this to my attention. Rebecca and I have spoken. Your concerns are valid and I'm sorry if we caused any discomfort. This story is FANTASTIC. Just what we're looking for. We will run it as is. More from us very soon!"

MY VICTORY felt great. But as I waited to hear more in the next few days, I couldn't get Gio out of my mind. I texted him a couple of times because I actually did want to hang out. Not to talk about the stuff that I'd written, which I figured he probably wouldn't have an interest in. But because I was still troubled by our last interaction. I was troubled by the fact that he thought of me as having fundamentally changed in some way—and not in a good way. There was the ego blow. But also, I wanted to know how I had changed. Before Gio's release, there wasn't really anyone around who knew me before and after. Who could, like Gio could, point back to historical references.

Gio never responded to the texts. I remembered the little burner-looking phone he was using. I called and finally got him.

"Yo," he said.

"Yo."

I felt awkward. Asking to hang used to be so simple that I never even really had to say the words. It was just assumed. "Want to grab something to eat?"

Gio was silent for a few moments. I could hear the cushions of the couch fold in on themselves under his shifting weight. "I'm a little busy right now. I'm looking for jobs and stuff."

"I could help," I said. "I could write you an amazing résumé and cover letter. I know a thing or two about making yourself sound good."

"That you do," Gio said, seeming less than enthused. "I'll think about it. But anyway, let me let you go." *Click.*

For the next day, I thought about that conversation. I progressed from wondering if there was something wrong with me to being angry at Gio. *Who the fuck does he think he is? Pretending like I don't exist or something. He should be begging for my help.*

My anger only dissipated when I finally got a response from Nic about the piece, declaring that a longtime dream of mine was about to come true.

"I've decided this is going on the cover of the next issue," he wrote. "In a big, big way."

Sixteen

LOOKING BACK, I'm still blinded by the speed with which it all happened. The day the print edition came out, I went to a newsstand in Harlem—the closest place I could find a copy. I held the magazine in my hands and stared at my name and the title of my essay—"A Friendship Marred by Injustice and Redeemed by Kindness"—in glossy large black letters on the front. The rest of the cover was swallowed by an illustration of two boys standing on either side of a dim hallway. A chalk line separated them. One boy was dressed in a cap and gown and holding a diploma. The other wore baggy clothes, a titled fitted cap, and a gold chain. The two reached out to touch each other. Their fingertips nearly connected for what seemed like a brief moment, just like in Michelangelo's painting.

I stood on the street corner marveling at the physical object. I felt a rush just knowing that others all around the country were doing the same. They would see *my* name next to the story. For a few minutes, they'd be consumed by me and *my* words. They'd be blown away. I wish I could have lived in that moment forever. Feeling that peace. That sense of accomplishment. But it was, almost instantly, interrupted by a crush of incessant chatter.

By the time I got home, my inbox was overflowing. My phone was basically moving on its own because of the constant buzzing of notifications. I'd been here before. But then it kept on going for days.

I was getting even more attention than when I wrote about Anais. That story had also been a catchy tune. But this story about Gio was received differently. Nas *Illmatic* shit. It struck a chord. It blasted through some unseen wall and became one of those things everyone on the internet seemed to know a little something about, even if they really knew nothing at all. People said it was a "must-read" and had "fundamentally changed" the way they thought about education, gangs, and prisons. They said it was clear that I'd been appointed the "voice of a generation" and that my talent was "the type that only comes around once in a while." It was a different kind of high. Not just attention. Validation. A big stamp was pressed into my forehead. I was certified by the Twittersphere. But also by my metrics app, where the numbers kept jumping and jumping.

Roller coasters are tired clichés for a reason, dear reader. But so be it.

If my story, if *this story* that you're reading right now, were a ride, this moment would be right near the top. The part where you're climbing and climbing and it looks like you'll keep going up forever. But instead you get just the slightest, teeniest glimpse of the crest. And then comes that sinking feeling, burrowing deep into the pit of your stomach, as you begin the descent.

WITHIN A WEEK of the story's publication, an email arrived from a literary agent named Miles Lorenzo. An agent who represented the same "buzzed-about" writers I'd watch and seethe with jealousy about.

I see a fantastic book in you, and I know a few big publishers who would be willing to scoop it up rather quickly. Let's chat.

The next day, I found myself in the lobby of a glass building in Chelsea. The brick walls in Miles's office were lined with bookshelves and plants. Two puffy leather couches flanked a massive table. Miles, a white, late-fifties-looking, silver-haired man in a dapper suit, shook my hand. I saw him eye my hoodie. My ball cap. My skin. He smiled, just like I'd expected him to. "I have to say, I was thrilled by your piece. Your past stuff is excellent, too. The topics you write about, the breadth of your gritty experience and background—all of it is just so ripe for the moment. And, you should know, the market is hungry for it."

"Thank you. I am aware."

Miles smiled. He asked me to sit.

"I can tell you're smart, Javier. Which is why I wanted to bring you down here to pick your brain. Because, you see, there are a lot of options for you. A lot of ways you can play this—a professorship, speaking gigs, awards, and so forth. But it all starts with a book. With something that clicks in the way that your latest story has."

I might as well have been back in high school, sitting across from Ms. Rivas, listening to her tell my mother that I had talent. I felt that same stirring. "What kind of book?"

Miles shrugged. "Depends on what you'd like to do. There's fiction, which is okay. But right now what is really in, what is selling like hotcakes, is the sort of stuff you're writing. First person. Identity-driven. Descriptive. People eat it up. Especially when it comes from the right kind of person. And you seem to have a lot going for you in that department."

"Meaning?"

Miles straightened one of the framed book covers on the wall. "Oh come now, Javier. You know. You're young, good-looking, you've got a tough background, some street cred, if you will. The minority experience is hot, is all I'm saying. I hope you don't take that the wrong way."

I liked Miles. He didn't seem nervous. He was respectful, and he laid on just the right amount of butter. He didn't treat me like some golden calf. He knew the game and wasn't beating around the bush. Together, I thought, we could get something done. We could even make a lot of money.

We talked through possible first-person books he could see me writing. There was, according to him, the "made it out the hood" story about my life in the Bronx, my time at Donlon, and where I was now. "The form is pretty set," he said, sounding like a sage. "It's been done to death, if you ask me. But people seem to love it. Especially now." If I didn't want to go that route, I could zero in on my friendship with Gio. Expand my piece for *The Rag,* essentially. "People also love those 'what if' tales. You could lean into that, do some interviews with your friend, find out your ancestral histories, get some nice old photos to go along with them. That's a pretty simple one to write, too."

No matter what route I went, Miles explained, the most important thing was that the book be heavy on scenes, on imagery. "Just, whatever you do, don't write one of these tomes trying to convince people of something with statistics and data. Nobody wants to be convinced of anything. They want a good ride. Paint the pictures they want to see, and don't take too long doing it."

AS I WAITED for Miles to draw up the paperwork for me to sign with him, my phone rang. I silenced the call without looking at it. I wanted to live in the moment. I felt like an elite athlete on draft day. Like Kanye West signing with Roc-A-Fella.

The phone rang again. Miles entered the room with papers in his hand. "Get that if you need to," he said. "I know you're a busy man these days."

I saw a number I didn't recognize. When I answered, the man on the line hurriedly introduced himself as a producer for the Nightly News Network. Jackie Knox, *the* Jackie Knox, loved my story and thought it had "so many parallels" to our cultural moment.

The producer asked me a fateful question: Would Gio and I be willing to sit with her for an exclusive interview? "I know you kept your friend anonymous in the story. But we really think having the two of you there, side by side, would be something special for our viewers."

I stared at more of the framed book covers behind Miles, who was shamelessly eavesdropping. I imagined my own book there behind him. I imagined it at the front of all the bookstores in the city, all the bookstores across the country. My name, my image, on posters. My face on the NNN screen with a chyron underneath reading "Writer" or "Author" as the show was broadcast all around the world. It was a level of exposure that seemed improbable to me. And an opportunity that, for once, seemed perhaps too far out of my league. I wasn't so delusional as to not recognize the leap from being a name printed in small type in a magazine to being a face broadcasted on television screens in homes, airports, and bars across the country. The level of recognition that would bring was also an opportunity for cracks to start forming in my armor.

The producer cleared his throat. "If you're up for this, we'd need you both at our studio tomorrow evening. Can you make it?"

"And what if my friend isn't interested? Would it be okay if it's just me on air? I'm sure I can capture—"

"No, no," the producer said. "For this to work, it would have to be both of you."

My gut was telling me something again, trying to warn me. But my lust for knowing what this level of fame could be like, what it could afford me, was far too strong.

"Yes," I said. "We'll both be there."

I JUMPED ON A TRAIN back to the Bronx. Everything seemed to be moving at hyperspeed. The only thing tethering me to reality, to the fact that all of this shit was really happening, was the one big hurdle ahead of me before everything would, I thought, fall into place.

When Gio answered the door, he looked annoyed. I felt like a pest. Like the kid that doesn't get the fucking hint. Still, Gio motioned for me to come inside his grandma's apartment. Clearly, not because he wanted me to. But because of our history together, because of the fact that I was essentially family.

I followed him into the living room, the first time I'd been in there since he'd been released. The first time I'd been in there since we were kids. Another air mattress—not the same one he'd used as a kid, but a newer version—was on the floor, just like old times. Other things mostly looked the same: Mercedes's hutch with plates and silverware she never used stood in its rightful place, although the paint seemed more faded than I'd remembered. Her couch, which also looked considerably older and less fashionable, was still cloaked in plastic, as if it were being preserved for viewing by some future civilization. The only real difference I could discern was that instead of Gio's corner of the room resembling the aftermath of a hurricane, it was neat and orderly. His clothes were perfectly folded in a bin. His bed was meticulously made. His shoes were lined up against the wall and color coded.

"Are you a serial killer now?" I asked.

Gio didn't laugh. "You don't get much in prison, so you learn to take care of what's yours." He leaned up against the radiator and crossed his arms. "What do you want?"

"There's something I need to tell you."

"I know you wrote that dumb story. I read it."

"You did? You bought a copy?"

"No, man. That magazine is not worth buying." He gestured to a laptop the size and width of a briefcase. "I read it on the internet."

"Do you follow me on Twitter?"

"That social media shit? Nah, I don't fuck with that. Too much information out there. Last thing I want is to give free crumbs to the cops."

"So how did you know, then?"

"Because I knew you were gonna write it. I knew as soon as you left that day we hung out. I could tell by the end that that was what you really wanted. So I just checked a few times until it was there. Just like I thought it'd be."

"What do you mean, you knew that was what I really wanted?"

"Come on, Javi. I known you too long. You weren't trying to see me on some homeboy shit. I peeped game. It is what it is."

"I'm sorry," I said. "I was just excited. About the story. About my job." I wanted us to have some deep conversation. The moment was ripe for us to really talk. To really be those kids again. But the clock was ticking. My future awaited.

"So what did you think?"

Gio stroked his beard. "You want my real opinion, Javi? It was a piece of shit."

The words stung. They weren't coming from some random person I didn't give a fuck about on Twitter; they weren't written in goofy red Comic Sans font in my email. They came from someone real, someone I cared about.

"I get that maybe some of it made you uncomfortable. But did you read the whole thing?"

Gio chuckled at my audacity. "Of course I did, Javi. It was about me. It was about you. And that's why I hated it."

"Because you didn't want me to write about you?"

"No, motherfucker. Because you make me seem like some kind of fucking idiot. Like I'm some pussy who is going around crying all day and begging you for help. I already told you I don't need you. I don't need you to 'unlock' me like I'm a fucking Pokémon. Whether you're here or not, I'ma get my shit together." He shook his head, patted his pocket, and took out a crumpled pack of Newports. "You had me tight with that shit. Writing this fairy-tale stuff. That's really what people want to read? Don't make no sense to me." He lit the cigarette and took a drag. He pointed the ember at me. "Thank God you didn't put my name in that shit. Then I'd really fuck you up. No lie."

I'd like to say this jolted me awake. Made me realize I wasn't hurting someone who didn't matter. But it didn't. As Gio said this, I was too busy thinking about the fact that I really needed to shave. I needed to track down my dodgy barber and get a haircut. I needed to practice what version of Javi I wanted to present to the world. But first, before all of that, I needed to make sure Gio would be there sitting next to me on television. Saying the right things. Making the ruse work.

"Listen, Gio. I'm sorry you're upset. And I'm gonna fix it. I'm gonna make it so that we're boys just like before, with none of the bullshit. I promise. But first, I really need you to do something for me. You see, the thing is, we've been invited on television. Do you know who Jackie Knox is?"

Gio's eyes widened. "J. Knox? From NNN? Hell yeah. We used to watch her in the rec room. She's bad, bro. I love that mouth of hers. The things I would do—"

"Okay, well, don't say that to her. You can't talk like that anymore. But yes, she wants to interview us."

"What's all this 'we' and 'us' shit, motherfucker? That's your story. What do I have to do with it?" He flicked ash out the window.

"It was a hit, Gio. You might have hated it. But guess what? Everyone is reading it and talking about it. And now I've got an agent and I'm gonna write a book, and on top of that, Jackie Knox wants to interview me. To interview *us*."

Gio shrugged. "Aight, cool, Javi. Good for you. You want a fucking cookie? Still don't sound like shit that has to do with me."

I felt my leg tingle with a notification. I whipped out my phone and looked at it. Another mention about the piece. "I'm in tears . . ." I swiped it away before I could even finish savoring it. I rubbed my temples. "Do you want money? I'll pay you."

Gio laughed. "Pay me for what, Javi? What the fuck you talking about?"

"It's nothing crazy, Gio. The producer told me Jackie will ask about our childhood, probably ask you about prison. About the story, obviously. But it will be quick. In and out. Five minutes, tops. On television, that moves like five seconds," I said, pretending I knew what it was like to be on television.

Gio looked incredulous. "Didn't I just say I don't want to be associated with this shit? You really not listening to me, Javi."

"But you'll get to be on television," I said, thinking this might be a winning argument.

"Yeah, telling the world I'm an ex-con who was so dumb I needed you to help me figure out my life. Not sure how that helps me. It's already hard enough finding a job with a record like mine." He flicked the remains of his cigarette out the window. He lit another within milliseconds. "Did you know I spent the whole day yesterday going door-to-door looking for a damn job and the only thing anyone wants to let me do is wash fucking dishes? I'm about to just do it, honestly."

"'Cause you need money, right? So why won't you let me give you some?"

Gio took a drag on the cigarette and looked at me closely. "I didn't think you had this in you. You really have changed."

I should have stopped right there. Really thought about what he was saying. But to tell the truth, it barely registered with me in the moment. "The thing is, you're just not understanding, G. This is important. This is my life we're talking about. If this interview goes the way it's supposed to, my new fancy agent is going to sell the book I'm gonna write for a whole lot of money. I'm gonna get invited back on TV, get bigger gigs, and then after that—"

"Yeah. And then . . . what? What happens next?"

"And then I'll have money and fame and a book and be closer to where I want to be."

"Which is where, Javi?"

In my mind all I could see in that moment was this magical door that would lead me to the perfect life. A life in which I could just glide. No more grinding, no more pitching, no more trying to sell a story, any story. I could work on what I wanted to. Whatever that was. I could be a "creative," an "artist." Maybe I wouldn't even have to use social media. I could eventually be big enough that it would be cool for me to be off it. But I knew I couldn't be that person yet. Not until I achieved a certain level of validation. And that is what I really thought this interview would do for me. Stamp me. Just like being the first Latino columnist at Donlon had. Just like getting into *The Rag* had. But this would be a bigger stamp. The one I needed to finally breathe a sigh of relief.

"I'll pay you a thousand dollars," I said.

Gio laughed. "You're a piece of work."

"I'm asking you now as your friend, Gio. As your boy. From way, way back. Come on, please? I know I haven't been the greatest friend recently. But I need you right now. Listen, we fell off when I was in college and all that, but you know I was always there for you. Always writing to you. I never abandoned you, right? You don't have to do it to—"

"Alright, alright. Stop with the bitching. I get it. Drop the guilt trip." Gio gestured the crumpled pack of cigarettes my way. I took one. We smoked for a while in silence.

"Would *I* have to lie?" he asked. "People might see that shit. That could follow me around."

"You think people in the hood watch NNN?"

Gio blew a ring of smoke in my face. "Who says I care about what people in the hood think?"

"Fine. No, you don't have to lie. Just follow my lead. They just want you there to make themselves feel better. So it's more 'authentic.' Don't say much; act shy. I'll do the talking. It'll be fine and over before you know it. They're not going to ask hard questions. They just wanna lap this shit up."

"You sure about that?"

"Just trust me, okay."

Gio mulled. He finished the cigarette. Tossed it and closed the window. "Two g's," he said. "Won't do it for nothing less."

The price seemed steep for five minutes of work. It would also pretty much wipe out my entire savings. But it seemed like an investment worth making. With the cigarette in my mouth wobbling the way Pops's used to, I stuck my hand out.

"Deal."

Seventeen

THE INTERVIEW was set to happen at 8:00 p.m. at the NNN studios in Midtown. I woke up that morning at eight, though "woke up" is the wrong phrase. It implies that I had slept the previous night. And "sleep" would imply that I shut my eyes for a long period of time, or at least a few consecutive hours.

What I actually did was lie in bed and stare at the ceiling, trying to visualize how things would go. I fought off doubts as to whether I should be going through with it at all. Whether lying in front of a prime-time audience of three million people was really a good idea. *I'm fine. I got this. I'm just nervous, right?* I picked up my phone. I scrolled through Twitter. I read replies to my previous tweet the evening before, in which I announced my appearance on Jackie Knox's show and asked everyone to "tune in." The responses brought me comfort. "Congrats!" "About time!" "Will be watching."

As I read, I half listened to the homies outside, who by 3:00 a.m. had dwindled from a group of a half dozen to only two. I listened as the two left held something like a confessional. One of the men, who, earlier in the night, I gathered from the conversation, had been talking shit about some girl, was now revealing that he was in fact sweating her. "I was just saying that. But to keep it real, shorty has me kinda sprung." I heard a belch in response. Then something like real comfort from his friend. "It be like that sometimes." It was a tender moment. The kind of moment I remembered having with Gio, even with Anais early on. Being vulnerable. Admitting something real. *When was the last time I did that?*

I shook off the thought. Tried to sleep. Woke up again around 5:00 a.m. and turned to look at my alarm clock, as if it were possible for me to oversleep by over twelve hours and miss my opportunity. Nonetheless, I convinced myself it could happen and did not sleep for the rest of the morning.

My living room still felt empty. After Anais left, it never stopped feeling bare. For a while there, I considered brightening it up by hanging some of my stories from *The Rag,* but I thought better of it. Even as I was preparing for a national television interview, and telling people to "tune in" to me, I still couldn't see the problem: I wasn't proud enough of the stories to hang them. I was proud of the reaction.

For the rest of the morning, I fielded pretend interview questions from myself. I practiced answers for what I believed to be every possible question I could be asked. I thought carefully about word choices. I'd use *hostile* and *dangerous* to describe my background and, by extension, Gio's background, rather than *underprivileged* or *tough*—those were too vague. I'd point out to Jackie that the word *underprivileged* didn't suit the true description, tell her, "The word only serves to hide the real violence and trauma that some people experience . . . only sweeps the dirt under the rug without dealing with it." I recalled some of the amazing performances I'd witnessed at the LTC. I practiced where I would insert my own dramatic pauses. I even thought about including a moment of tears, but I scrapped that plan when I realized it was too difficult for me to cry on command, and that even attempting to do so only made it seem like I was trying to take a shit.

AT 6:00 P.M., I met Gio in front of my building. Underneath his open coat, he wore the blue shirt and tie I'd hurriedly bought him the day before atop dark baggy jeans. With the Yankees cap on his head, he looked like the perfect contrast to me in my blazer and white shirt with dark slim jeans. I felt confident. We looked, I thought, like what people might imagine us to look like after seeing the cover illustration for my story. We fit the description.

As we rode down the West Side Highway in a town car paid for by the studio, I noticed Gio's knee bouncing up and down.

"What's wrong?"

Gio looked out the window. "I don't know if I can do it."

I had already given him half the money up front, per his demands. I'd spent more buying him clothes. And here we were in the car. "It's too late to back out. Everything will be just fine."

I watched him pound his fist into his other hand.

"What are you so worried about?"

"The last time I was interviewed, it was, you know. When everything went down. Part of why I got so much time. They had this recorder in front me, took all these official notes and shit. Then later on, in the courtroom, they went and pointed at the shit. They made it seem like my words were written in fucking stone and not some shit I said when they had me in a cold room in front of screaming detectives talking about how I was going to spend the rest of my life locked up." He sighed. "I just get nervous when people start asking too many questions."

I put my hand on his knee. Held it down until it stopped bouncing. "This isn't prison, Gio. These aren't the cops. This is the media. A whole different ball game. A game I happen to know like the back of my hand. I mean, look at this. We're riding in style. We're getting the celebrity treatment. Just enjoy it."

The driver opened the door for us, and we walked into the kind of lobby where the sounds of hard-soled shoes reverberate like an opera singer's vibrato. When the elevator doors opened, we were greeted by Scott, a tweedy man with a big pilot's headset on his dome and a clipboard pressed to his chest. On the phone, Scott had talked about how he and Jackie "adored" my writing and found it "incredibly moving." And even though I hadn't been a full-fledged staff writer at *The Rag* for very long, he said they were still keen to have me on. "Not only because of your writing but because of all that you represent. It's important for our audience."

But Scott's demeanor as he stood there in front of me seemed different. Frazzled, but also oddly cold. "Glad you could make it," he said. I followed as we were led to a greenroom with a table in the center filled with fruit and snacks. "You two hang out here," Scott said. He whispered into his headset before giving me a tight smile and taking off. A two-woman hair-and-makeup team entered soon after and asked Gio and me to sit in chairs facing mirrors on the wall.

"Nah. Pause. I don't do makeup," Gio said to the woman who approached him.

She looked to be in her fifties, with rouged cheeks and a smoker's rasp to her voice. "Oh please, hunny. You too much of a tough guy? I'm not going to put lipstick on you, baby. Just going to take care of those blemishes on your forehead."

Gio looked at her askance. "What blemishes?"

We sat still as they layered on creams and powders. The woman working on me styled my hair as Gio sat in his chair and chewed on an apple. Despite protests from the other woman and Scott, Gio refused to take off the baseball cap. "Javi didn't give me time to get a line-up. It ain't happening. Deal with it."

When we were all cleaned up, Scott walked us through the stage area and an army of people: cameramen, stagehands, assistants. They yelled directions. Buzzers and bells went off. Scratchy dispatches were shared on walkie-talkies. Jackie, meanwhile, sat at her desk reading through papers, looking as calm as a queen.

"Damn, she's even finer in real life," Gio whispered.

Jackie looked up for a moment. Glared.

She *was* fine. In her early forties, slender and tall, glasses hiding her intense eyes. Eyes that seemed to look right through you. I waited for her to say something, but she glanced back at the paper in front of her as the crew shuffled around. The man sculpting her hair deployed a cloud of mist.

Scott led us to our seats. Two comfy chairs oriented to face Jackie at her desk for the opening-conversation portion of her show. In the past, I'd watched on television as she'd interviewed Pulitzer Prize–winning reporters and writers, politicians, chefs, rappers, activists. Illustrious guests. Now I was joining their ranks.

"Thirty seconds!" someone yelled.

The man doing Jackie's hair skittered away. Jackie put her papers down. She smiled, curtly. "Nice to have you both. What an incredible story you seem to have here."

The word *seem* struck me as odd, but I decided, with the seconds counting down, not to overthink it.

"It's *very* nice to be here, Jackie," Gio said, sounding like the excited one now. "You look amazing. I used to watch you in prison. Had something like a crush on you. A little one. Aight, maybe not that little."

Jackie pushed her glasses up her nose and straightened the papers on her desk.

"It's a true honor," I said, kicking Gio's leg under the table.

Scott stepped before the camera and began counting down from ten. When he hit zero, Jackie sat straight up and stared into the blinking red light. Her face contorted into something inherently different from how it had looked moments ago. Her voice shot up several registers.

"Welcome back. I have here in the studio with me Javier Perez, a budding writer from the Bronx whose work you may have read in *The Rag*. Well, his last piece, the December issue's cover story"—she held the magazine up for the camera—"was a breathtaking read about his best friend, Giovanni, and how their paths diverged in their youth, when Giovanni was arrested and sentenced to prison for the sort of inane drug charges that too often befall young, poor men of color."

I noticed Gio wince. I hoped no one else had seen it.

"It reads as a heartbreaking story about injustice, systemic racism, and the very real obstacles facing Black and brown youth in this country. But rather than me going on about it, Javier, could you please tell us more?"

I sat up straight and delivered the spiel I had practiced. I told her about the two of us growing up with single moms, about losing a parent young, about facing trying times, about our bad influences and our failing education system. When I was done, Jackie contorted her face again, this time into a serious expression. Like what she was saying was the most grave and important thing ever said in the history of human civilization.

"That *sounds* so dreadful," she said. She stopped and sighed for effect. "So how does someone make it out of that, or perhaps not make it?"

"That, I think, is the crux of the story." I'd practiced using the word *crux*. "What I'm getting at in my story is what an uphill climb it is. How *lucky* you have to be to escape. The different paths that Gio and I took, despite the fact that we were basically the same kid, is *emblematic* of that."

Gio drummed his fingers on his chair's armrests.

"Let's talk more about those paths you say you took," Jackie said. "Javier, you write that after high school, you went on to attend Donlon—a *fantastic* school, by the way. And Gio, Javier writes that you went to prison."

"We had some decent teachers there, too," Gio said.

"Right. So how did your paths take you there? Gio?"

Gio flicked his nose with the edge of his knuckle. He stared at me.

"I'll take that one, actually," I said. "It would appear, from the outside, that it was pretty simple. I did my homework, studied, kept myself on the straight and narrow, and Gio here, let's say, fell in with the wrong crowd, perhaps didn't focus as much as he should have. So we each got what was fair, right? That is what the *world* would have you believe. That this is simply about one person who worked hard and did what he was supposed to and another who didn't. But, of course, that isn't the case. There are other, bigger, unseen forces at play."

"Say more about these forces, Javier. Please."

I unleashed more big words I'd been storing up. The ones that had always, in my experience, made white people like Jackie slink into themselves, feel guilty, and, eventually, retreat. "A myriad of things, Jackie. Systemic racism, unequal educational opportunities, the war on drugs—"

"And what do you make of this, Gio?" Jackie interrupted. "After all, Javier writes beautifully in his story about the 'transformation' you experienced as a result of learning more about all of this."

Gio pursed his lips. "Yeah," he said, with no enthusiasm. "I mean, you know, Javi knows what he's talking about."

"Is that all, Gio?"

"Gio is a little nervous to be on television," I said.

"Of course." The grin on Jackie's face is what, looking back, was the first real sign. The moment I realized I wasn't kidding myself. Wasn't overthinking things. Something was up.

"I find it very *interesting* the way you describe things in your story, Javier."

I started to get a sinking feeling in my stomach. The roller coaster was in its full descent.

"You see, before your appearance tonight on my show, my team and I received a tip in regard to your recent history with Gio, as well as allegations about your other stories. In our reporting, my team and I found a *mountain* of pretty damning accusations about you and your writing, stretching back to your days even before joining *The Rag*." Jackie turned to the camera again, no longer speaking to me, but to the audience. "After an initial investigation . . ."

Gio stiffened at that word. Looked at me, concerned.

". . . we found the tip and many of the accusations regarding the accuracy of your writing to be credible. And now, since we have you here, there are some questions we think you really need to answer."

I looked at the red light on the camera. All those millions of people.

Gio cleared his throat. "I think we should probably bounce now," he said. He started to take off his microphone.

Even though I felt like I was in free fall, I was determined to double down. Determined to fight. What could Jackie really know?

"I'm not sure what sort of 'investigation' you're talking about, Jackie. But, I have to say, I think you're mistaken."

Jackie's eyes narrowed, and I could tell I'd fucked up. I was on the other end of things, the gun in my face now. She read from the papers in front of her, the ones she had been studying all along. "Well, let us start with something small, shall we? It says right here in your story that you and Gio reunited when he was released from prison, what, eight months ago. Is that right?"

Gio shook his head.

"Javier?" Jackie asked.

"Yes. That's right."

"Except that it's not right. In fact, prison records show that Giovanni was released less than a month ago. But eight months is what you wrote in your story, correct?"

I tried to think of an angle to work. "Well—"

"Do you admit that you made up the date of Gio's release?"

"I may have played with the timeline a little bit. But that didn't fundamentally alter any—"

Jackie was in bulldog mode now. "So if you admit to fabricating that part of the story, which it sounds like you are doing, my question is: What else did you fabricate, Javier?"

Gio, struggling to unhook himself from the microphone, snapped his fingers at the stagehands behind the camera. "Hey. Can one of y'all help me? I'm gone. I ain't getting in trouble again."

"Take a seat, Giovanni. Please. We'd love to hear from you, too," Jackie said.

"Nope, nope. Don't have nothing to say. I told Javi. I told him I didn't want to do this." He ripped the microphone cord out of his pocket and threw it on the ground.

"Gio, please. The audience deserves the truth."

Gio twisted his face. "The audience deserves deez nuts." He

stuck a middle finger at the camera and walked offstage. Scott tried to put an arm on Gio's shoulder, but he shook it off. "Touch me again and watch what happens." Scott moved out of the way. Gio stalked toward the exit.

The cameras kept rolling. Jackie said, "Javier, again, I ask: What else did you fabricate?"

The word *fabricate* felt excessive. More serious than what I thought I was doing. I was taking advantage of a lane. Capitalizing on an opportunity. You know the deal by now.

"I didn't fabricate. That's not what's happening here . . ."

"So what *is* happening here, Javier? Because our investigation suggests that this story is not the first one in which you've taken some quite dramatic liberties with the truth. In fact, it suggests that this story is just the culmination of a budding career built on lies."

She turned to the camera. "Yesterday, viewers, NNN received a tip from a woman by the name of Anais Delgado. Your former girlfriend whom you wrote a popular story about, correct, Javier?"

"Uh, yes."

"Though you kept her anonymous in the story?"

"I was trying to protect her. So yes."

Jackie smiled wider. "Well, Anais said the exact opposite. She actually outed herself and claimed that your story is completely false. To prove it, she provided us with her correspondence with the police department, which shows that in fact there were no arrests made the night she simply called the cops on some rowdy neighbors. Another verifiable falsehood. She also claimed that you have a history of fabricating your stories and connected us with another source, a Ricardo Diaz, who said the same."

Ricardo and Anais. Of course. "Jackie. Listen. This is just hearsay from two people who are obviously jealous of me. I don't even know why someone of your caliber would even entertain that—"

"Jealous of you? Or on to you?"

"They're lying. All I did was tell compelling stories that people wanted to read."

"But were they actually true, Javier?"

"Well, they were based in truth."

I saw Scott pump his fist behind the camera. Jackie would have if she hadn't still been performing. But they both knew what they had. Gold.

" 'Based in truth' that you made more compelling how, Javier? By making things up? By taking advantage of others and their actual trauma and passing it off as your own?"

"I didn't take advantage of anyone. I didn't hurt anyone."

Jackie gestured toward the exit. "What about your *supposed* friend, Gio. You didn't take advantage of him? He seemed pretty upset just now."

I looked at Gio's empty seat. "No. That's not what's going on here."

Jackie motioned to someone behind the camera. "Well, Javier. Since you don't seem to be interested in sharing much, we have some news to share with *you*. After conducting our investigation into the allegations about you, we reached out to *The Rag* for comment . . ."

"Allegations" felt so formal. Like "charges." I thought about Gio alone in that courtroom at age seventeen. Had he felt as hot sitting there as I felt sitting in the studio? Had he had the same sinking realization that shit was hitting the fan for real? I suddenly thought past the people who might be watching this live. Thought about the millions who might see it on YouTube. Thought about the clips that would be posted on social media, that could follow me, seemingly, forever.

"We spoke to an editor who has worked closely with you since you began writing for *The Rag*. When we shared with her the information we'd obtained from Anais, she revealed correspondence between you and her in which you lied about contacting Anais before your story about her was published. This editor also showed us proof that you gave her a fake phone number and email account to use in contacting Anais. You even *posed as* Anais using that fake email account."

Jackie paused and sighed, as if I were the worst criminal in the world. "After hearing the totality of these allegations and learning of *numerous* verifiable lies, Nic Ossof, editor in chief of *The Rag*, provided the show with a statement. We have it here." Jackie gestured to the camera.

I looked up at a screen on the wall, which was playing the live broadcast. Overlaying it was an animation of a ripped piece of paper with words on it attributed to Nic. The same Nic who had been oddly quiet in the twenty-four hours since I'd emailed him to let him know about my appearance.

"*The Rag* says they are 'saddened to hear these allegations' and 'take seriously any potential fabrications in stories' because 'they compromise the magazine's editorial integrity.' They added that they will be promptly looking into further infractions you may have committed during your time writing for them. As of now, however, you're suspended."

"Suspended?"

"Yes. We're breaking that news tonight, in fact," Jackie said to the camera, reminding her viewers.

"So, Javier, anything you'd like to say?"

I thought about Pops. About how he would have reacted with his back to the wall. Even in his final moments, he wasn't scared. If he'd had a chance, if he hadn't been caught so off guard, I knew he would have fought back.

"I'd like to say that I'm feeling very targeted. Is this how you treat all of your guests? Or just some of us? Seems pretty racist, if you ask me."

Jackie was impressed, I could tell, by my fight. But there was something I hadn't known about her. White as she was, she was far more skilled in the dark arts than I was.

"I'm doing my job as a reporter, which is, in case you weren't aware, about telling the truth. And the truth is that you've been trading on emotional damage, Javier. Using it for leverage. It is, frankly, a disgusting breach of trust and journalistic integrity. And now you won't even take a shred of responsibility."

"You wouldn't understand. You're just a white woman working in a system designed to bring me down."

Jackie smiled. "So this is your shtick, isn't it?"

"What?"

"This, right here. Painting yourself as the victim. Don't you see how harmful that is? To people who have *actually* been through the things you write so flippantly about?"

"You don't speak for my people, Jackie," I said.

"Well, apparently, you don't either, Javier."

She pointed at the camera. On the screen in the back I saw the statement from *The Rag* replaced with live comments from Twitter.

"It's clear that despite your misleading accusations against me and *my* journalistic integrity, other people see your actions just the same way we do."

This fraud going up in flames in real time is the best television I've seen all year. Get 'im, Jackie.

This man has set us all back. Jackie Knox is doing a public service by roasting him.

Suspended? Please. This manipulator should never be allowed to touch a keyboard again!

The tweets kept coming in. An endless scroll, like the one I was used to on my phone. But now the tenor was all wrong. Where were my defenders?

I don't even really remember what I said next. But you can find the online clip for yourself. You probably already have. I was truly at a loss for words. At a loss for spin. There were no more strategies. It was just me. My naked, real self, exposed for the whole world to see. For me to see. This *is who I am,* I thought. *A fraud. And now everyone knows.*

Finally, I stood up. I ripped the microphone from my shirt.

"Where are you going?" Jackie said.

I tried to run off the stage but tripped down the small set of stairs, rolling on the floor. When I looked up, a camera was in my face. I looked at the screen displaying the live show. My mug there on the wall, looking like the face of a deranged man.

I got up and ran as the camera chased me down the hall. I had watched the scene many times. On daytime television, a man learns he's a father or not, and runs. On news shows, a politician or some evil swindler is confronted outside their apartment building, and runs. I'd laughed at these clips and thought, *What an idiot.* But now I understood.

I threw open the exit door and ran down the stairs. After a few flights, I realized that the cameraman had stopped following me. I turned on my phone. Immediately, it buzzed, and kept buzzing. Emails from my agent, from Nic. Missed phone calls. Mentions, comments. A bombardment of numbers and words on my screen.

I pushed my way out to the street and disregarded the alarm sounding behind me. I ran through the alleyway to the corner of the block and stood there as people pushed past me. I still had a piece of torn microphone cord hanging from my collar. Everything felt as if it were spinning. And the buzzing just wouldn't stop. It kept coming and coming, like little electric shocks.

I looked up at the jumbotron on the side of the NNN building playing the network, as it always did. There were already clips of me running off the set. The chyron read, "Writer caught in his own lies storms off set." Jackie was now speaking directly into the camera. Although I couldn't hear what she was saying, it was clear that she was talking about what had just happened, shaking her head, looking disturbed, distraught. The master, reveling in her victory.

I tried to discern if others were seeing what I was seeing. If they understood what was happening. But everyone around me seemed to have somewhere to go. They seemed to be speeding past. A blur of colors and sounds. The only thing that cracked through was Gio's voice.

I traced it to the hot dog stand, where he was speaking to the vendor jovially, exchanging cash for a pretzel bedazzled with salt. Eating, as if nothing had happened.

"It's over. I'm dead," I remember saying, with all the seriousness in the world.

Gio said something in return, something about lying on his name, about getting him in trouble. I can't remember the specifics. Or maybe I couldn't even hear what he said. Maybe I couldn't hear anything. I could only feel the buzzing.

I looked out into the busy street. All the cars meandering past each other. The honking. I didn't see chaos. I saw calm. Peace. That's all I wanted. So I walked forward.

Eighteen

A FAINT, CONSISTENT BEEP. Blindingly bright lights. I felt my arms. Saw tubes in them. Saw a white sheet over my torso and legs. I thought perhaps I was dead. That is, until I saw Mom slouched uncomfortably in a chair, one arm under her head. She opened her eyes slightly. "My baby," she said, in a voice that made me feel like a child again.

I couldn't remember the thudding impact of the sedan, Gio's desperate 911 call, the blocked-off street, Mom holding my hand.

The only thing that came back were the emails, the phone calls, the texts, the tweets. The only thing I could think about was the nurse who told me I'd been out for three days. So much time. How much had been said? My reputation, everything I'd worked for, where was it now? What was left?

I patted the bed in a frenzy.

Beeping noises picked up. Mom looked at a monitor.

"Whoa, relájate, nene."

"My phone. Where's my phone?" I wanted to respond. I

wanted to explain. I desperately wanted to hold on to the world I'd built, the life I'd created.

Mom pointed to her purse, hanging from the chair. "Whatever is left of it. I'm pretty sure it's dead forever."

"It's dead? Like broken? No. Ma, I need—"

Mom pushed me back onto the bed and held me there. Her face was serious. "You need to relax. That phone got you here. Gio said you were looking at it and talking crazy about that interview and then you walked right off the curb. That's why—"

I lay back.

Mom's face twisted. "That's what happened, right? It was a mistake? That's what it was, right? You weren't looking where you were going, right? You weren't trying to—"

She broke down in tears. She stroked my cheek with her thumb. "You know I love you, right? I'm sorry if I don't support you enough. I'm sorry I don't read your articles. I'm just trying to do my best. It's not easy. But I'm proud of you. I just want you to know that. I am." She waited for me to say something.

I decided that, this time, one more lie wouldn't hurt.

I WAS RELEASED with crutches, bruises, and lots of stitches. It wasn't until I was at Mom's place, set up in my old room with pillows and ice packs, that I finally got access to my laptop, a coveted device with Wi-Fi. Once Mom left my room to make sancocho, I whipped it out.

I started with Twitter. I was greeted by gigantic blue numbers of mentions and messages. I scrolled all the way to the bottom and read from beginning to end, like a masochist.

Many of the messages are still online for all to see. As are all the articles and blog posts written about me from outlets of various persuasions: "How a Young Writer's Skyrocketing Career Was Quickly Popped"; "Up-and-Coming Writer Busted for Making Up Lies"; "Race-Baiter Exposed as a Fraud"; "Light-Skinned Dude Gets Exposed for Being Mad Light-Skinned." All of these pop up whenever you google my name and will likely continue to do so for as long as I live. I don't need to recount them all here.

I was naively shocked to see the same people who had once praised me and my work burning me at the stake. People who had regarded me with great admiration called me a "purveyor of poverty porn," a "bad POC," a "bad brown person," a "Puerto Rican Uncle Tom." They were but one faction of those coming for my head. Another siege came from other writers and pundits I'd never heard from before. People who said they'd never liked my work and had been waiting for me to fall, had always known it would happen.

Despite the avalanche of people turning on me, banishing me, and cursing me out, I kept scrolling. News of my suicide attempt had apparently hit the media within hours of it happening. But there was no sympathy as far as I could tell. In the tweets that came after the news was shared, there were no hotline numbers, no calls for increased access to mental health. Instead, I was called a coward, scum. It was said that the world was better off without me. That finally, I had done something responsible. "Can anyone tell me if that clown Javier Perez is dead? I could use good news today."

I felt sick. I kept scrolling. Addicted. So committed that despite my overdose, I couldn't stop going back for more, for an even shittier version of the hits that had taken me sky-high and nearly ended me.

The only thing that finally stopped me was a knock at the door.

Gio was the last person I expected to walk in. But there he was, sighing, flicking on the lights. He stormed over and ripped the computer out of my hands. "Seriously? You almost died. Do you understand that? I saw you laid out on the ground, all bloody, your eyes closed. You weren't fucking moving, Javi. I thought you were gone."

He closed the computer and threw it on the floor. I watched it bounce, heard a cracking sound. To my surprise, I wasn't angry. It reminded me what a computer really is: aluminum, plastic, some cables and chips; an accumulation of pixels.

"Will you stop thinking about the fucking internet for a second? Imagine if you hadn't woken up, Javi. Think about that. Your moms? She'd be done for. It'd change her forever. And for what? For your phone? For that bullshit on the show? Get a fucking grip."

The emotion in Gio's face shocked me the most. Made me pay attention to what he was saying, really listen, perhaps for the first time since he'd been out.

"I'm so tired of your ass, bro. I don't know why I bothered coming here. What I should do is fuck you up for what you did. I told you that shit was a stupid idea."

Gio sat in the beanbag chair next to my bookcase. The same chair he'd sit in when we were kids. When he'd make up dumb excuses to come over and just hang out, just be in my space. It took me many years to figure out why he did that, to figure out that it probably brought him some comfort that I hadn't even realized he needed.

I looked at him and remembered when the chair would completely envelop him like quicksand. And even though he now looked massive in the chair, sitting there before me, the child version of him was the version I still saw.

"I'm sorry," I said. "For everything. Really. I fucked up."

Gio nodded. Sighed in relief. "Thank you, bro. *Finally*. See, now that's a good fucking start, Javi."

I leaned back against the wall behind my bed. Looked at the cast swallowing up my leg, the dark purple bruise on my wrist, which the doctor said caught my fall after the car's impact, saving my life.

"I'm fucked up, Gio. I don't know when it happened, but I was so far gone I don't even know what's down or up anymore."

"Hey, man, it happens. Sometimes you need to get your shit rocked. Sometimes you really can't learn something until you got a judge banging on a gavel, some iron on your wrists, or, in your case, I guess, a bunch of people talking shit about you on the internet. To be honest, it don't seem all that bad. I'd take that any day of the week over prison."

I thought about Gio as a kid. Always reminding me of what I had, always reminding me it could be worse. "The things they've said are wild, though. And they're not going anywhere. The internet never forgets, Gio. I have no career. I have nothing."

Gio shook his head. "How you gonna say you have nothing, Javi? You still got your life, right? Your freedom? Your moms? She still cooking up some fine-ass food, as far as I can tell. Whatever she's making now smells amazing. Don't come at me with that, Javi. You got plenty, son."

"You don't get it, Gio. I mean, yeah, sure, you're right, in a technical sense. But I was on live television. YouTube. My reputation is ruined. I'm not sure I can ever come back from it."

Gio shrugged. "Yeah, but it's still internet shit, Javi. Nothing gonna happen to you in real life. What they gonna do? They ain't gonna come to your block and yell your name out the window so they can fight you. They ain't gonna press you, pull a gun on you. Look around you. All those people yelling, but where they at? They ain't here, right?"

I looked at the computer on the floor. "I guess."

Gio chuckled. "Man, that internet shit ain't nothing. Matter fact, I was on the train just yesterday and some white dude with shades came up on me like, 'Bro, weren't you on television?' He really said 'television,' not 'TV,' which was weird. But anyway, nothing happened. I was just like, 'Nah, fuck outta here, lil bitch, don't talk to me,' and he looked at me all shook and changed cars. Normal interaction. It wasn't nothing."

"So people *have* noticed you? In the Bronx?"

"No, man. I was on my way back from an interview at Applebee's in Times Square. Same shit, different story. 'You can only wash dishes.' 'Your tattoos scare the customers.' Pussies. Anyway. My point is, you take this internet shit too serious. Trust me, your rep ain't worth your life. Focus on you. Your own problems. Because *clearly* you got some to deal with. That shit on the show. Yeah, that was pretty bad."

"I was desperate."

"Obviously. Out here bribing me. Speaking of which, I'm gonna need that other g. I already made plans for it. So, uh, whenever you figure your shit out, break me off with that, you heard?"

From outside my window, the music, the car honks, the train screeches, and the police sirens down below seemed to all carry up to us at once, like a beautiful symphony.

It all reminded me of my old life. When Gio and I were just kids. When he would annoy me, remind me of what I had. When everything was simple. When the computer was this clunky thing we messed around with, played solitaire and pinball on, but would drop just as quickly for a football, or a tip that some girls we were crushing on were hanging at the park. Before the followers and the likes.

My bedroom came into full view. I saw myself as a kid, sitting on the radiator near the window, which clanked every five minutes as if a little man lived inside and was reminding me he was alive. I saw myself there eating sugary cereal again. Staring out the window at my block, at the world. Mom was there. Gio was there.

And now, they were still here. Despite everything. I realized Gio was right. I was pretty damn lucky.

"Why do you even still care about me?" I asked him. "For real. That was some messed-up shit I did to you."

Gio smiled. "You know, I asked myself that same question, Javi. I figured I should just dead your ass. Drop you like I dropped Manny and everyone else. But then I thought about it. You were trippin'. Trippin' hard. And I know a thing or two about that, remember?"

He stuck his arm out for a pound, a real one, the first real one we'd exchanged since he'd been out.

"Not many people kept it real with me like you did way back when, Javi. Like you tried to, at least. So I guess we're even now. Well, after I get that bread you owe me. Then we'll really be even."

"Fair enough. Though I don't know when. I sort of don't have a job now, remember? Banished from media, probably society."

"Please. *I'm* banished from society. You just need a job, bitch. That's your problem. But a deal is a deal." Gio sniffed the air. "In the meantime, what's good with that food, though?"

"That's why you're really here, isn't it?"

"You already know."

I called out to Mom a few times. Eventually, she burst into the room with a dripping spoon in her hands. "What? What? You feeling okay? Your legs go out? You fainting?"

"I'm fine, Ma. Relax. My legs are fine. I'm alive."

She seemed relieved. "So what, then?"

"How much longer will that sancocho be?"

She twisted her face up, pointed the spoon at me. "The nerve. That's why you called me like that? Mira, nene, you're hurt and all, but don't get it mistaken. I'm no slave. Your food will be ready when it's ready. Until then, siéntate ahí y cállate." She looked at Gio, incredulous. "You believe this boy?"

She turned and shut the door.

Gio and I looked at each other.

We laughed. A real, hearty laugh. Just like when we were kids.

Nineteen

YOU PROBABLY DON'T believe me. But I didn't intend to write this book. It's the truth, for what it's worth. In fact, at the very moment that this book even became a possibility, I was writing something completely different. I was writing about how to attach the legs to a lounge chair.

It was two years after my cancellation, downfall, moment of shame, or whatever buzzword you'd like to use. The point is, my misdeeds had long stopped trending. Reporters had long stopped calling me for comment. My name had been replaced by those of others whose reputations were being torn to shreds, for better or worse.

I, meanwhile, had long stopped trying to reach Anais to apologize and make amends. I lived with the short statement she'd given to one outlet, the only one that had been able to reach her after the suicide attempt went public: "Not interested in speaking. I've said what I have to say. I am sad to hear about Javier's accident, and I hope he recovers." Whatever anger I had about the interview had long since faded. I had, after all, done her dirty. What she did in retaliation, I thought, was only fair.

I hadn't written a word for public consumption since I'd hit Send on my story about Gio—a story that had since been scrubbed from *The Rag*'s site, as had all of my stories. Look up my name now. The only thing you'll find from them is the statement they wrote upon my official termination. A statement that I imagine Rebecca—who is now the managing editor—read with great joy.

> *A recently hired staff writer for* The Rag *committed frequent acts of fabrication in his stories while writing about important, and often traumatic, experiences. The blatant disregard for the truth is something we at* The Rag *disavow completely. The writer, Javier Perez, has since been terminated. His stories have been completely removed from our site. We apologize profusely and vow to do better moving forward.*

I was nearing the end of my shift at my new job. Gio had been right, yet again. Finding work hadn't been all that hard. Especially when it was the sort of work I was looking for, which is to say, anything that had to do with words but was as far away from the media and literary apparatus as possible. My search had led me to a position as a remote contract technical writer for a massive international furniture company that couldn't have cared less about my past on Twitter as long as I submitted my work on time. It was the furthest thing from the type of writing I once did: cold, dry, boring, straight to the point. No persuasion involved. No room for unnecessary details or flourishes. It was perfect.

I'd managed to build a quiet little life for myself, and one day after work, I was looking forward to going for a walk, which I'd started doing to clear my head and take up some of the time I'd once devoted to social media.

But my flip phone buzzed.

I saw a number on the screen I did not recognize, a number that was not one of the handful of numbers I actually kept stored in my new phone. So I let it ring, figuring it was a telemarketer. Then I got the text: *Javi, it's Miles. Call me back.*

I thought it had to be a mistake at first. A prank. But just in case it wasn't, I called back. It was odd to hear Miles—the same man who'd voided our representation agreement within forty-eight hours of my appearance on NNN, while I was still in a fucking coma—suddenly ecstatic to hear from me. He tried to do the niceties—"Javier. How the hell are you? So good to hear from you"—but I didn't want to bother with that bullshit again.

"Why you calling me? You didn't even call me after you dropped me. You do remember you dropped me, right?"

He coughed on the line. "Alright. Listen, kid. Don't take it personally. Nature of the biz."

"What do you want?"

"Have you been writing? Anything about, you know—"

The truth was, I had been writing things. Things for myself. Entries in a spiral notebook, just like my old journals in school. Nothing with structure or a purpose. Nothing meant for public consumption. Just little things to try to make sense of what had happened. To make sense of how I'd gotten there. To make sense of all the hate and how quickly it had all dissipated. What was I to do with that? How was I to move forward? I wasn't sure. Writing, I figured, might help me get there. But my intention was to stay quiet. To fall into obscurity.

"Why do you care if I've been writing? You're not even my agent."

Miles sounded annoyed. "Sure I am, kid. I mean, I can be. It's just a piece of paper. Another one can be printed and signed. It's a formality. But I'm still here to help you."

"You don't wanna help me. You want something from me. What is it?"

I listened as Miles told me about a deal he'd gotten wind of. A large publisher who'd given nearly seven figures to a person who'd become a persona non grata with the public. "I can't name names yet. It'll hit the news soon. But that's not important," he said. "What's important is that I've been sniffing around, and there's a real market for this sort of thing. Sure, you're not a celebrity like this guy, but people are interested in what happened to you. I've even gotten some queries from publishers asking, on the sly, if you've been up to anything. They remember it. Which means they think people will read about it. Which means they'd pay you to write about it."

"I'd rather them not remember. I'd rather nobody remember, actually."

Miles sighed. "Why not? It's over now. The story is back in your hands. And you could take it in a lot of different directions. The right wing will love the revenge angle. They'll buy the book just to give the finger to the left. Then there's the repentance angle—you talk about the therapy, the nights you cried, the reflection, the agony. That plays really well with the lefties. You could probably even win an award or two. Make a documentary. After a while, if you wanted to, you could probably work your way back into the fold. Write for the pubs again. It's up to you." Miles paused. "I just figured I'd give you a call, kid. I always took you for a smart one. Okay, maybe not that smart. But ambitious. I *know* you have a memoir in you about all this. I just wanted to see if it's something you've given some thought to. That's all."

I won't lie. That's the point of this, right? Despite all the work I'd done to tell myself that attention was stupid and harmful, that I didn't need it, that I was better off in obscurity, better off with my small little life—working, going to the movies, seeing Mom, seeing Gio every now and then, trying and mostly failing to date, to let someone in, for real this time—I still felt a little flutter in my stomach hearing Miles speak. But I had grown enough that I didn't say yes right then and there. "I need to think about this."

"Sure. Just don't take too long. If you want to make a comeback, if you want to have your say, now's the time. Strike while this is hot. You might not get another window."

I hung up. I thought about his big question: Did I want to make a comeback? After everything, did I want to peek my head out from under the sand? Stir it all up?

YOU'VE PROBABLY wondered something similar: Why did I write this? What am I getting at here? Do I want redemption? Forgiveness?

I think it's only natural to want to explain yourself. To want to share your side of things. In the hopes that, at the very least, someone will understand. Someone will see you're not just some villain. Not just some psycho.

Despite my Google results, I'm not a scumbag who deserves death—albeit a cultural one. I'm a fucked-up human who made fucked-up mistakes. I lost my way. I valorized the wrong things, did some things I really regret, and hurt people I never wanted to hurt.

I stopped myself from sharing these feelings for two years. I stopped myself from responding to anything because I told myself it would only do more harm. I told myself that no one would want to read my side of things. No one would take it seriously. No one would care. But despite these seemingly good excuses, the real reason I never responded to anything, never had my say, was much simpler.

I realized it after hanging out with Gio following the call from Miles. We were living in different neighborhoods again. I was back at my apartment, and he was still at his grandma's, despite his constant swearing about how he was saving up for his own spot. It's not that I didn't believe him, it's that I also regularly saw him with new pairs of sneakers and fitteds, which made me wonder if he really was saving any of the money he made as a barback at a nice Italian restaurant in Riverdale.

That's beside the point. In the months and years after the interview, we repaired our relationship slowly—for real this time. We picked up where we left off as kids. But because we weren't kids anymore, life got in the way. Plans took more effort. And by the time we met up the evening after Miles's call, it had been a couple of months since we'd seen or even spoken to each other.

We met at a dive bar and ate wings as Gio told me stories about his restaurant. After a year of working behind the scenes, he said, he was finally beginning to get some shifts as a server. "I think they finally got over the neck tattoo," he said. "I know it's only because two of our regulars quit, but I'll take it."

"Congratulations," I said. "Sounds like things are going well."

"In that department." He scratched his head and told me about two servers who loved confiding in him about their problems and how he was currently managing a situation in which he was messing around with both of them at the same time without either of them knowing. "Pretty sure one just found out about the other, though." He looked at his phone. "Things are gonna get interesting."

"What did I tell you about bringing that baggage to your job?"

"What did I tell *you*? I don't take advice from you no more, man."

When a lull finally descended over the conversation, after we were well into our second round of beers, I decided to tell him about what Miles had described. The market, the opportune time. Gio worked on a wing, slurping until it was bone white. I still wanted a stamp of approval. But instead of *The Rag*'s or Twitter's, I wanted his.

Gio belched. He realized I was waiting for him to say something. "So? What? You gonna do it or nah?"

"I don't know. That's why I'm asking you."

"Asking me? I can't tell you what to do. You a grown-ass man, Javi—even if you do act like a little bitch sometimes."

"Well, then give me your opinion, at least. Would I be fucking up if I did it?"

Gio sipped his beer. "Depends," he said. "The bigger question is why? To make some money? To get famous?"

"No. I mean, at least I think that's not what I want."

"So you *do* want to do it?"

"Part of me does. Even if just to tell my side. To try to write something real this time."

Gio's phone buzzed on the table. He'd switched to an iPhone but still didn't mess with social media because of what had happened to me and because of his (largely irrational) fear of the government. Still, he was becoming savvy enough to send pics, videos, even emojis. He started to type something out, then spoke to me casually, as if saying nothing of importance.

"You want my opinion? Life is short. You wanna write a book, then write it. As long as you're doing it for the right reasons, then you might as well at this point. What's the worst that can happen? What they gonna do that they didn't already do?" He put down his phone and hit Send on a long message written to one of the servers. *It don't mean nothing, girl . . .*

What he'd said sounded so simple. So offhand. But I can't overstate the importance of it.

Gio left the bar in a hurry soon after. He'd gotten a response, a "sliver of opportunity," as he called it.

I paid the bill, went home. I opened up my laptop. I realized he was right. I'm not a prisoner. I'm free.

I HAVE ALWAYS WANTED to write something true. Something real. Honest. I was afraid before. I cared about the "audience." I cared less about what I was writing than about what the people reading it might think. I figured I had to do that to get anywhere, because anywhere to me was that stage. Madison Square Garden. My fists in the air. And all the applause seemed to be pointing me in one direction, to one kind of story.

But now I see that I was wrong. I don't have to conform to anyone else's vision of myself. I don't have to care about what my editors want. I don't have to try to smooth over the gap between what they imagine my life to be like and what it is actually like. Fuck them.

I'm sorry for what I've done. I know it was wrong. I'm owning that. But I'm not sorry about how things played out. Believe it or not, what happened to me was a gift. It freed me. It taught me the truth: Life ain't fucking neat. No one among us is righteous. And pretending to be for some attention, for some validation, will eventually just blow up in your face.

The high really does feel nice. All those retweets, likes, and mentions used to comfort me like a warm blanket. My community online, my army, seemingly ready to tweet for me until their thumbs bled, made me feel like a king. But they didn't really have my back. None of you ever did. I was a star in your eyes until I wasn't. A useful puppet saying all the right things until you realized I was no longer useful.

But that doesn't matter anymore. Here's what does: I'm alive. I've still got an apartment. I make a decent salary doing something easy and boring. My mother still loves me. And although I don't have many friends to speak of, Gio, surprisingly, still answers my calls.

That is enough these days. It was always enough. I just wish I would have understood that sooner. Understood that when I had the chance to save myself. But sometimes you have to eat rocks and taste asphalt. Gio taught me that.

So as you draw your own conclusions about my life, about my rise and fall, as you perhaps find your favorite passages to tweet and make fun of, or as you play the video clips of me over and over for fun, just remember one thing: You're not innocent either.

I'm not some mastermind. I'm just a two-bit hustler. Just what you might expect. I'm responsible for my indulgence, but you're responsible for creating me.

That's right. I said it. You created me.

Say I haven't learned a thing. Say I probably shouldn't even be allowed to write this. Say whatever you want. Maybe you're right.

I wasn't trying to be a victim until the world taught me how powerful victims are. Now I understand that my life circumstances just were what they were. The hand I was dealt, and so on.

So I went too far. I played with the truth. I hurt people.

Fine. But just remember, there was a point when you were along for the ride. A point when you were willing to believe. When you wanted to believe more than anything else. Everyone forgets that now. Except for me. I haven't forgotten.

Acknowledgments

First and foremost, thank you, God, for your blessings and for your perfect timing.

Thank you to my mother—my rock and my biggest champion. Thank you for making sure I believe in myself as much as you believe in me. Thank you to my beautiful wife, Marcela, for seeing me through countless drafts, being my first reader, and telling me the truth. Thank you to my children, Milan and Luna. You've made me more patient, loving, and empathetic—all of which bleeds onto the page.

Shout-out to my family. My sisters Sydney and Gaby. Izzy. Abuelita, Chiki, Titi Nelin, Tío Jon, Tío David, and the rest of my Tampa family. To my family in El Barrio: Titi Lourdes, Chuki, Padrino, Joan, Ralph, Titi Sandra, Emilio, Christian, Eric Williams. My Colombian family: mis suegros, Cata, Rosa, and Etel—may she rest in peace. To Travis, for reading I don't know how many versions of this and always being there. To Danny, Fab, Ariel, and Boston for keeping me grounded. To Andy White. Mi familia en Loíza, te amo. To my family that didn't make it: Tío Pillin, Tío Joe, and Johnzue—RIP. Bits and pieces of you all are in here.

Shout-out to P.S. 86, M.S. 118, and Mount Saint Michael Academy. To Ms. Alvarez, Mr. Pape, Ms. Stein, Mrs. Negrin, Mr. Guffey, Hack, Mr. Jennings. Shout-out to the Princeton Summer Journalism Program and the *New York Times* scholarship. To my family at Achilles and at Cornell, especially Dick Traum, Joe Traum, Hope Mandeville, Monica Burke, and Katherine Reagan. To the University of Miami MFA program, where I did a lot of growing as a writer.

Thank you to the incredible writing teachers, editors, mentors, and co-conspirators who've poured into me along this journey. Thanks to the OG Big Homie David Gonzalez, Ernesto Quiñonez, Helena Maria Viramontes, M. Evelina Galang, Chauncey Mabe, Patricia Engel, Chantel Acevedo, Mat Johnson, Henri Cauvin, Miguel Pichardo, Candace Mays, Thomas Colon, Daniel Peña, Marin Cogan, Jordan Blumetti, Alex Perez, Lucas Baker, Dagmawi Woubshet, Stephanie Vaughn, Maureen McCoy, Michael A. Gonzales, Pastor José Víctor Dugand, and Aliya Ismail. Special thanks to Paul Beatty, Victor LaValle, and Leigh Stein for reading this early and giving me game when they didn't have to.

Danielle Bukowski, agent extraordinaire! Thank you for all the time and effort you put into making this stronger and getting it out into the world.

Cara Reilly, thank you for your beautiful editorial vision—which never once felt imposing. You're the perfect shepherd for this project, and I'm so glad we worked on it together. To Victoria Sieczka and Emily Mahon for the stunning cover illustration and design.

The entire Doubleday team, thank you for believing in the book, and believing in me. It feels amazing to come out the gate with you all behind me.

About the Author

Andrew Boryga grew up in the Bronx and now lives in Miami with his family. His writing has appeared in *The New York Times, The New Yorker,* and *The Atlantic,* and been awarded prizes by Cornell University, the University of Miami, *The Susquehanna Review,* and the Michener Awards Foundation. He attended the Tin House writers' workshop and has taught writing to college students, elementary school students, and incarcerated adults.

Bookmaking Team

EDITORIAL

Cara Reilly, *Editor*

PRODUCTION

Katherine Hourigan, *Managing Editor*

Kathleen Cook, *Production Editor*

Lorraine Hyland, *Production Manager*

Anna B. Knighton, *Interior Text Designer*

JACKET DESIGN

Emily Mahon, *Art Director*